INCENDIANT

VIRGINIA BLACK

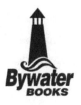

Bywater BOOKS

2025

Bywater Boooks
Copyright © 2025 Virginia Black

All rights reserved. No part of this book may be reproduced, stored in a retrieval system, or transmitted in any form or by any means, without prior permission in writing from the publisher.

Print ISBN: 978-1-61294-317-6

Bywater Books First Edition: June 2025

Printed in the United States of America on acid-free paper.

Cover design by TreeHouse Studio

Bywater Books
PO Box 3671
Ann Arbor MI 48106-3671

www.bywaterbooks.com

This is a work of fiction. Names, characters, places, and incidents are the product of the author's imagination or are used fictitiously. Any resemblance to actual events, locales, or persons, living, living dead, or dead, is fictionalized.

For Kate, always.

*And for those lost in the long dark.
Keep going—the light will come.*

PROLOGUE

NATHANIEL WAS FAMILIAR with pain.

His life before becoming a vampire had been one of violence and suffering, hunger and, yes, pain. This new torment, however, was unparalleled.

He clenched one arm—the only part of him that didn't hurt—against one side of his chest, his body hunched in on itself in an effort to keep moving forward. Splotches of blistered, swollen skin covered half his face, and twelve-day-old burns ravaged his torso from one shoulder down to his thighs.

Nathaniel navigated the shadows of the moonlit streets. When he hurt too much to take another step, when every touch of his suit's fabric against his skin felt like a new abrasion, rage powered him onward.

If his mission was successful and he managed to keep his head on his shoulders, some day soon he would find the bloodling who had marred his perfection. The fire from Leigh Phan's spell had burned through his clothes as he'd made his escape from his master's vineyard. No amount of swatting at the persistent flames had suppressed them, and neither had any of the water he'd splashed on himself from a trough near the vines. The fire wasn't extinguished until he'd tripped and fallen face down in a pool of mud.

The burns, though, wouldn't heal. In the days since, the blood from several feeds should have restored him to his previous flawlessness. These burns and that fire had been something beyond his understanding.

When he found Leigh Phan again, he would kill her.

Nathaniel dragged himself several more steps toward his destination. For days now, he'd traveled overland on foot and by night from the vineyard near Calvert, Oregon, to this understated mansion on the outskirts of Ogden, Utah.

The night wind blew against his face and new pain flared as he walked the garden path to the front entrance. In another life he might have admired the garden's design, the meticulous attention to each plant's placement and the obvious care taken in their maintenance. Tonight, other matters took precedence.

Ankle-high, solar-powered lights shone golden along the stone pathway. The concrete and glass house beyond the path was split-level, accented by sharp angles, and built into the side of a low hill at the base of the mountains.

The architecture interested Nathaniel about as much as the garden had—not at all. He sensed movement nearby—two humans, one far to one side of him near the long, winding driveway, and the other blocking the path ahead.

Not much security for a Guild First vampire.

Nathaniel gritted his teeth and pushed himself to his full height as he walked the last few steps toward the male before him. The human wielded a nasty cudgel with barbed wire wrapped around one end to dissuade anyone from approaching his master's house.

After one good look at Nathaniel's face, the man took a step back.

Nathaniel was aware of how frightening he appeared. He was taller than most men, and his broad shoulders and tapered body had once communicated the ease with which he'd walked through the world. He'd trimmed his unevenly burnt hair close to his scalp, and the polyester suit he wore was a hasty acquisition and not tailored as was his preference, but one did not approach a First without attempting a more formal presentation.

When last he'd braved a mirror, the burns on his face still smoldered. One eye had stopped seeping, though blackened skin and the ruined eyeball remained.

He was too proud to wear an eyepatch. If this is what he looked like now, he wouldn't hide himself.

The man smelled of fear, the same as every other human Nathaniel had passed on the streets to this house. Ogden was vampire territory, ruled by its lone vampire occupant. If the rumors were true, other vampires and bloodlings—those with some superhuman attribute or ability—weren't allowed in this territory.

All Nathaniel knew about the vampire who lived here was what he had overheard from traveling vampires who had visited his master, Victor. Arnaldus was rumored to be over six hundred years old and had settled in this country along with the first British settlers. His only Legate—a vampire master's first-sired right hand—had been killed in the eighteenth century, and he had never created another. Anyone who had tried to approach him to join his guild had never been heard from again.

Perhaps Nathaniel might be killed for coming here, but he had no other options. Inside this house lay a minuscule chance of exacting revenge against the Ruby Court, against the Legate Bartholomew, against the impudent war witch Joan Matthews along with the bitch who'd scarred him . . . any chance was worth the risk.

The human touched his own ear—no, a communication device tucked in its hollow. "Yes, my lord?"

Nathaniel's injuries kept him from hearing the other side of the conversation. In another moment, listening wasn't necessary. The man gestured to the door behind him and stepped aside to allow Nathaniel's passage.

No one greeted him as he stepped through the open front doors. The minimalist interior matched the modern exterior, and with most of the house dark Nathaniel followed a hint of light through the halls until he found the great room.

Arnaldus, First vampire of the Hall of the Reverent Word, stood near the fireplace.

He was over seven feet tall and thin, his skin a pallid brown in the firelight, and his attire was as mid-century modern as the architecture. He wore a brown V-neck sweater, tan slacks, and trim loafers, the casual guise of a technology billionaire. For all Nathaniel knew, that might be close to the truth. Most Firsts were wealthy, and with no other vampires in his guild all the spoils of his territory would belong to Arnaldus alone.

The room was warm from the swollen fire. A crack from a splitting log broke the silence, and Nathaniel flinched. How anyone could stand so close to open flame was beyond him.

Nathaniel bowed at the waist, though it pained him to the point of blurring his vision. He took a deep, settling breath before he spoke.

"Lord Arnaldus, I apologize for the unannounced intrusion. I am—"

"Nathaniel. Former Legate to a vain adolescent with delusions of supremacy."

His assessment of Victor, Nathaniel's former master, was harsh though accurate.

"Yes, my lord." Nathaniel slowly straightened, his breaths sharp so he didn't groan.

Arnaldus narrowed his eyes, noticing the movement. "Not quite as dashing as I was told."

Nathaniel didn't rise to the bait in reply.

Arnaldus looked disappointed at the loss of a verbal challenge. "Satisfying my curiosity is the only reason your head hasn't been separated from your shoulders. You and Victor were bloodlings in service to one of my peers, one who died under mysterious circumstances.

"The next I heard of either of you, Victor—that egotistical rodent—had created a false court in the wilds under Elizaveta's nose, and you'd thrown your lot in with him. Judging by your appearance, Elizaveta has rendered punishment. Either your master is dead and you've come to me for aid I will not give, or you serve Elizaveta, in which case I'll kill you where you stand."

His ill will towards Elizaveta was a good sign, if Nathaniel lived long enough to take advantage of it. The mention of Elizaveta's punishment, however, was confusing.

"Victor is dead, my lord, killed by a war witch, and I wanted to offer—"

"Your wants are irrelevant. You will answer my questions and die quickly, or I'll break your legs and toss you to my thralls for their entertainment until I remember to kill you."

The concept of more pain wasn't frightening, but Nathaniel had endured enough. He hadn't wanted to serve Victor, though there had been many advantages. Now, he had to work to make sure he allayed hints of weakness enough to make a positive impression.

"I am embarrassed to admit Victor misled me when we served together under our previous master. One evening, I believed we were leaving the grounds to hunt when, in truth, Victor went off alone soon after the hunt began and circled back. He seduced our master into changing him and killed him without my knowledge. When I returned, Victor changed me, and made me his Legate."

That Nathaniel had not offered his consent didn't change the outcome.

Arnaldus folded his arms over his chest. "So you chose to align yourself with the rubbish."

"I did." Adherence to duty might be considered an admirable trait. "He was my new master, and it was my duty to serve him, whatever the cost to my own fate."

No matter what Victor had asked of him, Nathaniel had been compelled to deliver it.

"Yet for all his aspirations," Arnaldus said, "he was put down by a common war witch."

Not common, but no need to disclose that yet.

"She was aided by Bartholomew, Legate to Elizaveta."

Disapproval and disdain twisted Arnaldus's face into a sneer. "Elizaveta formed a treaty with another coven?"

Something was going on between the vampires in Black Rose City and the war witch of Calvert. Whatever it was didn't matter—Nathaniel only cared that Joan Matthews didn't get what she wanted.

Nathaniel stilled himself as another wave of pain passed through his body. He hoped he could hold himself upright long enough to make his case.

"I don't believe so, my lord. Elizaveta is collaborating with one war witch in particular and sent only Bartholomew. The Ruby Court does not follow the true path as you do. They negotiate with the living instead of conforming them to the enlightened and experienced will of a First like you."

Arnaldus stared at him in frank appraisal. Perhaps Nathaniel had over-embellished. He must be careful and stick to as much of the truth as possible. Arnaldus might be one of those who could sense subterfuge as well as insincerity.

Nathaniel took another breath and willed his wounded leg to stop trembling. "After my master's unjust death, I knew I must seek you out. I understand you may not want my service here—"

"Get to the point."

"I do not wish to serve in another unsanctioned court."

He would not serve those like Elizaveta and Bartholomew, vampires who would not acknowledge their true place in the world or their power over others. Though Victor had lorded himself above those in his pretense of a court and over the humans he'd stabled, he had cared most about exacting his vengeance against those who had affronted him in his previous human life. He hadn't been the master Nathaniel longed to serve, and Victor's court would never have provided the kind of opportunities a formal guild might.

Once he'd killed Matthews and Phan, Nathaniel still had a bright future ahead of him, even if he wasn't in the shape to enjoy an endless life the way he'd planned.

"I am not yet well enough to travel alone to one of the other guilds. The Ruby Court has aligned themselves with a war witch and does not honor the old ways. I beseech you—direct me to a Court with the resources to hold them responsible for allying themselves with our enemies."

Arnaldus' measuring glare was cold. "The so-called Ruby Court and its presumptuous leader are abominations. We are meant to rule, not barter deals with humans and witches, or offer terms to our stabled feeds."

His voice took on a professorial tone. "We who live forever have a true understanding of how this world can be shaped, not these irascible children who preen and bicker when they're only here long enough to ruin what they touch before they shuffle off to death."

He raised a hand and drew it over his immaculate black hair as if one were out of place. "Their territory could be put to better use. Elizaveta is a young fool who proclaimed herself First, no different from your Victor in that she did not earn her position. And one as old as Bartholomew should know better than to throw his lot in with such an impetuous—"

Arnaldus paused, calming himself.

"Despicable as they are, they have procured enough of a base to make colonization or annexation expensive and foolhardy. And you are in no condition to serve anyone."

The implication was insulting, though Nathaniel did not take it personally. Such was the nature of politics, vampiric or otherwise. Arnaldus did not see his value.

"If I may, my lord, perhaps you might hear what else I have to offer."

Arnaldus scoffed, a gesture foreign on his ageless features. "What could you, a petty backwater air mage from a country most have forgotten, who served a false lord in squalor and now comes to me hiding the full extent of his wounds—what could you possibly offer anyone?"

He was well-informed. Even Victor had not known of Nathaniel's origins—had in fact never once inquired where he was from.

Nathaniel bowed again, the better to sell his proposition. Arrogance would not sway a First. Best to remain deferential, though the pain was harder to ignore.

Arnaldus's history wasn't the only information Nathaniel had gleaned from the visitors to Victor's court.

"If you want the Ruby Court to fall, I can deliver the means to destroy them."

CHAPTER 1

One year later

IF JOAN MATTHEWS was outdoors, the crows were nearby.

The sound of the wind was faint beneath the chatter and squawking. Dozens of them darted and danced in the evergreens and the thin, bare branches of trees left naked in the February chill.

Joan shoved their distraction aside to focus on the woman holding her hand. Despite the cold, Leigh Phan was clad in fewer layers than Joan, and strode along the composted path as if she had memorized every step.

Joan glanced askance at Leigh then back to the overgrown trail. "You sure this is okay? Just the two of us, I mean?"

Leigh's frown conveyed exasperation, but her eyes were alight with something akin to joy. Her straight black hair fell free past her shoulders instead of being twisted in her habitual messy bun, and her golden-brown skin was flushed with eagerness. The irises of her tiger stone-brown eyes twinkled gold, the sclera gleaming yellow without the glamour spell she often cast to hide her other-than-human nature.

When she was like this—alone with Joan and free in the outdoors—she was uninhibited, unashamed. Beautiful.

"How many times do I have to tell you?" Leigh asked.

So perhaps Joan had been a tad redundant, but only because she wanted Leigh to have no reservations. "Doesn't make it any less official as far as I'm concerned."

Most people would have chosen to have a few friends or family present. Neither of them had much beyond each other. Leigh's only family, her grandmother, had passed years ago.

All of Joan's family was dead. As both binder and war witch, Joan was the most powerful protector their hometown of Calvert had seen in generations. She knew plenty of people, but only one or two might have merited an invitation—not that they'd been invited.

Leigh squeezed her hand. "Joan, I only care about you."

That was probably true. Leigh was a natural recluse—understandable after all she'd been through—and spent her time in the house or in the gardens. Lately, she'd been spending more time in the woods near the Matthews homestead—at least during daylight hours.

Leigh was always indoors by sunset, though a bloodling didn't have much to fear in the dark. No one in Calvert knew she was more than human, and what keeping such a secret might mean in the long run was a problem for another day.

Today was for the two of them.

The first rays of morning sunlight painted the scattered clouds above them pink.

"Ready?" Joan wasn't nervous. A simple handfasting was an everyday event. Were her hands clammy?

Leigh raised Joan's trembling hand to her lips and kissed her chilled fingers. "Long past, lover."

Joan hoped her dark skin hid her blush.

The trail through the pines, cedars, and firs ended in a clearing. Fog lingered in the shadows, and the ground rose to a knoll thick with overgrown grass, slick from the overnight rains. Joan treaded carefully up the rising earth—neither of them was likely to be hurt from a fall, but no one wanted wet jeans in winter.

When Joan reached the rounded peak, she turned to face Leigh.

Here was where Joan had surrendered the whole of herself to the land, claiming the responsibility of its protection, and here was where she wanted to give herself to Leigh. She felt more at home here than she did in her own house.

Sunlight passed through the trees and shimmered in Leigh's gaze before she looked down and kicked off her boots.

Joan did the same and hissed as her warm feet touched the ice-cold grass. The moment her skin touched the earth, a vibration tingled through her toes toward her ankles, surging up her legs into her body.

She straightened her spine as she clasped Leigh's hands. The ley lines hummed beneath the knoll. The earth's power filled her, intertwining with capabilities she'd inherited from the long line of Matthews binder witches, all of it mingling with the joy of being here with Leigh.

Joan breathed deeply, the crisp air burning in her nose and lungs.

"In perfect love and perfect trust," she said, her racing heart calming as she began the ritual. "I have come to bind myself to you, to bind my life and path to yours."

Leigh smiled as she spoke. "In perfect love and perfect trust, I have come to bind myself to you, to bind my life and path to yours."

They shared a deep breath. A few crows circled, one of them brushing against the back of Joan's head. Too close for Joan's comfort.

"Trying to get married here."

"Be nice," Leigh said. "Maybe they're happy for you."

This . . . affinity Joan had with the crows was irritating at best and a menace at worst. What good were they to her if she wasn't fighting? Another distraction getting in the way of the moment.

"Yeah, yeah." Joan slid one hand inside her coat to reach into a pocket. "Show me what colors you chose."

Leigh rocked back on her heels, her visible excitement keeping her from standing still. "You first."

"You're just scared we chose the same colors."

"Quit stalling, Matthews."

After pulling them free from her coat, Joan hid her strands of leather laces where Leigh couldn't see, then selected one and raised it in the space between them.

"Black. For protection and purity." Above all else, Joan would keep Leigh safe.

Leigh tugged a matching length of leather from one of her front pockets. "White. For peace, truth, and devotion."

All true heralds of Leigh's personality, and not surprising in the least. Joan hummed in agreement before lifting another strand.

"Blue," Joan said. "For unity, harmony, and fidelity." Each based on honesty, something Joan was determined to share with Leigh.

"Brown," Leigh said. "For grounding, home and hearth. For the earth."

The Matthews homestead was the heart of Calvert, and the heart of their relationship. Joan had once walked away from her home, from Leigh, and her soul had been crushed by the loss. No way would she ever let that happen again.

She dangled the last strand with a grin.

"Red. For strength." Joan lowered her voice an octave. "And passion."

Leigh pulled a matching red strand from her back pocket, and bit into her lower lip, which was sexy as hell. Joan would bite that lip back later.

The wind shifted as they took turns weaving the strands together before binding them around each other's wrists in a loose knot, tugging each other closer.

Joan summoned a burst of wind, thinning the streams of air, bending and tightening them until they were snug against the ends of the loose knots, and pulled them taut—a blatant demonstration of the power she possessed as binder of the land beneath her.

When the knots were secure, Joan winked at Leigh. What was the point of being a powerful witch if she couldn't show off once in awhile?

Leigh leaned forward and rested her forehead against Joan's before pulling back, nodding for Joan to begin the next stage of their handfasting.

Joan closed her eyes and took a deep breath, pulling more energy from the ley lines and the earth into herself, fueling her words. This was a time for her highest truths, spoken without reservation.

"For as long as I breathe, I will be your constant friend and partner," Joan said.

So much might have been different for them all those years ago if she had stayed in Calvert instead of running away. If she had chosen back then to put their friendship above all else, they might have worked out their problems instead of being torn apart by them. They were stronger now for overcoming the challenge.

"As will I," Leigh said. "For as long as I breathe, I will shoulder your burdens."

"As will I," Joan said. "I will comfort you in sickness and grief, and share your health and joy."

And offered acceptance of Leigh as she was—not only a giving, compassionate, beautiful woman, but also a bloodling who hid her true self from the world. A human half-breed, turned by vampires into someone more than she'd been, though not yet vampire.

Never a vampire if Joan had anything to say about it.

"As will I," Leigh whispered. "I offer you kindness and compassion."

They still fought. Not the way they once had, and Leigh was always the one to fight fair. Joan didn't, and the words she wished she could take back were many.

"As do I," Joan whispered back, clutching tighter to emphasize her promise. "I will share your pain and seek to ease it."

"As will I. And I will love and cherish you always." Leigh squeezed back, though Joan already believed her.

"I will love and cherish you always."

Joan reached into her front jeans pocket and pulled out two matching rings crafted from filigreed gold and blessed with protection charms. She handed one to Leigh, who slid it onto Joan's ring finger before Joan did the same for Leigh with the other.

The wind died down, the sun streamed warmth on Joan's face, and for a heartbeat even the crows were quiet.

"So mote it be," Joan said, and the earth beneath them trembled and stilled as she settled herself, melding her power once again with the magic below as the wind rose again. With a sweeping, cacophonous swell, the crows rose from the trees and swirled overhead.

Electrifying energy pulled at her, the binder in her wanting to feed the magic back to the earth, the war witch itching to shape the flows into spellcraft. She pushed both urges aside, focusing instead on the bond she was strengthening between her and Leigh.

The magic in the knoll receded, the tingling in her limbs replaced by the force of the energy swelling between their bodies as Joan reached for Leigh.

Leigh cradled Joan's face in her hands, her kiss tasting as it always did—of light, and warmth and home, of smoke and honey, of need and want and all the things making Joan ache for her, even through the years they'd been apart.

The kiss changed, too—also predictable, because Joan

couldn't help herself. Leigh slid her hands from Joan's face to her shoulders to the back of her neck. Her grip was tight enough to bruise, her bloodling strength uncontainable as she gave herself over to Joan's desire. Leigh's lips parted and Joan deepened their kiss, clutching at Leigh's hips to pull her closer.

Leigh's hand on the back of her head tightened, her palm hotter than fever, her kiss passionate enough to keep Joan from minding the burn.

CHAPTER 2

WHEN JOAN SHIFTED her shoulders, Leigh read it as the discomfort it was. Her hands were too hot again.

She pulled her hands away and deepened the kiss.

"I love you," she whispered when Joan stopped to breathe. She could have held her breath a little longer, but Joan's chest heaved.

"Love you back," Joan said. The wry twist of her lips almost made Leigh smile.

"I'm sorry about—"

Joan shook her head and planted another firm kiss on Leigh's lips. "Don't worry about it."

Leigh worried anyway and stepped a few inches away to collect herself. Her touch had been too hot for Joan more than a few times, yet another thing different about her now.

She bent over to pull on her boots, staving off the feeling that wasn't embarrassment or shame exactly, and more like discomfort at the things about herself needing to be allowed for.

On the other hand, Leigh felt like she could climb a mountain without extra effort, like she could run for hours and not stop, like she could wrestle someone twice her size into submission. Maybe it was the excitement of the moment, the joy of now being bound to the woman she loved, or perhaps it was something else—some aspect of her other-than-human nature.

Joan pressed one hand to Leigh's shoulder as she slipped her feet back into her boots in turn, and pulled Leigh with her down the knoll. "Let's go celebrate."

It was exhilarating and terrifying. Every day, Leigh felt like she was changing in some small way into someone new, something difficult to define. One thing she knew for certain was that she loved Joan more than ever, and Leigh clung to the normalcy of it.

Joan waved her free hand, casting a cantrip for floating sparks of light like fireflies dancing in the morning sun. Such magic used to require Joan to speak. She'd grown more adept at using her newer powers.

The best time to watch Joan was when she wasn't looking back. Her shoulders were broad and strong, her torso lean and hidden by the coat until the flare of her hips. Her hair was combed into a thick ponytail under a knit hat a few shades of brown lighter than her skin.

Dark brown eyes darted from the trail to the crows to the path ahead—always searching for the next threat. Joan was protecting them, as always. Protecting Leigh.

"I swear," Joan said in a grumble. "There's more damned crows every day."

Joan appeared annoyed at their presence, but also at their proximity, which was closer than usual.

"Maybe you could befriend them," Leigh said.

Joan grunted and kept walking. She claimed she couldn't tell them apart. Leigh could—that one had a scar on its beak, and this one was missing a few tail feathers. Rufus circled closest, so named because one side of his chest was always in puffy disarray, giving him a ruffian appearance.

At least Leigh thought he was a "he." Rufus never landed close enough for anyone to handle him.

"Trying to . . . connect . . . with them just gives me a headache," Joan said, irritation lacing her tone.

"Such an old grump," Leigh teased.

Joan's frown cracked. "You love me anyway."

"I really do. What does that say about me?"

"Good taste."

"True." Leigh tried to swing their clasped hands between them, but Joan resisted, not one to give in to idle playfulness.

She was always so serious.

The trail ended at a back road bordering the Matthews homestead. Leigh sensed hidden squirrels skittering away from them, small heartbeats racing as Joan and Leigh got closer. Something bigger—a rabbit?—froze until they crossed the road and stepped onto the official parcel of Matthews land.

As they meandered through the spacious garden, weaving between rows of raised beds, Leigh trailed her free hand over the stems, the stalks, and the leaves of herbs flourishing despite the winter cold. The rosemary was so healthy tiny unseasonable purple blossoms nestled among its leaves.

Each touch made Leigh happier than she already was on this day of days.

"Probably have to build up the fire again," Joan said as she stomped mud from her boots on the back porch of the two-story Craftsman farmhouse.

Leigh stopped herself from responding, unsure of how to explain she could sense the fire was low and the coals still hot. Thinking of the fire made her fingers itch. Yet another quirk about herself she didn't understand.

She paused to wipe her feet in the mudroom before they entered the house proper, then walked through the kitchen to the dining room. An oak table with seating for ten was half-covered by books and journals. Some of the piles were Joan's, in her ongoing search to find some mention of an ancestor with powers like hers. The rest was Leigh's research in an attempt to learn about how she knew the things she knew, and did the things she did.

Leigh didn't like to think of the name for what she was—*bloodling*. Calling herself so put her too close to the monsters still walking her nightmares.

She had fewer of those since she spent her nights in Joan's arms.

"Hungry?" Leigh asked, though she herself wasn't. Still, she liked to make sure Joan had everything she needed. Joan tended to focus on what needed to be done, and not always on taking care of herself so she had the strength to do it.

"Not exactly," Joan said, arching one eyebrow in clear suggestion as she tugged Leigh closer.

A buzzing broke the silence.

"Thought you took the day off," Leigh said.

Joan's scoff spoke for her as she answered her phone. She turned to one side to be polite. Leigh with her heightened senses heard every word.

"Joan, it's Dayton," a deep voice said, as if Joan wouldn't recognize the voice of the watch leader.

"I'm busy," Joan said, glancing at Leigh.

Leigh hid her discomfort at Dayton's voice. It wasn't the man himself making her uneasy, but rather his position on the town watch. No one whose work it was to fight vampires would accept Leigh hiding her true nature from them, even if she had no intention of hurting anyone.

"I know," Dayton said. "But we've got a situation."

"There's always a situation," Joan said. "I'm busy."

Joan rarely took time for herself. She'd spent several busy days working with the coven to fortify future crops by blessing the land before the spring plantings, and busier nights teaching her war witch combat skills to the town watch.

Dayton ignored her and pressed on. "We've got another group at the northern checkpoint. They want to talk to you."

"Tell 'em to take a number."

Leigh gave Joan's hand a tug, a reminder to be nice.

Joan rolled her eyes and softened her tone. "Let 'em camp in the square. I'll check in first thing tomorrow."

"They're . . . insistent. I wouldn't call you, Joan, honest, but they're twitchier than the usual bunch."

Visitors were common to the Calvert borders. Word had spread throughout the region that Calvert was one of the safer places to live since no vampires or human thralls had been seen near the town for months.

"How many?"

"Three women," Dayton said. "And they've got a kid with them."

"What the hell?" Joan muttered.

Leigh agreed. Why would such a small party bring a child onto the open road? Calvert might be safer than most, but beyond the limits of town watches or the walls of bigger cities, bandits, vampires and their thralls preyed on travelers.

"They say where they're from?"

"They claim to be from Arock," Dayton said.

Leigh raked her memories until a reference manifested. Arock was small enough to be considered a village, most of a day's drive away in the southeastern part of Oregon.

"What the hell are they doing way over here?"

"Said they came to talk to the Calvert binder, and only the binder. Hence my call."

Joan bit back an obvious curse. She cast a sorrowful, apologetic glance at Leigh. "Take 'em to the library. I'll be there in half an hour."

As Joan disconnected the call, Leigh wanted to curse with her since it was now their wedding day. She kept those thoughts to herself. Having just married someone equal in stature to the town mayor, she couldn't complain when duty called.

Then again, she didn't want to be away from Joan either.

"Why don't I come with you?"

Joan appeared as shocked as Leigh felt at making the

suggestion. Leigh didn't travel into town unless necessary.

"Yeah? Even though . . ." Joan stopped herself, no doubt holding back on bringing up the thing they didn't talk about.

They never spoke of the glamour spell Leigh used to hide her appearance from the other residents of Calvert. Only Joan had seen the countless scars of vampire bites, or the yellow sclera of her eyes revealing her as a bloodling.

It had been Leigh's idea to keep using the spell, but she'd become increasingly uncomfortable administering it, and instead chose to remain at home, unobserved and unglamoured.

Leigh brushed her thumb over the newly seated ring on Joan's finger.

She knew what Joan was really asking. Leigh hadn't worn the glamour in days. No one came to the house, and Leigh had found herself using the spell less and less as she spent her time in the back garden or alone in the house.

She also never told Joan how much the spell hurt.

"Any chance Willy will be there?" Leigh asked.

Joan shook her head. "Shouldn't be, and if he is, I'll ask Dayton to put him outside. I told him you're afraid of big dogs. Kind of insinuated they'd used them at the vineyard."

Leigh had been subjected to cruelty and torture in the vineyard where she'd been held captive by vampires, but no dogs had been involved. She loved dogs, but Willy, Dayton's enormous Siberian husky, might sense her otherness, and his attention would lead to questions she didn't want to answer.

Joan had once again lied in some way to protect her. Would a time come when Joan thought it was too much?

"Give me ten minutes," Leigh said, shoving aside any thoughts beyond the immediate.

"I'll go warm up Luther." Joan grabbed the keys from a hook by the door. Her customized Range Rover, an enchanted mobile fort despite the scratches and dents in its faded black paint, was parked in the gravel driveway in front of the house.

Leigh kept the necessary herbs tucked away in a bathroom in the back of the house, far from their communal bed on the second floor. She washed herself, mixed the ingredients, and added her blood before finishing the ritual of preparing the solution.

When she rubbed it into the required locations on her body, she forced herself not to hiss. The glamour burned against her skin more than it used to, a necessary pain.

If this was the cost to stay by Joan's side, she'd pay it.

CHAPTER 3

THE MORNING FROST had melted by the time Joan led Leigh by the hand to the library's front doors. In the parking lot, Willy whined behind the half-upraised window in Dayton's pickup truck. Joan squeezed Leigh's hand, hoping it felt reassuring.

Calvert's small-town library had double duty as a community center. Bigger than the century-old City Hall, the library contained half a dozen conference rooms, each of them often reserved by one local organization or another as needed. Calvert's coven met weekly in the largest room. The town watch used the same space.

Speaking of the town watch, Dayton nodded in greeting. Before Joan's return to Calvert the previous year, Dayton had been the town watch leader. He now deferred to Joan as both binder witch to Calvert and seasoned war witch.

He loomed a full head taller than the handful of watch members clustered next to him, and his wavy dark hair fell past his broad shoulders and thick beard.

Dayton managed to appear apologetic to Joan and threatening to the newcomers, a group of strangers standing inside the doors.

Though no one's stance was hostile, the tension was thick.

Three women and one kid. The women shared a gaunt, haggard appearance, their clothes loose and hanging where they should have been snug. One of the women was younger, late 20s maybe, with dirty blond hair and eyes a little too close together. The other two women were gray-haired, though they might not be as old as they looked.

None of them had the stance of fighters—those who stood with their hands free and centered their weight in case they had to defend themselves in an abrupt conflict. The youngest woman had her wringing hands clasped in front of her. Another had her arms crossed as she glared at anyone who caught her eye.

The boy, who stood the farthest back, must have been about ten years old. His black hair was unevenly cut and his shoes were too big for him. His gaze wavered between Joan and Dayton, never staring for longer than a second or two, trying to determine which of them was a bigger threat. He must have been forced to run for his life more than once.

None of the adults were physically foreboding, yet there was a rangy desperation to them, twitching the small hairs at the nape of Joan's neck. Desperate people were unpredictable, and until Joan found out what they wanted with her she'd best be on her guard.

Then again, wasn't she always on guard?

"I'm Joan Matthews, of the Calvert coven." Joan offered her hand to the woman standing before the others.

The woman ignored the gesture and didn't introduce herself in kind. She was a head shorter than Joan, and the lines on her face suggested her frowning expression was permanent.

Fine. Since they were going to skip the pleasantries.

"What's so important it couldn't wait?" Joan asked.

"We want answers."

The business-like nature was welcome. The tone was not.

The woman glanced at the people she'd come with before speaking again. "Word reached Arock you've claimed all the land to the east of here, all the way to Idaho."

The claiming happened over a year ago. These folks from Arock weren't the first to come to Calvert for a blessing or protection or who knew what else from Joan. It had been a long while since someone had claimed they'd only just learned about the greater binding.

And this was the first Joan had heard about the binding extending that far east. Much of the terrain was empty, most of the smaller towns overrun and eradicated decades ago by vampire lords. The people who had survived had banded together to form something akin to city-states—areas easier to defend with a sturdy watch or a coven, if not both.

Arock was so small, she'd only heard of it in passing years ago. Something about it being so far out in barren territory, it wasn't likely to survive on its own.

Joan called from memory her usual spiel.

"I didn't then and don't now have the intention of affecting any community's autonomy. My only hope is to share my strength with the land, to repel the influence of any vampires in the area who seek to claim the land for themselves."

She looked at them all in turn, hoping her sincerity and conviction would persuade them she was no threat.

None of them looked convinced.

"Well, our land is blighted, and our people are starving," the woman said, her tone flat despite the severity of her words. "What are you going to do about it?"

That was the rub, wasn't it? Having claimed all that land, wasn't she in some way responsible for all of it?

Then again, if she ran all over the place putting out fires and shoring up farmland, she was bound to piss off the Portland High Coven. Unincorporated territory like Arock fell under their jurisdiction as the regional governing body. Covens like

Calvert's were supposed to stick within their own established boundaries.

She'd already received two strongly worded missives to tend to her own business in Calvert, and when she requested an audience to discuss the situation, the High Coven had informed her—again via message—they would be in touch. So far, there'd been no further word.

In the meantime, dozens of representatives from all over the region had visited Calvert inquiring, like these folks, about Joan's intentions.

"What exactly do you expect me to do?" Joan asked, matching the not quite respectful tone, but not outright rude either. When in doubt, equivocate.

"Come to Arock today and bless the land."

A binder witch's blessing instilled power in the land, improving growth and shoring up plants against pests or disease.

"Why not request the Portland High Coven?"

Joan held back from mentioning how her binder skills were needed here in Calvert, not off in the sticks somewhere, and that she was in enough trouble with the Portland witches. Not to mention the fact that she didn't want to be anywhere today but home with Leigh.

As if Leigh had heard her thoughts, Leigh moved closer, resting her hand on Joan's lower back.

One of the other women leaned forward to mutter in the speaking woman's ear. "I told you, Ronnie. She's not going to come. We're better off getting her to sever the connection."

Joan shifted her weight, not happy about the suggestion. Severing a connection to the land was serious business, and a horrid energy drain. Either way, she didn't relish the idea of traveling to unfamiliar territory and putting herself at risk for people she didn't know.

"You're the one, not the High Coven, who claimed the land without asking us," Ronnie said, answering Joan's question. "The least you can do is make sure we don't starve to death. Clear the blight from the winter crops. That'll be enough to get us to the spring. The blessing will hold into the planting season."

"Waste of time," the youngest woman said when Joan didn't answer right away. She dropped her eyes when Joan glared at her.

The leader, Ronnie, scoffed before she spoke again. "What's the point of binding to the whole damned state if you're not going to take care of it? May as well hand us over to the monsters if you're not going to tend to it."

If it was meant to be a dig, it hit bone. Leigh flinched beside her and Joan grunted, one hand twitching toward her knife at the woman's tone before she suppressed her instincts.

The kid moved behind one of his elders. Guess he'd decided Joan was the bigger threat.

Great. Now she was intimidating children.

"We should go," Leigh said, low enough only Joan would hear.

We? Leigh had never accompanied Joan on a trip out of town. Joan had never asked her to, and Leigh had never once offered.

"You'll come with me?" Joan asked.

Leigh nodded, though her expression was uneasy. "It's our day, right? Doesn't matter where we are."

On the one hand, the thought of Leigh on the open road, out where anything could happen and often did, made Joan want to break things. Leigh had been through enough these past few years and deserved a peaceful life.

On the other . . . sure, it was dangerous, but Joan could handle anything they were likely to run into.

"Out and back," Joan promised. She didn't want to ask about another possible issue out loud. "We'll have to crash there overnight."

The glamour spell should last that long, but only Leigh

knew for sure.

Leigh nodded, more certain this time. "Should be fine," she said, and Joan understood the implication. The spell would hold until they returned.

Joan turned back to the borderline hostile visitors, her eyes drawn to the boy though she spoke to Ronnie.

"Best to leave as soon as possible."

Though Joan was going to give them what they asked for, neither Ronnie nor any of the others expressed any thanks or relief.

Luther's huge tires hummed on the aged asphalt as Joan drove down a remote highway in Eastern Oregon. The high desert terrain was already sparse, and the winter cold made everything more desolate. Scattered scrub brush and arid rock formations stretched for miles, with no human structures to break the monotony.

Some song Joan hadn't heard in years played on the sound system, loud enough to add to the timelessness of the drive and low enough they could talk without yelling. Dayton's snoring added a relaxing counterpoint. He was sprawled across the backseat, his long legs folded into the space behind Leigh's seat.

"You said you'd never been this far east," Leigh said in a pause between songs.

Joan had traveled for years moving from place to place to combat vampires and their thralls. Most of the time she'd spent in small towns like the one they were from and the one they drove toward, but she'd also spent a lot of time in the cities up and down the west coast.

Joan shook her head while keeping her eyes on the road. "Not much reason to come out here. Just like everybody else, vampires want territory that's worth a damn, and most of this isn't of much use to anyone save a few persistent farmers. Sparse human populations don't make for a sustainable diet."

Damn. She shouldn't have said that. Leigh knew more about the feeding habits of vampires than Joan ever would. And she didn't want to hint at any of Leigh's history. Joan did that a lot—tried to modify the words she chose so she didn't mention anything that might remind Leigh of her past captivity.

"I spent most of my time up and down the coast," she said, keeping up the flow of conversation. "Maybe got as far inland as the east side of the Cascade mountains."

Better land, more people, more attractive for the kinds of vampire lords she used to hunt down and kill.

"Anyway, could be these folks decided to stay out here precisely because it wasn't attractive. I mean, people live everywhere, right? In unreasonable, unsustainable climates all over the world, I'm told. Maybe it was somebody's bright idea to stake a claim in the middle of nowhere, convinced that no one would come knocking."

It wasn't a farfetched idea. These Arock pilgrims were an odd bunch. Since Joan had agreed to come back with them, they didn't have much room to be so contrary. Maybe it was a character trait no matter what the situation.

They drove a ruggedly outfitted van. Another truck followed behind Joan with three more members of the Calvert town watch. Joan had told them they didn't need to come. They'd been emphatic about supporting her, providing backup even if she didn't think she'd need it.

They weren't the only ones. Dayton, too, had insisted on coming, and had cracked a couple of jokes at Leigh about making sure he was around to hold Joan's stuff—another attempt in a long line of them to try to get Leigh to relax around him.

It was obvious he sensed Leigh's discomfort—he was always conciliatory and funny, though that might be out of respect for Joan—and in a rugged kind of way, charming. So far, Dayton hadn't been inside the house, which was considered not only Joan's home territory, but also Leigh's.

Neither of them wanted anyone getting too close. Not with the secret they were keeping.

The golden hours of a wintry afternoon cast a sheen across the desolate landscape. Everything could look beautiful if you splashed enough orange and red across it, including this land far from any other civilization. Land now under Joan's protection.

"Can you feel anything here?" Leigh asked, as if she'd read Joan's mind. "They said the land was sick."

Joan's hands tensed on the steering wheel. "Not yet. Once I get out of the ride, though—touch the ground, taste the air—I might be able to get a better feel for this blight they're talking about."

All the power Joan had claimed by binding herself to the land, on top of the skills she'd acquired as a war witch, not to mention her own innate abilities, should be more than enough to treat anything affecting the crops.

The scrub gave way to barren fields. Leafless trees broke the monotony of flat brown farmland. A few farmhouses poked up from time to time, their paint long faded, their structures sagging under the weight of time and poor maintenance. Nothing moved, and she saw no other people.

"Why would anyone live out here?" Joan muttered to herself, though they'd already speculated on the subject.

The highway ended, and a sign at a T-shaped intersection pointed left toward town. Dayton shuffled in the backseat when Joan decelerated, yawning like a bear when he woke.

"Jesus," he said. "What a pit. You can sure tell they don't have a binder."

The land was open, with few barriers to mark a border. Arock had only a couple of blocks of buildings, most of them abandoned. The only two-story building was the boarded-up town hall at the end of the street in front of them.

As they approached, several people emerged from the main door armed with rifles and shotguns, though none were aimed at Luther. Not exactly a welcoming committee.

"Joan," Leigh said in warning.

"I've seen worse, but yeah," Joan said, and reached across the space between them to squeeze Leigh's thigh. "No need to worry yet, but you might want to stay here. Luther's new enchantments will keep you safe."

Joan had spelled a few nasty surprises for anyone who tried to take a shot at her ride.

She parked at an angle for easy egress, in case they had to make a run for it. If this was all some kind of trap, these people would regret it.

The van parked near the building and its occupants joined their townsfolk. Another handful of people materialized, outnumbering the Calvert group four to one. They were all rangy, with heavy eyes and untrusting faces. The child hugged one of the women, then ran inside the building.

Joan stood at the head of her own group a few steps in front of Luther, with Dayton and the others assuming positions that implied they wouldn't settle for any drama.

Something here was odd. There'd been no checkpoints or town watch to stop them from coming into town, and Joan hadn't noticed anyone keeping lookout on the roads. A place like this shouldn't have been able to survive on its own without a binder or a watch for protection. A small community like this would attract a lone vampire.

"About time you showed up," the lead man said. He was older than Joan by maybe a decade, and though he didn't raise his rifle, his hands tightened on its butt and forestock. His salt-and-pepper hair was cut close to his pale skull, and his clothes were ill-fitting and stained by dirt.

A few others grunted in agreement.

"You've got a lot of nerve," one woman said. She was shorter than average, with a broad body despite her gaunt face. "Laying claim to land without warning, without talking to anyone about it. Who does that?"

"Didn't care to check on anyone after?" someone else said.

The voices started to overlap, the general content the same. A couple of the bigger men started to step forward. Dayton and his companions followed suit until Joan raised a hand and motioned for them to stay put.

"You people asked me to come here," Joan said. "I understand what I did affected you, and I'm here to do what I can to make that right, but don't think you have the right to question or challenge me."

She knew how she appeared to these people. A Black woman covered in weapons and driving an armored vehicle. Most of the time when she came to a remote place like this, assuming she hadn't been invited, the locals thought she'd come to take over.

Joan almost smiled at the thought that she probably could. And those weren't the only ways she captured attention.

The moment the thought passed through her head, a warm shiver crept up her spine to the base of her skull, not pleasant but familiar. Shadows created by the waning sunlight danced on the building and on the faces of the townsfolk.

One by one the people stopped glaring at her and turned inquisitive—or wary—glances towards the west, back the way she'd come. She kept her eyes locked on the man in the lead and watched his face as the realization hit him.

Joan, Dayton, Leigh and the others had covered over four hundred miles since leaving Calvert. These wouldn't be the same swarm as back home, but wherever she went the crows answered a call she didn't know she was making.

The crows' cries were sparse at first, then swelled as hundreds of birds descended upon Arock, claiming any surface including the ground. They clustered in groups on the vehicles, the windows of the building, the roof. One tried to land on a man's head before he waved his arms to ward it off.

Only Leigh knew Joan hadn't a clue how to control or communicate with the damned things. Nothing in her father's binder journals or the coven's library held a single clue. Any reference to her ancestor, Agnes Matthews—Agnes of Crows, according to legend—mentioned crows were her familiars, yet didn't reveal how she'd interacted with them.

Guess you couldn't be a legend if you told everyone your secrets, but Joan would give a lot to have some answers. In the meantime, having murders of crows following her around did wonders for her reputation. Like now.

The bitching had simmered down to whispering as the residents of Arock muttered to each other.

"Where's your most hallowed ground?" Joan asked, eager to move this right along. It was bad enough they'd have to camp here overnight.

If she could get her part done, she and the Calvert folks could trade watches until it was time to hit the road at first light.

"We don't have hallowed ground," a woman said, so matter-of-factly it must have been the truth.

That gave Joan pause. Most places had identified a space as the primary point for binding spiritual energy to the land. Many towns like Calvert had built halls or churches over such spaces, the better for covens and communities to focus their energies on the land.

"What happened to it?"

"Never had it."

Most of the places not protected by some sort of blessing or binding with the land were more populated. This place was like traveling back into time or stepping into another dimension.

"Have you ever had a binder?" Joan asked.

After trading looks with a few of the people with him, the leader shook his head. "Never needed one."

Suspicion flared, though she sensed no immediate threat

from these people. They'd been cowed by her flying entourage. Those damned birds were good for something.

"So how exactly have you protected yourself from any vampire lords?" From what she'd seen so far, this place would be easy pickings for an enterprising vampire and a handful of thralls. Town defenses were nonexistent, with only one fortified building, and unless there was a bunker underneath it, all the vampires had to do was wait them out.

"We don't have anything they want," someone answered.

Stupid thing to say. Vampires wanted blood and power. This place would immediately supply one and de facto provide the other once they controlled everyone here.

Were these people lying? Could be subterfuge, or the usual propensity of small-town folk to keep their business to themselves. No time to get into it now, not if she wanted to perform the blessing before it got dark.

"All right then," Joan said. She'd ponder all this weirdness later. "Take me to the nearest place where this blight is affecting your crops."

Joan beckoned to Leigh, who climbed down from Luther and joined her. Dayton and the others trailed behind them.

The walk wasn't long before they reached a broad field a half mile from where she'd parked. In a patch of land framed by swaths of dry dirt, the remains of a crop of winter vegetables lay wilted and covered in a thick, white, pasty muck. Whatever it was, it didn't discriminate—though several different types of crops were planted, each had the same layer of blight on its leaves.

Once the destination was clear, Joan took the lead and stopped at the edge of the field. The others stretched alongside her to either side, her allies close by, the Arock residents farther away with all their eyes on her.

Dayton poked at a half-rotted, blighted squash with his boot. It collapsed in on itself, a pile of grimy dust.

One of his buddies thumped him in the arm. "Don't touch it, man."

Dayton, chagrined, scraped the toe of his boot through the dirt. "Never seen anything like this."

Joan had. A long time ago, she had once traveled with her father, Trevon, to a farming enclave near the coast. They'd been hit by a blight like this in the heart of summer, and a thriving community had been crippled by it. It had taken a full coven hours to heal the land.

Well, now it was just her, and she hoped she had the juice for it. She turned to the leader again, who stood several paces away watching her with wary suspicion.

"Magic or circumstance?" she asked.

He shrugged and frowned. "Ain't you the expert? You tell me."

Asshole.

She winced in advance at the thought of tasting the sickness, but she needed to know what she was dealing with, and how deep it went.

Joan offered Leigh a hidden wink—wouldn't want her to worry—before crouching down to one knee. She sank the fingers of her left hand into the dirt, closing her eyes as she opened her mouth to breathe in the air.

A dry, musty taste coated her tongue, and the spiritual residue on the earth—an unseen malevolence on its health—felt like she'd bashed her elbow into hardwood. Joan cringed, though she didn't pull away. Without moving she sank the essence of herself through her hand into the dirt, melding the core of her with the straining lifeblood of the land.

The blight hadn't sunk far into the roots, yet the earth beneath the field was ... tired. Joan didn't sense any nearby ley lines, or clusters of power where she could reach. This land was too far from the magic she lived nearly on top of, and after years of giving its soul to keep the crops alive, there was little left to replenish itself against what appeared to be a natural attack.

The sun was setting as Joan closed her mouth, pushing aside the need for something to wash the taste from her tongue. She could heal this on her own, though it would be taxing.

She glanced at Dayton and he nodded, perhaps sensing her true question. When this was over, she'd need to crash hard, which meant he had the first watch when she was done.

Leigh's gaze held everything else Joan needed—support, and strength. Love.

Joan sat in the dirt, closing her eyes. She envisioned a line from the base of her skull, down the length of her spine, through her tailbone, and into the earth. She pushed aside the noise of the people and their proximity, the birds and their squawking, the need from the townsfolk and the land.

She cast it all down, and summoned the power that pulsed in her veins.

Back home, the answering power of the earth would hum along her nerves, its resonance as deep and regular as a heartbeat. Here, what should have been a thriving pulse was a dull, tinny whine, the power a trickle where it should have been a river.

Every month the communion she shared with the earth via the ley lines on the knoll replenished the core of her own magic. Now, she would feed the same power into this patch of earth.

Soon, all was quiet, even the crows and the wind, or so it seemed to Joan as she gave back to the earth what she had been given.

CHAPTER 4

LEIGH WAS NO stranger to magic. Everyone in Calvert had seen spells cast, had observed or participated in one ritual or another. Growing up next to the Matthews family—not to mention falling in love with one of them—meant she'd been more familiar with binder magic than most of the other residents.

She'd never seen anything like this.

Joan sat motionless in the dirt. Forty-five minutes later, the sky had faded to purple, and Leigh noticed the changes in the field. In the shallow ditches between crop rows, the dirt darkened as if saturated with water though it remained dry. The muted brown earth slowly darkened until it was almost black, as if the soil had been mixed with a powerful fertilizer.

The sections with rotten vegetables decayed faster, collapsing in while falling apart. Ruined crops and vines and leaves disintegrated, sinking and intermixing with the dirt below.

Some of the other crops—kale, root vegetables—must have been salvageable because the blight receded from the leaves. One by one, each of the plants straightened as if bolstered from within, every leaf hearty and healthy.

It was slow, painstaking work, and Joan never wavered as

she delivered a miracle. Hours passed, and while Leigh could hear the wonder in the quiet voices of the Calvert folks and the stunned silence of the Arock residents, she watched Joan, who never once opened her eyes or took a break.

The spellcraft was impressive, yes, but not as much as Joan.

By the time Leigh noticed the chill, most of the people around her were shifting from foot to foot, jostling in place to keep warm. Joan's lips were purple in the cold, though she still didn't move until, finally, she did.

Joan pulled her hands from the dirt and brushed them against each other before wiping them off on her pant legs. She rose to one knee, took a deep breath, and pushed herself upright.

"It's done," she said, as brusque and businesslike as usual.

The fatigue in her slower movements was obvious to Leigh. Joan had pushed too hard. It didn't happen often, not with the power she drew from the land back home, but nothing here appeared capable of replenishing her. Leigh wished she could take her home immediately.

When Joan turned to the lead man who'd spoken earlier, he said nothing. Behind him, the rest of the people turned their backs and headed back to the town hall. The leader and Ronnie from the road group were the last to go, watching Joan and Dayton and the others as if ensuring they wouldn't follow.

Joan shook her head but didn't say anything.

"Seriously?" Dayton looked ready to spit nails.

Leigh couldn't believe it either. Sure, they might have been angry at the necessity of asking Joan here, which might have excused the lack of thanks for making the trip, but . . . all Joan's effort, and not even the civility of a goodbye?

"Forget it, man." Joan shrugged her shoulders, her movement slow and exaggerated. "I don't want to deal with them anymore."

Leigh stepped closer, ready to offer physical support if Joan keeled over. Joan only took her hand, her fingers freezing cold, and for once Leigh was glad her own skin was so warm.

"Let's camp in the open," Joan said when they'd walked back to their vehicles. "Four-hour watch shifts."

"As long as you keep your name out of the rotation," Dayton said. "Anything comes calling, we'll see it first."

After moving to a parking lot next to a half-burned-down former feed store on the edge of town, Joan and Leigh curled up fully clothed on Luther's folded-over backseat while Dayton joined the other members of the watch.

"You sure it's safe here?" Leigh asked.

Those Arock people had made a poor impression. Joan might be sure they were safe, but Leigh knew from experience people weren't always what they appeared. She was proof of that herself.

Joan's eyes were already closed. She looked comfortable and content, bundled in these close quarters. She'd probably slept here more times than Leigh could count.

"Luther's enchanted to warn me of any spellcraft," Joan said as she pulled Leigh into her arms. "And I'll wake up long before anything gets past the watch, so get some sleep. We'll head home as soon as it's light."

Joan's breathing steadied as she fell asleep, leaving Leigh alone to face the threat of the night. The dark outside could be hiding anything, and if a vampire got anywhere close to them—

Joan kissed the top of her head. Though fast asleep, she was trying to comfort Leigh.

Leigh sank into the blankets and the solace of Joan's embrace though she wasn't cold. She forced herself to close her eyes, to focus on what she could feel and hear.

Outside, the others prepared for the long night. With her better-than-average hearing, their conversations were as loud to her as if they'd been standing right beside Luther.

"I'll take second shift," Dayton said as he climbed into the front passenger seat of the other truck. "Don't fuck around, and keep your eyes open."

The others grunted in acknowledgement, one of them climbing in the backseat of the same truck. Ten minutes later, Leigh could hear Dayton's bass snores, proving he could fall asleep anywhere.

Two other men had taken the first watch and took turns walking the periphery of their makeshift camp.

"Those guys were assholes," one said when he'd rejoined the other. "If I had Joan's power, I'd show them a thing or two."

"Well, you don't, Rory, so keep your focus on your job." That was Huck, a big Caucasian man with patchy brown hair who didn't talk much. He always had a polite nod for Leigh, and as far as Leigh could tell in the few times she'd seen him, deferred to Dayton and Joan.

The fourth man tossed and turned in the backseat a few times before he, too, fell asleep. All was quiet for a while, and Leigh heard nothing until a lighter's flick when one of the men lit a cigarette.

"That Leigh's an odd one, yeah?" Rory said as he exhaled his cigarette smoke. "She don't talk much."

"Wish you didn't," Huck muttered.

"She doesn't come to town all that often or hang out with the other women. I mean, she's shacked up with the binder. You'd think she might, I don't know, participate more in the community or whatever."

"If you're stupid enough to say some shit like that around Joan about her woman," Huck said, "I'm not even digging your grave. Nice knowing you."

Rory didn't say anything else.

What would people like them do to her if they knew what—how Leigh was different? Few if any ever said people like her deserved compassion or understanding. Only justice or vengeance.

They would call her a monster.

Would anyone stop to listen to her explanations? That none

of it had been by her choice?

With those thoughts running rampant—whether people she'd known her whole life would either force her out of her hometown or kill her outright—Leigh didn't sleep at all.

Morning broke cold and dim, the sunlight hidden behind low gray clouds thick with an impending storm. The crows were quiet, as subdued as the scenery and the weather.

Not a single Arock resident came to see them off.

Once again, Dayton rode with Joan and Leigh as they headed back to Calvert. Leigh drove the first leg out of town, while beside her Joan tilted her head against the window and closed her eyes. To Leigh's eyes, Joan was wiped out.

"That was weird, right?" Dayton asked from the backseat. "Like those folks last summer from Estacada who wanted your protection but didn't want you to come visiting."

"Not so rare." Joan covered a yawn. "A lot of folks when I was fighting on the road—they were the same way."

"What do you think these guys are hiding?"

Joan stared ahead and didn't answer for a while. Leigh focused on the road, though she stole more glances at Joan the longer she stayed quiet.

"I don't know," Joan said.

The steady speeds and slow rocking of the SUV on the highway lulled Joan back to sleep. After another hour of monotonous driving, Leigh settled into the task and relaxed her shoulders against the seat.

"How much longer do you think you can hide?"

Leigh jerked her hands in surprise, and the SUV swerved before she got it under control.

"What do you mean by that?"

Adrenaline spiked by fear made her sit up straighter. Did he know? How had he found out? With Joan asleep, if he attacked her now—

"I don't know how much sleep you got last night," Dayton

said, his voice confused. "I can take a shift if you get tired."

Her heart raced so fast the beat of it thumped in her ears.

Drive. He'd asked how long she thought she could drive. She needed to calm down before she sparked his suspicion for real.

"I'm fine," she said, meeting his questioning gaze through the rearview mirror before she looked back at the road.

"Well, let me know if you change your mind."

"Okay," she said, though she knew she wouldn't. Anything she could do to appear normal now was crucial.

He didn't know anything. Her secret was safe.

Leigh turned up the music, hoping to dissuade any further conversation.

CHAPTER 5

JOAN USED TO think of herself as an early riser. Lately, even if she woke with the sunrise, Leigh's side of the bed was often cold.

Today, Joan had slept much later than usual since it was noon. Purging Arock's blight had taken a lot out of her. She dressed and set out to find her wife.

Five minutes later, she'd tracked down Leigh in the garden. Joan closed the back door to the house and ambled down the porch stairs.

"What are you doing?" Joan asked as Leigh stood next to a newly constructed bird-feeding platform, one topped with a flat tin roof. "Trying to train a wild bird?"

Leigh tapped on the tin until one bird, the one with the ruffled chest feathers, landed on the platform. She tossed a handful of nuts on the tin, clicking and tutting at the birds as they shuffled each other for position.

"Well, I wouldn't say I'm training him." Leigh brushed crumbs from her palms. "Let's call it striking up a friendship."

Joan scoffed. "You gonna make friends with all of 'em?"

The crows were intimidating. Her attempts to commune

with them had failed, and only in the heat of battle did they seem to understand what she wanted from them. Not that she wanted much more than for them to attack her enemies. What else would they be good for?

"Just starting with Rufus."

Was it odd Leigh had named one? Maybe not. Maybe it was just unsettling because Joan hadn't thought of it first. Hell, she couldn't even tell them apart.

Maybe it was another way Leigh was different. Even now, Leigh seemed preoccupied by thoughts she wasn't sharing, a pensiveness that happened with more frequency. When Joan had asked about it before, Leigh had claimed nothing was wrong.

A break in the clouds cast watery sunlight over Leigh's profile, and Joan was captivated as always by her beauty. After everything Leigh had been through, nothing could detract from the quiet strength reflected in the elegant lines of her face.

When was the last time Joan had shown Leigh how much she wanted her, no matter how much Leigh had changed?

She tugged at Leigh's hand, and when Leigh finally looked back, Joan tipped her head forward and offered a suggestion without speaking. Sometimes talking was difficult because they couldn't bridge the gap between them to get it all out in the open. Sometimes they couldn't talk because the words got in the way.

Leigh scoffed, with affection and clear understanding of what Joan was implying.

The first kiss was always a surprise, the heart-stopping, breath-stealing warmth and tenderness of it. Not a lot of things could kick Joan's ass or knock her off her feet. One kiss from Leigh weakened her knees.

Leigh traced along Joan's jaw with the tip of one finger, light enough to send shivers down Joan's spine. Sometimes, they didn't need words to say what needed saying, and other ways of communicating were much more fruitful.

Her offer extended and accepted, Joan led Leigh back towards the house. She took a moment inside the mudroom to kick off her boots while Leigh wiped down her bare feet before they made their way through the kitchen and the downstairs rooms to the stairs. Leigh led the way now, and Joan was pleased and eager to follow.

They passed the room that had been Joan's as a child, and the rooms belonging to family members long gone until they reached the master bedroom at the end of the hall on the south side of the house.

Joan and Leigh had changed a lot to make this room theirs, including all new furniture and a different color paint on the walls. What had once been a reading nook was now a meditation space they each used at different times of the day. A few of Leigh's older charcoal sketches adorned the walls, along with a few things Joan had picked up in her travels over the years, though there weren't many of those. Joan had preferred to carry little with her on the open road.

Joan saw none of it as she led Leigh to the bed. They didn't bother helping each other strip. The important part was to get naked and together as soon as possible, not waste any time with seduction. Joan's gaze lingered on every inch of revealed skin as Leigh removed her clothes. Leigh wasn't self-conscious about her scars—the marks of a dark experience—and the grace of her movement compelled Joan to ditch her clothes faster.

Leigh's eyes were hungry, matching the ache in Joan's belly.

The eyes were the hardest thing to adapt to, considering Leigh's many subtle changes. The love and want in her brown irises was the same, but the bloodling yellow sometimes captured the light in an ethereal, unsettling way, triggering warning instincts Joan knew rationally she didn't need to heed.

Making love to Leigh had always been a quiet joy. Succumbing to Leigh's pull, and the desire she always stirred in Joan had been as easy as sliding through water. Now, there was some part of Joan waiting for something to change, though so far nothing had.

The foreplay was brief—Joan was already wet, and ready. She brushed her thumb over one of Leigh's tight nipples, and Leigh grabbed her hand and pulled it between her own legs.

"No teasing," she said, and reclaimed Joan's lips before she lifted Joan bodily over her.

The strength wasn't as surprising anymore, and Leigh wasn't blatant about it. Instead, she'd press her advantage in more subtle ways—holding Joan in place while she had her way, or holding herself up with abdominal strength, putting Joan's to shame.

Or now, when she pulled Joan's arm in entreaty.

"Harder," Leigh said, and hissed when Joan complied. "So good."

And it was good, but it was also different, more fervent than Leigh usually preferred. Joan drove them both further, pushing her endurance, demanding more from Leigh with her touch, and Leigh never surrendered. It was like she claimed her orgasm as something hard-fought and hard-won.

"Again. Please."

Joan slowed until she found the rhythm again, one Leigh responded to with her hips, and then she drove Leigh higher. Leigh's limbs were taut in response to Joan's thrusts, her hands clamped against the slats of the headboard, her cries louder as she peaked again.

No sooner had she caught her breath than she flipped Joan onto her back, reversing their positions. Her kisses were consuming and deep until Joan broke to catch her breath. Leigh slid herself down the bed, planting kisses over Joan's breasts and belly until she kissed between Joan's thighs.

Joan didn't have to tell Leigh what she wanted. Leigh sank into Joan's body and took her fill. Relentless. Leigh was relentless, clamping her arms around Joan's thighs until the only give, the only place Joan could push back was against Leigh's mouth, and Leigh moaned every time she did.

Leigh loosened her hold, sliding her hands to clutch at Joan's hips, lifting Joan to her mouth. Joan surrendered, to Leigh, to Leigh's desire, to her own rapture as the joy of being with the only woman she had ever wanted filled her as it always did. The sensation in her thighs swelled, tingled in her limbs in tandem with the pulsing in her clit, all hinting at the climax Leigh was driving her toward.

The hands against her hips were warmer now, hot on her skin. The heat in them increasing along with the swell of her impending orgasm—the higher she rose, the hotter Leigh's hands until the pain mingled with pleasure, sweeping her away. Her vision flared white, and her ears rang with the power and potency of what Leigh made her feel.

When she could think again, the ringing faded to thunder as her heart beat staccato in her chest.

Leigh cried in dismay, a stark contrast to Joan's bliss. Tears filled Leigh's eyes, along with more than a ghost of fear.

"I—I didn't—I'm sorry." She sobbed and covered her mouth until she caught her breath. "I didn't mean to, Joan. I don't know how to—I'm so sorry."

Confused, Joan raised herself up to prop on her elbows, then hissed at new pain when she moved.

Blistered skin in the shape of Leigh's hands marred her hips.

CHAPTER 6

LEIGH BURNED THROUGH the first pair of gloves the next morning. Three days later, while she was digging out weeds in one of the herb beds, the second pair were reduced to ash before she smothered the remaining flames with dirt.

By the fifth pair, she'd learned to force herself to relax before her emotions brimmed to the point of overwhelming her. Meanwhile, the front yard, the flower beds on the sides of the house, the back garden, not to mention the hedges and bushes along the back road, had been pruned, mowed, and weeded to perfection.

This morning a flash downpour drove her inside. Some other time, she might have felt welcomed by the fire and by Joan's presence. Today the lack of sound and movement was too close to the feeling of stagnation she'd been trying to overcome.

Joan was focused on the meticulous cleaning of a disassembled pistol on the dining room table. Her breakfast dishes hadn't been cleared, only pushed to one side. Without a word, Leigh picked up the half-full plate of cold eggs and potatoes and carried it to the kitchen.

A long silence stretched between them, once a comforting

layer of peace affirming their connection, now a swirling chasm of things undiscussed.

"You missed training again today," Joan said, an abrupt end to the silence. Since the previous fall, Joan had been teaching Leigh some basic self-defense.

"We should . . . hold off on that for now." Leigh winced when her gloves slid against the juice glass she lifted from the table.

"You don't have to wear gloves around me."

"I'm not taking any chances," Leigh said. The gloves were annoying, a sensory-limiting barrier between herself and the world. If they kept her from hurting Joan, they would stay.

"Leigh, it was an accident. I understand. You can't—you can't help it." She set down a tiny scrub brush with an overtaxed sigh.

Her conciliation and loving tolerance made Leigh feel worse.

"Well, I don't understand," Leigh said. "I don't know how it happens."

"How long are you planning on shutting me out?"

Leigh's gloves creaked as she squeezed her hands into fists. "Until I figure this out, I'm not touching you, Joan."

Figuring it out was not going well. She'd been through all the journals in the house from every Matthews witch for the last hundred years—everyone except Trevon's. Reading Joan's father's journals would have been too personal, since he'd been a parent to her as well. Leigh hadn't found a single word to describe what was happening to her.

She wouldn't say it out loud, but she didn't think she was going to find any answers, either. And where did that leave her? She couldn't move forward without knowing how she did what she did, and she couldn't go back to the way she'd been before.

Pacing did no good, so she stretched along the couch in front of the fire—the fire she could sense with every breath. She knew when to add wood because she could feel when the flames lessened. Another mystery to solve with no path to an answer, and there were already too many unanswered questions.

The dishes were done. The house was immaculate thanks to Leigh's incessant cleaning. She picked up one of the logbooks on the table—one she'd already read, written by Trevon's grandmother—and flipped through pages she knew held nothing new to discover.

Joan worked in silence for some time until her task was complete, and the final step of loading the weapon broke the uneasy quiet in the room.

"Listen," Joan said, nonchalant enough for Leigh to gird herself against whatever came next. "This weekend is the Mist gathering, a couple hours drive from here."

Leigh rested her book on her chest. Joan's wariness was evident in her expression and her dark eyes.

"Okay," Leigh said, not understanding at all, but wanting to keep Joan talking if it would take that indecisiveness from her face.

"It's a conclave of witches—war witches, binders, some folks who don't exactly fall into either group. On neutral ground, with white flag protocols in place in case any covens or vampires—sometimes both—want to parley."

Joan took a deep breath as if gathering her strength, or her courage. "I think we should go."

Shock rendered Leigh speechless.

Joan wanted to take her into the heart of—of all the people Leigh had spent months trying to avoid. Months of hiding herself behind a spell that took a little more out of her every time she cast it.

Joan stood. "I know the people who host the gathering—two old war witches, Ollie and Medha—and they have a kind of roaming coven. Fought with them a few years back. I . . . I can ask them some questions about . . . about what's going on with you, without letting them know it's about you."

Leigh tried to calm herself before responding, for fear her hands might once again have a will of their own. "Doesn't seem like a good idea."

With so many witches and vampires in one place, the chance of being discovered was significantly higher and not worth the risk of exposure, of possible persecution, of having to run for her life. Again.

"It's as safe a place as I can think of to take you," Joan said.

"Safe? What if someone figures it out, Joan? All we need is for one person to sense the glamour and it's over for me."

The news that a bloodling was living with a binder—with Joan Matthews of all people—would spread like wildfire.

Joan crossed the room to clasp Leigh's gloved hands and wouldn't let go when Leigh tried to pull away. "I know you're scared. This is our best shot. Someone there will know . . . something."

She was the epitome of confidence in that moment, lending some credence to the words coming out of her mouth.

Leigh didn't share her conviction, but she would always believe in Joan.

Leigh folded her hands together in her lap as Joan guided Luther into the library's parking lot. The only sound in the car since they'd left the house was the windshield wipers. A light rain fell from patches of fast-moving clouds.

Dayton loped across the rain-soaked asphalt until he stood outside Joan's window.

"Pablo's not happy you skipped another coven meeting." He ran a hand through his hair, wiping some rain from his face before drying his palm on his canvas pants. "Says it won't be good if you miss another one."

"Well, he can call me and lodge a complaint," Joan said.

"Not today he can't. Phone lines are down. Just sent Huck and a crew to check on all the towers."

"Who's he got with him?"

Leigh ignored the rest of the conversation, too distracted by where they were going and what might go wrong to listen to coven updates or town watch news. As much as she feared discovery, another possibility was comparably bad. They might not find out anything.

What would she do then?

"What's in Mist?" Dayton asked, attracting Leigh's attention once more.

"An annual conclave on neutral ground," Joan said in a matter-of-fact tone. "I didn't get to the last one. "

A good reason for the trip, without hinting at their true need to go.

"We'll be back in a few days." Joan nodded her head at another of the coven members when he waved as he hurried through the rain to his own car.

"I could use a break," Dayton said. "Give me a minute to grab my go bag and drop Willy at the fire station. Pick me up on your way out of town."

Dancing around Dayton with half-truths in town was one thing. Doing it on the road—especially for this trip—was another.

Joan shook her head. "Dayton—"

He raised a hand to pause her before she got started. "I know what you're going to say, but you mean a lot to Calvert, and I'd like to think we're becoming friends. So I'm coming. Now, I can ride in Luther, or I can strap myself on top, or if all else fails, I'll follow you in my own damned truck if I have to."

Joan glanced at Leigh as if asking for approval. Leigh wasn't sure what to say, and Joan must have interpreted it as approval and nodded at Dayton.

"Leigh's not giving up her seat for your big bear legs," Joan said. "You can squeeze yourself into the back."

"Of course," Dayton said, with a warm grin at Leigh that might have been winsome to someone else.

Leigh couldn't muster one back.

After they picked up Dayton, Joan drove through the northern checkpoint, a barricaded entry point with three members of the watch on the road out of town. All three of them waved at Joan as Luther passed.

Leigh tucked her gloved hands in her jacket pockets and tried to focus on her breathing instead of where they were going.

Forty-five minutes into the drive, a sign posted at a fork in the highway pointed left to Mist and two other towns. Joan slowed before driving to the right.

Leigh didn't notice the significance, but Dayton shifted his weight in his seat.

"Boss?" Dayton asked.

Joan kept her eyes on the road. "We go that way and I'm going to have to stop at every checkpoint and spend hours negotiating passage with everyone questioning the land claiming."

Checkpoints also meant vehicle inspections and ultraviolet eye verification to confirm no vampires or bloodlings were entering human territory. Leigh's glamour might hold under closer inspection. Maybe Joan didn't want to risk it.

More reasons for Leigh to worry.

Dayton didn't appear to mind the excuse. He stretched out in the backseat as best as he could considering his bulk and fell asleep.

"Can he crash anywhere?" Leigh asked, somewhat impressed.

"He's got battle mentality. See food, eat it. See water, drink it. See something you can lie on, sleep."

Leigh couldn't imagine feeling safe enough around someone other than Joan to sleep without worrying about protecting herself. Maybe Dayton had never been through anything like she had, or maybe he'd become this person as a result of some traumatic experience—someone who could fight or sleep anywhere.

He was a good backup for Joan. Leigh would never mention she felt better knowing Joan had his support whenever she raced off into trouble. Joan was formidable on her own, to be sure, but a little extra insurance couldn't hurt.

Under normal conditions, the drive might have taken ninety minutes. With Joan taking the back roads, four hours had passed before they arrived at the Mist checkpoint.

Joan reached over to squeeze her leg, and Leigh stopped holding her breath.

Luther was fourth in line at the vehicle-only access point to a former football field surrounded by trees. The line of cars inched forward before them, each interviewed by a burly tan woman with a clipboard. Once she'd spoken with the inhabitants, she waved the car along.

Joan lowered her window.

"Name and affiliation," the woman with the clipboard said, a wry grin on her lips.

"You're a funny one, Yolanda," Joan said. "Hasn't been that long since we've seen each other."

A reminder to Leigh—Joan had lived years away from Calvert, and there was still a lot she didn't know about Joan's life during that time.

"I don't think we're running in the same circles anymore." Yolanda tapped her pen against the board. "Anyway, rules are rules."

"Joan Matthews, from the Calvert coven, with Leigh Phan and Dayton Just Dayton, both residents."

After leaning forward to confirm the occupants of the SUV, Yolanda nodded. "You all swear to attend this space under the rules of parley or face the consequences as determined by the conclave hosts?"

"We do," Joan said, speaking for them all.

"Then be welcome." Yolanda stepped back. "Been a long

while since we raised a pint. Find me later after the circle call."

"Will do." Joan drove forward, navigating between the hazard cones that marked lanes in the open field.

"Yolanda and I fought together against a vampire lord near Coquille a few years back," Joan said, answering the question before Leigh had a chance to ask.

Leigh didn't want to think about her own life a few years ago, back when she'd been addicted to whatever high she'd thought would keep her out of the clutches of vampires. Not that it had worked.

"What happens if you break your word?" Dayton asked, and Leigh was glad for the change of subject. "Magical consequences?"

"No," Joan said. "Your name goes on a blacklist, and you're declared anathema in the region—no white flag access anywhere—until you offer penitence, usually with some kind of payment to the hosts."

She pulled Luther into a parking space at the end of a row of a few dozen cars, squashing the grass on the edges closest the highway. Tents were pitched nearby, and more than one small camp had a firepit dug.

"They'll be calling the circle soon," Joan said as they climbed out of the vehicle. "After that, we can—"

"Incoming," a woman yelled from the next lane of cars. She stood at the top of a ladder to a single-story freshly constructed wooden lookout station. She was older than Joan and Leigh by about a decade, with silver crewcut hair, and she already had a gun in one hand as she pointed with the other. "Thralls on approach from the east."

Alarmed voices and a clanging bell sounded from somewhere closer to the center of the field.

"You gotta be kidding me," Dayton said.

Leigh froze. Should she get back in the car? Could they leave? "Joan—"

"Stay between us, no matter what." Joan raced to the back of Luther where her weapons were stashed and opened the back hatch.

Staying with Joan meant being in the heart of the fight. Joan wouldn't stand alongside and watch. "I—I can hide in the car—"

"No. I want you with me." Joan grabbed Dayton's axe and tossed it towards him. "Back-to-back, Leigh in the middle. I don't know who's here, but I haven't fought with any of them lately."

Dayton rested his axe against his leg and spared a moment to wrap his hair back in a ponytail before picking his weapon up again. "You lead. I've got your back."

Leigh stood unmoving while around them people ran between the cars, calling to one another to take positions or other actions Leigh didn't understand.

Everyone was preparing for a fight and Leigh had no idea how to help. She had no weapons, minimal training, and the only spell she knew she couldn't control.

Someone screamed, a bloodcurdling cry of pain and disbelief.

Fear slithered down Leigh's spine like ice cold water.

CHAPTER 7

JOAN TUCKED A loaded magazine into her coat pocket. "Nobody has been stupid enough to attack a conclave in over a decade."

She glanced at Leigh, and though she wanted to hold her hand, she needed both of her own free. "Stay close to me."

Leigh only nodded, eyes wide and bright.

The sun had sunk past the tree line, lengthening the shadows where several figures streamed from the forest on the far side of the campground. Some of them kicked over tents and knocked supplies into campfires, while others attacked the campers.

"Joan," Leigh said, fear in her voice.

Joan couldn't focus on that fear right now, on comforting Leigh. She weaved her way through the parked cars, Leigh close by and Dayton right behind them as Joan tasted the air, centering herself for the coming battle.

"Oh, shit," Dayton said. "Two o'clock."

Joan pivoted a step to the right, fingertips itching with power ready to be unleashed.

A flanking force of ten thralls spilled from the woods to the side of the campground. They were armed with clubs and knives, and though they weren't stealthy, they weren't making enough noise to be heard over the other louder conflict. They walked like humans—cautious and scanning for any threat. Not like the brazen confidence of bloodlings or the casual arrogance of vampires.

If no one stopped them, they'd sneak up behind the other witches and conclave attendees and pin them down.

No clean shots for Joan's gun, no clear paths for her spells. She needed to get closer.

Joan drew Dayton to her side with a glance, and they closed the gap between them and faced the new invaders.

Her caution with Leigh gave Dayton a head start. He took the first thrall out with a swing of his axe. The blood didn't surprise her—situation normal for her and Dayton—but Leigh gasped at the brutality of the attack.

Shit. No time to console her.

Joan shot one assailant in the head—a tall, gangly man with matted, filthy hair that might have once been blond. By the time he hit the ground, she and Dayton were in the thick of a wild, close-quarters fight with half a dozen thralls.

She had to keep them from getting to Leigh.

Joan pushed one palm forward, casting an air spell designed to pummel multiple targets with high-pressure pockets of air. She aimed for half of the attackers and only hit two while the others moved quickly out of range.

The two affected fell backward to the ground at the onslaught, and though one managed to rise again, the other didn't move.

Still, the rhythm Joan and Dayton had built together over months of fighting side by side and back to back was off with Leigh in the mix, and Joan found herself reacting more than taking charge of her own fight.

Four more people slipped through the trees. All around her, gunshots were answered by screams, shouts of positions and attack coordinates sounded over each other, crows shrieked as they flew in and out of the melee, and the spellcraft of countless war witches added to the madness of battle.

Through it all Joan kept Leigh's position paramount, and it changed how she normally fought. Joan couldn't seek higher ground on any of the cars because dragging Leigh up there with her would make Leigh a target. Any of the tactics she and Dayton had worked out between them wouldn't make sense to Leigh, and Joan didn't have time to explain.

And the thralls kept coming—a handful at a time as if someone were moving them forward like pawns in a chess match.

The crows above her squawked in warning—and how she *knew* it was a warning escaped her—right as a shadow materialized in her peripheral vision.

A new arrival. A familiar vampire in a charcoal suit that didn't match the camping or road attire of everyone else on the field.

Bartholomew, from the Ruby Court guild in Black Rose City. Legate to the guild's First vampire, Elizaveta.

A vampire wasn't unwelcome on neutral ground. Joan growled at him anyway. His slacks had a few splashes of mud, and his dress shirt was wrinkled beneath his coat. Otherwise, he appeared as if he'd just spent a day in office meetings. The only thing disturbing the impression was a pair of silver aviators covering his eyes.

Joan hadn't seen Bartholomew since that horrible night at the vineyard when he had joined her in her stand against Victor. She'd told him all bets were off if she ran into him again.

Guess tonight she could keep her word. If these attacking thralls were his, she'd slay him where he stood.

To her surprise, Bartholomew headed straight for the invading force. He grabbed a bear of a man by the throat and lifted him two feet above the ground in one smooth motion.

"Who sent you?" Batholomew's voice was cold and angry.

The man didn't raise an arm to defend himself. He stared blankly at Bartholomew and swallowed his tongue.

Beside her, Leigh cried out in horror. Dayton cursed.

Suicide rather than surrender? Who were these people?

As the thrall asphyxiated, Bartholomew shook him once and dropped him on the ground. He wiped his hand on his pants as if ridding himself of something vile.

Bartholomew joined the melee, though Joan wanted him anywhere else.

Options were now limited. Her preferred spells—walls of air, clouds of dirt, clusters of embers—were all ideal for close-quarters fighting. With Dayton and Leigh so close, she couldn't take the chance of hitting them.

Joan's gun was the best choice. She shot two men on the far edge of the enemy line, because taking them out was a straight shot with nothing in the way, and then flicked two fingers at an attacker. The lightning spell she'd perfected over her years of training no longer required a verbal trigger. Arcs of white-blue light crackled from her fingers to the assailant, hitting him in the chest, and he fell to the ground a second later.

Where were they coming from? Who besides the Ruby Court—and Bartholomew's presence suggested he and the rest of Elizaveta's guild weren't behind this mess—had the kind of resources to toss humans out like cannon fodder?

The crows darted among the bodies, in the way more often than not, pecking at the enemy combatants. Once again, she had no way to control them, to guide their assistance in any way worth a damn.

Bartholomew danced ahead, grabbing another human thrall. He attempted interrogation again with one, while four attackers split their forces to gang up on Dayton and Joan.

Joan shot the first of her two in the head and drew her tanto when the other one raised a tarnished sword. He wasn't good with it, but he was strong and solid as he swung at her head.

She blocked him, raising her gun arm to pause his swing before slicing her tanto under his arm across his axillary artery. Deep enough to slow him down, maybe not enough to kill him.

Leigh screamed, and Joan's blood ran cold. She risked a look behind her.

Another man, this one skinny and underfed, had grabbed Leigh and jerked her toward him. His eyes were wild, his pupils dilated, and he bared his teeth and growled as he dragged her back toward the woods.

Hell, no.

"Leigh!"

Enough of this bullshit. Joan took a step out of her next attacker's range. She raised her gun to dispatch him, aiming at his forehead but only hitting his neck. The crap shot was still effective. As soon as he dropped, Joan whirled around to help Leigh, who was still screaming.

With obvious panic, Leigh pulled herself from his grip, her superhuman strength wrenching his arm and dislocating his shoulder. The man screamed as Leigh planted her gloved hands on the man's head. In less than a heartbeat, flames burned through her gloves and onto his face, burning his skin and torching his hair. His clothes caught fire, but Leigh didn't release him.

Joan called out again, hoping to stop Leigh before she did anything else to reveal herself here in the open.

Leigh didn't hear her. Or couldn't.

The fire grew, scorching the man's skin, and still Leigh didn't let him go—not until he was engulfed in flame. The man's screams were faint, his vocal cords already damaged.

Leigh hauled him upright and lifted him over her head—something only a few human women might have been able to accomplish but a bloodling could do only too easily. With an agonized groan, she hurled his burning body to the bare ground fifteen feet away where he landed in a pool of churned mud.

The air smelled of burnt fiber and scorched meat.

"What the fuck?" Dayton yelled.

No, no, this was not good.

Leigh turned away from the carbon-scored man who lay dead yet still twitching, and vomited into the grass. She fell forward, heaving and coughing.

Joan glanced at Bartholomew, hoping against hope he'd missed the whole exchange. He killed the last of the human thralls closest to their group. One more thrall ran toward them from the woods, and after seeing the vampire, turned around to flee.

"You've been harboring a fucking monster?" Dayton's voice was a growl. The scowl he aimed at Joan was bright with betrayal.

"She's not a monster," Joan said as she pulled Leigh to her feet and checked her for injuries. Leigh was hyperventilating and shaking, her eyes full of tears.

Joan pushed Leigh behind her as Dayton approached them. "Can't talk about this now."

Beyond Dayton, Bartholomew stood motionless, facing in their direction.

Dayton clenched his hands at his sides. "Joan, how could you—"

"I said later, Dayton."

He caught on she was looking beyond him and gripped his axe like he meant business as he turned around.

Joan wished that axe could solve her problems. Not fucking likely.

Bartholomew strode toward them, relaxed in manner and gait. He stopped outside swinging range, the faint light of the evening shimmering on his aviators. He nodded in greeting like they were at a goddamned picnic.

"I am once again pleased to see you alive, Joan Matthews."

Bartholomew may have been speaking to Joan, but his head was faced in Leigh's direction.

"Can't say the same." Joan kept her hands free, loose.

Bartholomew hadn't taken another step toward her or Leigh. Didn't mean he wasn't a threat.

Not good. Not good that Dayton knew Leigh was a bloodling, not good Leigh was out in the open, not good that Bartholomew had Leigh on his radar. Too many variables, not enough options.

Had anyone else noticed?

All across the field, the battle had ended as quickly as it had begun. In its aftermath, the wounded were being carried to the medical tent. A cluster of war witches had conjured globes of water to hurl at the fires. Someone was adding wood to a makeshift pyre at the edge of the campground while several others dragged bodies toward the flames.

No, only these two were going to be a problem.

Bartholomew tipped his head forward in a measured bow. When he stood upright, he removed his glasses, revealing the milky white eyes of an ancient vampire.

"I am Bartholomew," he said.

"I know who you are." Joan gritted her teeth. The first time they'd met, he hadn't struck her as the overdramatic, introduce-himself-repeatedly type. She could have been wrong.

"I did not take the opportunity at the vineyard to make the formal acquaintance of Leigh Phan."

Joan's heart stopped, then restarted in double-time. Leigh made a sound like a whimper.

Things had gone from not good at all to terrible.

Joan shifted her weight and adjusted her grip on her gun. She didn't raise it.

Not yet.

Bartholomew's head tilted an inch toward Joan, though he made no other movement. Good. Better he focus on her than Leigh, even if it turned into a fight. She hadn't taken down a vampire as old as Bartholomew before, but she had to believe she could if it meant saving Leigh from—from whatever this might be.

"What are you doing here?" When in doubt, change the subject.

He didn't answer immediately, and the pause stretched long enough for her to realize she was holding her breath.

"I received word this swarm was headed toward the conclave," he said, his tone of voice not changing.

She'd have to unpack that later.

"Who's behind them?" Keep him distracted, focused on the specifics of the battle. Maybe it would give her time to think of an escape plan.

"Unknown. I will find out in due time. Other matters are more pressing." He nodded at Leigh. "I see you are a bloodling with rare skill."

Leigh still hadn't spoken. Her true face was still hidden, but the glamour wasn't useful if Dayton and Bartholomew knew the underlying truth.

"Perhaps," Bartholomew continued, and if Joan didn't know better, she might think he was being excessively kind as he spoke to Leigh. "We could have a private conversation to discuss your . . . circumstances."

Oh, hell no.

Joan took Leigh's hand. Leigh's grip tightened to the point of painful. "She's not going anywhere with you."

"I'd imagine she can speak for herself."

Leigh's teeth began to chatter, which meant she was trying to form words and failing. Joan had to get her away from Bartholomew, and out of here altogether.

"Joan—" Dayton interrupted.

"Later, Dayton." He needed to take a hint. His input was not welcome.

"Seems like a now thing."

Bartholomew raised a hand in conciliation. It might have been more effective if not for the inch-long talons at the end of his fingers. "I assure you, Joan Matthews, I—"

"Enough." Joan's stomp, one boot against the ground, should not have shaken the earth, but enhanced with her power, the ground rose and fell in jilting waves. She stood fast while the others wobbled as they secured their footing.

"Dayton, we're not talking about this here in the open. And you." She pointed at Bartholomew. "We're not talking to you at all."

For the first time, Bartholomew's expression lost its blankness and he frowned. Joan's stomach swooped. This vampire might be over a thousand years old, and pissing him off without certain backup could be a death sentence. He was too close, none of the other witches were nearby, and Dayton and Leigh were in no position to help had they even been willing.

"Soon, neither of you may have a choice," Bartholomew said.

Right now, Joan needed to get the hell out of here. Leigh was shivering, and she *never* got cold.

"Neutral ground, Bartholomew." Joan backed away, keeping Leigh behind her as she did. "If you attack us, you'll break the treaty."

He might not care, but many of the regional treaties had been hard-won with a lot of bloodshed all around—vampires, witches, thralls, noncombatants. Much of the neutral ground in this region had been established for generations.

Breaking a treaty had a lot of impact, and Joan was betting Bartholomew would honor it. Or at least pause long enough to allow them time to escape.

In any case, the distance between where Bartholomew stood and where Joan, Leigh, and Dayton were moving was growing by the second.

Dayton reclaimed his spine as they walked. "Joan, I need some answers."

"I don't owe you any," Joan said. "Not for this."

And it was true. She hadn't put Calvert in any danger. Leigh was no threat to any aspect of Calvert's safety, and Joan would stake her life on that. She already had, every night she slept beside her.

"You serious with this?"

"Bet me."

Bartholomew wasn't following, and Joan took advantage, pivoting Leigh toward Luther. She kept the vampire in her line of sight as they stepped over the churned ground and the fallen. Any other time, she would have helped, but Leigh was bordering on hysteria, and Joan needed to get her somewhere safe. "No talking. We need to get back on the road."

Dayton's scoffing was loud, and Leigh flinched.

"We can't go back to . . ." Dayton cleared his throat and tried again. "We have to talk about this. You can't take a bloodling back into town."

"We're not staying here." She pulled Leigh along with her as she walked as quickly as she could manage without drawing attention from any of the other war witches. They might not attack, but she couldn't take the chance.

"If you want a ride, Dayton, decide now. I shit you not, you'd better not pull anything because I will secure it with extreme prejudice."

His expression darkened to one she'd never seen aimed at her, and his knuckles whitened on the handle of his axe.

"Don't test me," Joan said. She centered her weight, her body ready to cut him down if needed. Goddamn it, she didn't want to.

Could she? Could she kill him after all the times they'd fought alongside each other? He'd had her back more than once, but if he thought for one minute Joan would let him treat Leigh like the thralls they'd just killed, he had another think coming.

She hated to lose Dayton as an ally, if that's what was happening, but Leigh came first.

The stare-down was a short one. Dayton lowered his eyes,

though his expression didn't change.

When they got to Luther, Joan finally took a moment to turn to Leigh and groaned at what she saw.

Leigh's face was wet from crying. She was still sobbing, her red tear-filled eyes darting from place to place as if searching for threats. Her hands were covered in burns.

"Joan," Leigh cried, and Joan couldn't resist. She pulled Leigh into her arms.

"It's going to be okay. We'll figure it out." Joan glared at Dayton, and kept murmuring in Leigh's ear though she knew he'd hear her. "No one's going to hurt you, baby. I promise."

Dayton's face had been a combination of anger and consternation. Now it changed to confusion.

Maybe he'd figured out Leigh wasn't the threat he might think she was. As long as he didn't do something stupid to take matters into his own hands.

Joan loosened her hold on Leigh as she spoke to Dayton. "The axe goes in the gear case. No arms in the car. You ride shotgun."

She didn't wait for his response. "You'll be okay in the back, right?" Joan said to Leigh.

Leigh collected herself enough to stop sobbing, and wiped the tears from her face with her sleeve. She nodded.

"Good," Joan said. "Let's get out of here."

"What about the conclave?" Dayton asked, a bite to his words as he spoke to her through the door before they both climbed inside. "I thought you wanted to get information from the other witches."

Joan glanced at the field where they'd fought moments ago. Bartholomew hadn't moved, still faced in their direction. No way she could get to the hosts without dealing with him again, and Leigh was in no state to be left alone while Joan tried to talk to someone about her.

Joan claimed the driver's seat and slammed the door. A

moment later Luther's engine roared to life.

"There aren't any answers here," she said, but it didn't feel like the truth.

CHAPTER 8

CURLED UP IN the backseat, Leigh clutched at her own thighs, needing something to do with her aching hands so she didn't claw out her eyes.

She'd killed that man. She'd killed someone *again*.

Was she one of the monsters she tried so hard to hide from?

No one had spoken a word since they'd left the campground, and the revealed truth was a fourth companion in the SUV.

Where was she going to find answers now?

Every time Dayton shifted in his seat, Leigh wondered if this was when he'd let loose and . . . would he try to kill her? Force Joan to leave her behind? Most people killed bloodlings on sight, or tried to anyway. The legends were full of stories of people who'd disappeared and returned under cover of night, mistaken for human when they showed up at the door before kidnapping their own families, offering them as blood donors to their new masters.

Bloodlings were the reason the people bolted their doors at night. And Dayton could tell their whole town one had been living in their midst for months.

The vehicle swerved too far to one side as Joan took a curve in the road faster than the recommended speed.

"How could you do this?" Dayton said, as if the jarring had shaken him from his silence.

He wasn't speaking to Leigh.

"I haven't done shit," Joan said. "And neither has she."

"You let a bloodling within the town limits." His shoulders were as tense as Leigh's, as if anticipating an attack.

Leigh wasn't going to hurt him—or at least, she didn't plan to, but could she say that without a doubt when she couldn't control what she did?

Joan growled. "Her name is Leigh, and she's more of a citizen of Calvert than you are."

"She's still a danger to—"

"You know damned well she isn't a danger to anyone."

But that wasn't true, was it? A man was dead, and it wasn't the first time. After months of torture and captivity, Leigh had killed Nathaniel, the vampire in charge of the donors at the vineyard. When last she saw him, he'd been consumed by flames, though afterward she'd never seen his body.

And only a few days ago she'd hurt Joan.

"I don't know a thing, so start explaining," Dayton said. "How long have you been hiding this?"

"I don't owe you an explanation, Dayton. This isn't your business."

"Are you kidding me?"

He spun in his seat to face her, and Leigh pushed herself back against the door. "Who's that vampire to you? What did he want?"

Leigh shook her head because she didn't know, but the words wouldn't come out.

"Hey," Joan said, her voice harsh and hinting at the possibility of violence. "You talk to me. Leave her alone."

"We're not going to talk about how she burned that thrall to a crisp?"

"You saw what happened," Joan said. "It was self-defense."

"That's not the point. Jesus, Joan, what kind of binder are you? Trevon never would have—"

Comparing Joan to her father wasn't a way to win an argument with her.

"He wasn't a damned saint, Dayton," Joan said. "And he knew. Hell, this was all his idea."

Dayton leaned back as if slapped. "What?"

Calvert's northern checkpoint came into view. Barring their path into town, three armed figures stood in the road. To either side of them, barricades blocked passage.

Joan slowed, flashing her lights. Was it some kind of code?

"Dayton," Joan said, "we're working on it, and you and I can talk about this later. We need more time."

"So this was why you wanted to go to Mist."

"Yeah." The vehicle slowed. "And no one else can know."

He scoffed.

Leigh didn't believe for one minute he'd keep her secret. She slipped one hand through the door handle, ready to leap out and run if she had to.

The silence stretched as the distance got shorter until they came to a stop. Dayton's breathing was tense, rough in the front seat. He appeared seconds away from revealing everything.

"Please," Leigh said, her voice cracked from all the crying. "I just want to go home."

He stilled, rigid, his jaw locked.

All the watch people—a woman and two men—were built like sturdy farmers. The woman, Piper, had a day job as a manager at the grocery store and always offered Leigh a smile.

She'd shoot Leigh if she knew the truth.

Piper walked toward the rig as Joan lowered the window.

"Hey, Joan. Y'all are back early." She nodded a greeting at Dayton, and peered into the backseat at Leigh.

Leigh didn't meet her eyes.

Joan tilted her head back against her seat, suggesting she was tired when Leigh knew she wasn't tired at all. "Thralls attacked the conclave. We got it sorted, and left when the show was over."

"No shit?" Piper's eyes widened in surprise.

"Yeah. I could use a damned meal."

"Of course. All clear, boss?" She asked Dayton, an affront at Joan, but understandable considering the late hour.

The passing seconds felt like years to Leigh.

"It will be as soon as I shower," Dayton said, his gruffness laced with anger.

Piper picked up on his irritation and laughed nervously. "I'll let you get to it."

She waved them through.

Dayton didn't wait for a ride all the way home. The moment they turned into the main stretch of town, he leaned forward.

"Just drop me at the end of the block."

"I know you want an explanation," Joan said.

"You're damned right I do, but I'm done with your bullshit for one night."

When the SUV slowed at the curb, Dayton opened the door before Joan had come to a full stop.

"I'll come find you tomorrow," he said without looking back. "Just let me get my shit."

To Leigh's surprise, Joan didn't push back on him for his tone. Instead, she shifted Luther into neutral while Dayton reclaimed his axe and gear bag and slammed the tailgate closed without another word.

Joan pulled away, picking up speed as she navigated the town streets until she got them back to the homestead and parked in the driveway.

"What is he going to do?" Leigh asked, though she knew it was a foolish question.

"I don't know."

"Will he summon the watch?"

Joan growled. "It'll be his last mistake if he does. I don't think he'll be that stupid."

"How can you be sure?"

Joan snapped. "I can't, but what choice do I have?"

Leigh trusted only Joan, though a tiny voice she wanted to ignore reminded her this whole trip had been Joan's idea. Could she blame Joan, though, for wanting to help her find answers?

They didn't speak until they were inside the house, after Joan cast a spell to reset her magical wards protecting the homestead.

Joan approached slowly as if Leigh was a wounded animal. Then again, wasn't that how Leigh felt? Wounded, damaged, like the shadows were moving in on her—

"Let me see those burns," Joan said, her voice over-gentle.

"You shouldn't touch me. You saw what I did."

"C'mon, Leigh—"

"I killed him."

She took a step backward. Joan was getting too close.

"He was going to hurt you, baby. You had to fight back."

Not like that she didn't.

Leigh turned away, headed for the downstairs bathroom. "I'm going to get cleaned up."

All Leigh wanted was to crawl into Joan's arms and try to forget everything that had happened over the last few hours, but she needed a bath. A shower wasn't going to get the smell of burnt skin out of her nostrils.

Joan let her go, and Leigh was grateful.

In the bathroom where Leigh had applied her glamour earlier in the day, she stripped out of her clothes, piling them on the floor. They belonged in the trash, but not before she removed every trace of—

She didn't want to think about it.

Leigh ran the hottest bath she could stand, climbed into the old clawfoot tub, and let the water rise to her shoulders. Steam curled above the waterline, and Leigh exhaled, an attempt to center herself, to breathe in some measure of peace.

Closing her eyes was a mistake.

The man from the campground—his face flashed in her mind. He'd had the haggard, hungry madness of a thrall in his eyes as he'd dragged her away from Joan, bringing back unwelcome memories. Leigh had been like him once, and the reminder of her time as an unwilling vampire donor had sparked her terror.

Then flames had erupted from her hands, igniting his clothes, burning through to his skin. His face, twisted in horror and pain at her scorching touch, changed from one of a vicious thrall to become Nathaniel, who for months had held her captive and drained her blood to feed himself, his peers, and his master.

She couldn't hold it all inside anymore. The tears became sobs and she pressed her burned hands against her face to muffle the sound or she might scream.

Leigh slid down until she was submerged, blocking out the world for as long as she could.

When she came up for air, a new sound broke the quiet.

"I meant what I said." Joan was talking in the other room. "Now, fuck off."

Leigh's hearing was more sensitive, another new development, though Joan's voice was muted by the walls. Was someone with them in the house? No, there was no response.

"I'm not meeting you anywhere." The stomp of rhythmic boot heels signaled Joan was pacing, like she often did while on the phone.

Who was she talking to? Leigh couldn't make out the other side of the conversation.

Maybe Dayton had changed his mind about being done for the night.

"She's not coming, either. We already told you—she doesn't want to talk to you."

The heat of the bathwater couldn't keep the chill from Leigh's bones.

Joan was talking to the vampire. Bartholomew.

Whatever they'd left behind them at the campground wasn't over. What did he want with Leigh?

"Leave the coven out of it," Joan said, her voice a threat. "None of this is anyone's business but ours."

The pause in the conversation was long and Leigh's hands ached from gripping the side of the bathtub. She leaned her head toward the door, hoping to hear more.

"One hour. I'll text you the coordinates." Joan didn't sound defeated, but she wasn't pleased at conceding. "Just to talk, Bartholomew. I mean it."

That couldn't be good for either her or Leigh.

Leigh finished her bath—the urgency of finding out what Joan had agreed to wasn't more pressing than cleaning the ash from her skin—and dressed.

The house was quiet, the crackling of the fire in the living room the only sound. Joan sat at the kitchen table, staring out the window.

At Leigh's arrival, Joan tapped a fingernail on the case of her phone where it sat on the table.

"Bartholomew has sent a formal request for parley."

Leigh bit back a hiss when she clenched her hands too tightly.

"What does that mean?" she asked, then stopped Joan from speaking the obvious. "I mean, I know what a parley is. What I mean is, what if we say no?"

Joan studied her palms as if they held the answers.

"Rejecting a parley without good reason when there's no active conflict is an insult." Her voice was flat, measured, a sign she was nearing her limit.

When backed into a corner, Joan didn't always make good choices.

"If we don't show, he says he'll make a formal request to the coven. Not sure how far he and Elizaveta will push it. I've heard stories about town covens rejecting parleys and finding themselves eliminated from treaties. Calvert runs the risk of insulting the Black Rose Guild, and I don't know how that might play out."

Leigh had seen Joan worried, angry, hurt—any number of emotions, but never wide-eyed with bald fear.

"Some guilds in the past have retaliated." Joan stood and crossed the room. "If we meet him, we might be able to keep Calvert out of it."

Leigh didn't want to talk to terrifyingly powerful vampires, and she didn't want the town to pay the price, either. She'd tried running once before and had ended up back at Victor's vineyard, the place she'd been trying to avoid.

No matter which way she turned, sooner or later the truth would always catch up to her.

CHAPTER 9

ONCE AGAIN, JOAN drove the back roads out of Calvert. This time, she avoided checkpoints she'd made herself.

By the rules of engagement established long before Joan or Leigh had been born, they had the right to select the location since Bartholomew requested the parley.

The best place for them to meet would have been the vineyard. She and Bartholomew had fought there against Victor, and the fields beside the burned-out manor house were neutral ground close to Calvert without being under constant surveillance by the watch.

Dragging Leigh back to the scene of her trauma, though, sickened Joan's stomach. She chose a similar site ten miles away—an old farm surrounded by trees, long ago abandoned and only checked periodically to make sure no new threats had come to roost.

Some other time, she'd consider filling all these holes in her security since she might not be the only one taking advantage of them.

Bartholomew was waiting in the designated glade when they arrived.

The helicopter he'd flown sat quiet and idle. Before the circumference of the looming helicopter blades, he stood placid and nonthreatening, with no apparent armaments besides the talons visible from this distance.

The waning moon cast some light between the clouds, enough to lengthen his shadow on the overgrown grass. His milky eyes were uncovered, making his accountant-like attire less inconspicuous.

Joan parked several car lengths away from him and his transport and turned off the engine. The motor clicked as it settled.

"I won't let anything happen to you," Joan said, unstrapping the pistol in its holster and loosening the knife in its scabbard. Weapons weren't allowed by parley rules, but no way in hell was she going into this unarmed.

Leigh reached for Joan's hand, then changed her mind and pulled away. "I know you'll try, but please be careful."

"Always."

They climbed from the car. As they walked toward Bartholomew, Joan shivered in the crisp night air, and not from the cold. Wings fluttered in the trees. Guess the crows were already here.

She stopped far enough away from Bartholomew to speak without shouting. "You pull any shit, I swear I'll gut you where you stand."

He only tilted his head, suggesting he was more entertained than offended. Bastard.

"I mean neither of you harm, Joan Matthews, and will honor all terms of parley. I only want to have a conversation. You are in no danger."

"Heard that before," Joan said. "Let's hurry this along. We've got places to be."

He nodded, a slow measured movement. "I am here to extend an invitation to you, Leigh Phan, for an interview."

An interview?

"For what?" Joan answered before Leigh could speak a word.

Bartholomew took his time responding, his eyes on Leigh. "To assess your powers and determine what training you require to control them."

Leigh made a noise, something like a cough or a whimper.

"She doesn't need your help." Joan said, and Leigh could be pissed at her later for speaking on her behalf. "Neither of us needs your help."

She'd ignore the fact that they needed someone's assistance since they hadn't found any answers themselves. Not from him, though.

"That wasn't always the case, was it?" he asked, glancing at Joan. "We've fought alongside each other before, not too far from here."

Joan's fingers twitched toward her gun though she didn't draw.

"I take no offense at your breach of common accord," he said. "I can even understand how you might feel about this . . . situation, but the circumstances must be addressed."

"We're not consenting to some interview."

"The invitation is for you alone," he said to Leigh.

Leigh didn't speak. Joan didn't dare look at her—not when this vampire might take advantage of the distraction.

"Absolutely not happening," Joan said. "She's not going anywhere with you."

He tilted his head in Joan's direction. "I implore you to be reasonable. An unchecked bloodling of unknown power falls under the guild's purview, and if unaddressed, will attract undue attention."

"She's not—" Joan bit back her words. He wasn't wrong, and it ate at her to have those terms apply to Leigh, to have them spoken out loud. Bloodling. Unchecked power.

Under the guild's purview.

What was worse was that they were probably true. Joan might have claimed the territory, but all the vampires within the region fell under the governance of the guild. Was it a stretch for such oversight to include bloodlings?

Bartholomew shook his head in what might be pity. "Though I understand your concern in this matter, Joan, you cannot speak for her. Leigh Phan, you are not the only bloodling who has ever had these gifts. I'm sure you have questions, and I can provide answers—ones you will not find elsewhere."

To Joan's surprise, Bartholomew softened his voice.

"The interview is not invasive. It is merely a test of your powers. While you are in my company, you will be safe and under my protection. And though I will offer you the choice, no one will turn you without your consent."

Joan scoffed. "Since when do vampires care about consent?"

Bartholomew frowned at the interruption.

"Do not pretend you know all there is to know of our world, Joan." His tone was a hair short of condescending. "This offer is made in good faith, on my word. That you chose this place, so near to where I came to your aid, should be proof of what my word is worth."

"I don't want to . . . to come with you," Leigh said, her voice trembling but clear. "I don't want your help."

"There you have it," Joan said. "Guess we've covered the key points of this little meeting."

She took a step back, maneuvering herself into Leigh's space and hoping Leigh took the hint they needed to move toward the car.

Bartholomew sighed, a deep heavy sound of disapproval.

"I apologize for breaking faith," he said. "This situation is unprecedented and dangerous, and must be resolved."

He turned to one side, and Joan gripped the handles of her weapons, ready to draw if he so much as leaned in their direction, but he didn't move again.

Instead, the door on the far side of the helicopter opened and the short hairs rose on the back of Joan's neck in warning.

Another vampire stepped into the night.

Elizaveta, First vampire of the Ruby Court guild, strolled across the grass.

CHAPTER 10

LEIGH'S HEART POUNDED so hard in her chest she couldn't hear anything else. She felt lightheaded. Whatever was about to happen, she wasn't ready. It was too late to flee. If she did, could she leave Joan to face it alone?

This vampire was tall—taller than Bartholomew, taller than Joan—and her skin was so pale it glowed. She wore the dated attire of a statesman or a businessman, with creased pants and an open-collared dress shirt under a double-breasted waistcoat. A watch chain hung from one pocket.

She wore no jewelry besides a ruby glinting from one ear, and her dark hair was pulled back into some kind of twisted bun behind her head.

None of this captured Leigh's attention as much as one final detail. Her shirtsleeves were rolled to her elbows, and her hands were covered.

She studied Leigh while tugging her gloves more tightly against her fingers.

Did this vampire have a power like Leigh's?

Leigh didn't feel the cold the way she had before she'd been changed into a bloodling, but the knowledge she had something in common with this—this predator chilled her.

Bartholomew raised an open palm in the new vampire's direction.

"Leigh Phan, allow me to introduce Elizaveta, First vampire of the Ruby Court guild of Black Rose City."

A First. Leigh didn't know much about vampire politics, but everyone had heard of vampire Firsts. They were immensely powerful—enough to keep other vampires in line.

"Ah, yes," Elizaveta said with something akin to delight. "The bloodling who brought the legendary war witch to heel. I must say I'm impressed."

What? How did this—how did she know anything about Leigh?

Joan leaned forward, her anger leaching into the air.

"This isn't what we agreed." Joan stepped further in front of Leigh. "Since you didn't come to this parley in good faith, we are leaving, and you're not stopping us."

If they did, Joan would have to take on two vampires by herself. Leigh would be of little help in that department, judging by Elizaveta's gloves.

Elizaveta rolled her eyes in impatience. "Bartholomew's terms didn't specify he would come alone, only that he would meet with you on neutral ground. And you're one to talk, as armed as you are, so let's not quibble over minutiae."

Joan took a step backward. "I'll be sure to mention your deception when I report this to the High Coven."

"A poor feint, warbinder," Elizaveta said, not unkindly but not mincing words either. "We both know you aren't on the best of terms with that coven. You are also outnumbered, and you won't do a thing to put your beloved in danger."

In the dark of the nearby woods, the rustle of birds broke the natural quiet. A few squawks edged nearer.

"Oh, your devoted crows." Elizaveta arched one eyebrow, then let it fall. "Do keep them in check."

"Well," Joan said. "Stop pissing me off."

Leigh prayed these vampires didn't push past that bluff since Joan had no control over the birds.

"Enough." Elizaveta's tone was more serious. "Your attempts to derail the conversation won't make the need for it disappear. We're wasting time."

"Not anymore." Joan turned half toward Leigh to beckon her away.

Could they leave?

"We can't allow that," Bartholomew interjected. "Not until we've had this discussion."

"There's nothing to talk about," Joan said, taking another step. Leigh got the hint and stepped backward as well.

Elizaveta frowned, her expression like that of an impatient teacher. "Belay your nonsense for five minutes, Matthews. And let's stop this interminable prancing around the issue."

Her gaze was back on Leigh. "You killed a man in combat with the power of flame. As no one has seen you participate in a single altercation before that, not even in Victor's little fiefdom, I presume this is the only time this has happened."

So they didn't know about Nathaniel, about how Leigh had killed him. About how this hadn't been the first time.

"You wield this power," Elizaveta continued, "but are untrained, which makes you dangerous. Unchecked, these abilities manifest themselves unconsciously, doing untold damage by accident."

It was as if Elizaveta could hear Leigh's thoughts. Could she? How terrifying that would be.

"How many times have you inadvertently set something on fire, hmm?" Elizaveta's tone turned dark, painful . . . seductive. "How many times have you burned someone?"

She lowered her head, emphasizing her thick, brooding brows. "How many times have you burned Joan?"

How did she know?

Joan exploded. "That's none of your business!"

The echoes of Joan's scream rang in the glade, her response only proving Elizaveta's point. Leigh shrank in on herself, the shame warring with the fear.

Elizaveta didn't so much as twitch at the interruption. "The answers you seek exist, as do the ways to keep those incidents from occurring."

By ignoring Joan's outburst, Elizaveta had stripped her of power, of influence, of importance. Joan's shoulders trembled, her fingers beginning a slow pattern that would no doubt summon a spell.

Bartholomew tilted his head. One of his hands twitched.

What powers was he hiding?

Leigh rested her hand at the base of Joan's back in an effort to stop her, to keep her from getting them killed, but she didn't take her eyes off Elizaveta.

Elizaveta's gaze was more piercing when she spoke again.

"You can learn to control it, but not in Calvert, and not from the witches."

Joan scoffed. "She's not going anywhere with you."

"That is precisely what I'm offering. Accompany us to Black Rose City, and learn what you need to know."

Ice formed along Leigh's spine. Black Rose City was infinitely worse than Victor's manor house had been. Hundreds of vampires, countless bloodlings, human donors everywhere—not a small enclosed environment, but an entire city and all of it vampire territory. Not a single witch or coven was allowed on guild land without invitation, or so Joan had said, and no one could protect Leigh from vampire influence, their desires, their whims.

Every horror she'd endured under Victor's rule flashed across her mind, terrifying her anew. Chained below ground in spaces more like dungeons than basements. Barely able to stand while detoxing from the drugs she'd consumed in an effort to make herself less palatable. The vampires hadn't cared. They fed her only enough to keep her alive between blood draws. Tossed into dark rooms with young vampires who'd tormented her as they sank their teeth into her skin—

Joan cast a cantrip, one making the wind rise and swirl through the trees and grasses.

Bartholomew raised a fist and then spread his fingers.

The wind died in the space of a breath.

"This is not a fight you can win," Bartholomew said to Joan. "Do not make it into one."

Joan recovered before Leigh did.

"You're just gonna turn her," she began, but Elizaveta cut her off.

"I shall swear to you both on whatever you require that I will not harm you, Leigh Phan, or allow harm to come to you in any way. I will not change you without your consent. Once I'm assured you can control your abilities, I will take you wherever you want to go, even if it's back to that hovel you call a home."

Leigh bristled despite her fear. When Elizaveta's lips curled into a faint grin, she realized she'd been baited.

"There's some fire," Elizaveta said with dark amusement.

Had that been a pun?

"Who are you to say what she has to do?" Joan asked.

"You harbor a bloodling of unknown power near my guild. Were this another time, many in my position would kill her where she stands, a barbaric practice I am glad to see has fallen from favor. I offer safe passage—"

"You're not offering for free, Elizaveta."

Joan's courage would have been admirable under any other circumstances. Right now, Leigh thought it might get them killed.

"You want something," Joan said. "What is it?"

Elizaveta didn't answer immediately, and when she did, she offered her response to Leigh instead of Joan. "Answers, a desire

I'm sure you share."

"You don't know a thing about what she wants," Joan countered.

That wasn't true. Leigh wanted—needed answers, and these last few months of searching had yielded only new questions.

Joan spoke over one shoulder at Leigh, her eyes still on the vampires. "You don't have to do this. They can't make you."

It was a lie. They could take her whether she wanted to go or not. They could subdue Joan or kill her outright and take Leigh captive in a heartbeat.

Instead, they had requested a parley, met Leigh and Joan on neutral ground, and offered her an invitation. Elizaveta's presence made it clear they wouldn't take no for an answer. They had, however, extended the illusion of consent and were persistent in it.

Why? Why did she matter to them? What weren't they saying?

Two options, both awful. Agree to the interview, and be dragged back into a world that still ruled her nightmares. Decline, and they might kill Joan.

Joan's stance shifted, and Leigh saw the hairsbreadth of a moment standing between where they were now, and how they would die in seconds when Joan attacked.

Leigh grabbed Joan's arms. "No, love. Don't . . . you can't stop them, Joan. Not both of them. They'll kill you."

She thought she heard Elizaveta mutter something about the ridiculousness of their response, of not taking her at her word.

Leigh ignored it for now. The word of a vampire meant nothing to her.

"I won't let you—" Joan growled around a sob.

Only one path would keep Joan from harm.

"No." Leigh's voice trembled as she spoke. "This is my choice, Joan. You can't help me with this."

The heartbreak in Joan's eyes was hard to bear, but Leigh would have to carry it. This wasn't the first or even the hundredth difficult choice she'd made in her life.

She'd left Joan once before to save her.

"If anything happens to her," Joan said. "Nothing will stop me from finding you, and I will end you, however long it takes."

A dangerous threat to make at two aged vampires. Joan was nothing if not courageous to a fault. Leigh tried not to think about how much that was one of the reasons to love her.

"Consider your favor repaid, Joan Matthews." Elizaveta spun on her heel and walked back the way she'd come, as if the matter was resolved.

Bartholomew waited as Leigh turned to Joan, who was glaring daggers at Elizaveta.

"What favor, Joan?" What could Joan owe a First? And why hadn't she told Leigh about it?

"It doesn't matter now," Joan said.

Another secret between them they didn't have time to discuss, and if Leigh was going to do this, best to do it now.

She kept her words, her embrace, her kisses to herself. Nothing about her relationship with Joan was any of their business. Instead, she tried to convey everything she felt for Joan with one final look because she couldn't pretend she'd be back, either.

Joan didn't respond in kind. She glared at Bartholomew like she was plotting war.

Leigh took a step toward the unknown before she lost her nerve.

Bartholomew gave her a wide berth as he escorted her to the helicopter. Leigh's knees shook as she stepped past Elizaveta to climb through the open door, relieved when the vampires took the front seats. She pressed herself into the compact seat in the back.

As the helicopter rose from the ground, Leigh allowed

herself one last glance at Joan, who stood alone below them, eyes wet with tears, fists clenched in rage.

CHAPTER 11

WARBINDER.

The word echoed in Joan's head as she raced along the back roads, swerving into the oncoming lane on the curves so she didn't have to lower her speed. If she did, if she slowed down enough to acknowledge the hole in her chest, she'd lose her mind.

Kind of like she was losing it now over a word she'd never heard but that described her perfectly. How had the vampires known it but not any of the witches she'd ever met?

A blur of brown and white leapt across the road in front of her and she slammed on the brakes, her body crashing forward into the steering wheel. The deer disappeared into the trees while Joan caught her breath. Too close, but the interruption snapped her from her spiraling frustration.

Focus.

She had to get Leigh away from them. Elizaveta had sworn she wouldn't turn Leigh into a vampire, but there'd be ice in hell before Joan trusted a First.

The most advantageous location for Elizaveta to take Leigh would be her home. Joan had been in Black Rose City once, and few details of that visit would be helpful now. Bartholomew had escorted her from the riverfront to Elizaveta's manor, but it had been dark, and Joan had had no time to recon any of the layout.

Joan had no reinforcements she could rely on for a rescue attempt from the heart of vampire territory. None of the war witches Joan knew and had fought with before she'd come home to Calvert would be likely to join the effort. Dayton was still pissed at finding out Leigh was a bloodling. No way in hell would he accompany Joan into the lion's den—again, since he'd gone with her the first time—for someone he wouldn't think was worth saving.

No matter who Joan thought of, the overarching problem was that they would view Leigh as one of the enemy, not a captive.

Joan was on her own and couldn't just walk through the gates—she was too recognizable. Lately, she was damned near notorious. She'd have to be more circumspect, and she suspected they'd be on the lookout for her.

Luther was a liability. Though the fortified vehicle offered a range of protections, from bulletproof glass to enchanted tires, it was the only one of its kind and everyone who'd ever seen it knew it was hers.

No, home first to switch vehicles and arm herself before finding a way into Black Rose City.

The tears on her cheeks itched until she wiped them away.

Half a mile from the southeastern gate into Portland, Joan rode her motorcycle into a fueling station. The day had dawned bright and clear considering the season. After filling the tank, she pulled around back and locked herself in the single-occupant bathroom.

She hung her pack on one side of the two-prong hook on the back of the door and shed her unnecessary outer rain protection layers. She dug out a small case from inside her pack.

The glamour kit was basic and familiar, though Joan hadn't used one since she was a teenager. Back then, she'd heard warnings from her father and her teacher, Gretchen Wilson, about the dangers of glamours. Making and using one were part of her lessons and not to be repeated outside those conditions. Glamours were addictive, they'd said, tantalizing misrepresentations that led to untold damage when people grew attached to what they'd imagined and lost touch with what was real.

Joan had convinced herself Leigh's case was different, that Leigh's choice to hide her true self was the only way to keep her safe.

How safe was Leigh now?

The herbs and salt were already mixed, and she'd waited until now to add a pinch of iron filings. She gave the ingredients a quick shake in a thumb-sized vial before she added the concentrated rosewater from another bottle.

She couldn't take a bath in here, so she settled for a wipe-down with hand towels and gritty soap. She drew a knife and pricked a fingertip, adding a few drops of her blood to the solution.

When Joan applied the compound to her wrists, the backs of her knees, the junctions of her thighs and both sides of her neck, the ointment burned her skin. Pain was no hardship to her, not with the kinds of wounds she'd withstood in her many fights over the years. This was different, like someone had found a way to mute the feeling of rubbing alcohol across an abrasion.

Leigh did this every day? Her respect for her lover—her *wife,* damn it—grew as she considered what Leigh endured all the time to keep herself hidden.

Joan closed her eyes and visualized how she wanted to appear and, to be sure, held the image in her mind for longer than the thirty seconds she'd been taught.

When she opened her eyes, her jaw slacked in surprise, though she shouldn't have been shocked.

In the scratched and cracked mirror, her cheeks hollowed, her pupils lightened to a flat brown, her nose narrowed, and a jagged scar ran from one brow to her ear.

A good disguise, but it wasn't enough.

She drew a knife and tested its sharpness with her thumb.

Forty minutes later, Joan climbed onto her bike and slid her helmet over her newly shorn scalp.

By late morning, she'd backtracked twice on her way to Portland. Chances were slim anyone was following her, but the twists and turns made her feel safer, more invisible on her journey to a familiar three-story brick building in the no-man's land outside the Portland city gates.

Though old and worn-down, Loufield's way station was more formidable than it appeared. All kinds of local powers were represented here: gangs parleying on neutral territory, war witches adding grist to the rumor mill as they passed through. Even the Ruby Court kept a permanent room here.

Lodging was available at an inflated price, and a hungry traveler could grab some sustenance in the pub, though few would visit a place that vampires and war witches frequented.

Joan had visited several times over the years she'd spent as a roaming war witch. She couldn't say she'd enjoyed any of those visits, yet this way station had its uses. She parked her bike in the lot, and chained it to a grid-lined metal frame welded to the side of the building.

Joan banged on the entrance, shaking the midday rain from her pants and jacket as she did, and tucked her helmet under one arm. Loufield, the neck-bearded proprietor who owned and managed the joint, wouldn't man the door until dark though he wouldn't recognize her through her glamour.

A brawny man with thin, patchy black hair, deep-set eyes, and a gravelly voice hollered through the grated cutout in the door. "Who are you here to see?"

"No one. Just passing through," she lied. Most folks came here to meet someone. Joan didn't know who she was looking for yet.

He bought it and opened the door to let her pass, though he did glower at her and issue a warning.

"No bullshit, no fights, no spellcraft on these premises."

She grunted her acknowledgment, and walked the long dark hall to the pub.

At first, Joan spoke little to the other customers, not wanting to draw attention to herself by being too eager or invested in any answers. She needed to get into the city and approach Elizaveta's manor without detection, and intel came at a cost. Trading in cash was too visible, attracting attention and more questions, which left only information in trade or personal favors.

Joan was in no mood for favors. Not since her most outstanding one had just been paid.

Soon she bought a few drinks, traded innocuous chatter with the other patrons—news of treaties in exchange for the same about supply lines, of alliances forged or broken in recent months. Minute by minute, Joan settled into the old role of a traveling war witch, inviting idle conversation to hear how the world fared.

Much of it she already knew, thanks to all the folks holding her to task since her claiming. She pretended it was valuable in order to gain what she still needed to learn.

After a few hours, she hired a room though she didn't plan to sleep here. She talked with the bartender, the staff—or at least those willing to talk to her—and heard more murmurings and whispered fears about the rise of thrall attacks in the area. No vampire or bloodling support was mentioned, but small groups of humans had disrupted some of the supply lines and smaller towns throughout the coastal region. No pattern emerged other than the similarities between the attacking forces.

Problems for another day. Hours passed, and she was too wired from worry, anger, fear, and caffeine to give in to any urge to sleep. Customers rotated in and out, a few more arriving when the evening's entertainment—a crooning songstress with a beat-up guitar—captured most of the room's attention.

Joan sat still for one song before she struck up her next conversation. Someone somewhere had eyes and ears inside Black Rose City and knew who the key players were, or where the double agents were working. Vampires weren't immune to human nature, and Joan wasn't the only fool willing to take immeasurable risk for personal gain. Her gain was a person, but still.

No matter how much a town or a coven or a city government thought they had everything locked down, people always found a way past barriers to spy, to share information, to trade in black market goods.

"Slim pickings around here." The man beside her broke into her thoughts. They'd struck up a conversation in the pause between the performer's sets. He was wiry with short blond hair and three days of unshaved beard on his face and let his guard down after Joan bought him a beer.

"Gonna head south," he said. "Some folks in San Francisco are joining up to deal with some smaller band of monsters wanting to form their own guild."

Joan faked a laugh. "Didn't you just say there were more thrall attacks? Sounds like more than enough work for everybody."

He wiped beer foam from his upper lip. "I mean vampire lords. People pay more if they're hunting nearby, and since that Matthews witch claimed a bunch of land, most of the lords have moved on."

She let that pass without comment.

He eyed her like he was trying to figure out how to get a cut of her business. "Where you from? You on a job?"

"Tracking down a vamp who might be hiding in Black Rose

City." It was the best excuse she could imagine for why she was searching for intel. No one sane would want to offer to help, no matter what the bounty might be. "Gotta get in without pissing off the coven."

"You're crazy, but I heard about someone even crazier than you." He made a show of tapping his pockets for a wallet Joan got the sense would never appear.

"You want Fiona," the man said, nodding in thanks when Joan paid for another beer. "War witch from back east somewhere. Word is, she's set up shop within Black Rose City itself. If you want to know what's going on without involving those more invested in above-board communication, she's your best bet."

He gave Joan a code phrase too banal to be made up and took another pull from his glass. "Fought with her once, down in Grants Pass. She's a tough one, I'll give her that."

He drained the last third of his beer and leaned close enough for Joan to smell his stale breath. "Good luck. Hope you don't get killed. I promise not to bet against you."

He winked and spun on his stool to get a better view of the singer, ending their conversation.

Some of the tension bled from Joan's shoulders since this Fiona might have the answers she needed.

Now all Joan had to do was get to her.

CHAPTER 12

WHEN THE PANIC came close to making her scream, Leigh drove her fingernails into the palm of her hand. She stopped shy of drawing blood for fear of how the vampires might react.

Yet Elizaveta and Bartholomew said nothing to her the entire trip. Maybe now that she'd surrendered to them, she was beneath their notice. Unlikely, but . . . so was this tense limbo where they barely acknowledged her presence.

The blur of the trees below them as they traveled overland was not enough to capture Leigh's attention as she stared at the backs of her captors' heads until lights drew her gaze outside.

Portland lay ahead of them, brightening the night.

Once, years ago, Leigh had visited, and she'd spent most of the trip high. Back then, it had been winter, too, and the short, rain-soaked days had been broken only by the lengthy drug-filled nights. Every day, she'd hustled for a place to crash, for the next meal, for the next bump of whatever she could get her hands on.

She hadn't noticed the height of the outer walls, the armed guards, or the people camped outside the gates. How had she managed to get into Portland in those dark days?

The helicopter flew over the river, low enough for Leigh

to make out figures in boats below them, on the shore, on the city walls. Beyond Portland, Bartholomew veered the helicopter north toward a green bridge with towering spires rising a few hundred feet over the banks of the river.

The streets of Black Rose City were well-lit and, unlike Calvert, where most people took to their homes after dark, this city was full of pedestrians, a thriving commotion despite the late hour.

Of course, vampires had no need to hide from the dark. This was where they ruled. And she was flying into a nest five times the size of Calvert.

The sound of the helicopter was drowned by the ringing in her ears. A city full of vampires. She couldn't get enough air. They would use her, drain her, and spit her out. Leigh would be chained up again, left in the dark, used for someone else's entertainment and sickening desires, and she wouldn't be able to escape this time.

"I gave my word, Leigh Phan," Elizaveta said, breaking into Leigh's thoughts.

They had landed. The helicopter blades were spinning down, the engine quieted, and Bartholomew had already disembarked. How had she not noticed?

Elizaveta did not turn toward Leigh, instead speaking without shifting her gaze from the lot before them. "You are safe under my protection, and no harm will come to you. You will not be turned without your consent."

Elizaveta climbed from the helicopter without waiting for a response and stepped clear. She stopped beyond the door to hold it open, leaving an unobstructed path for Leigh to disembark.

Leigh closed her eyes and got her breathing under control.

Once she was sure she could move without sobbing, she wiped the tears from her face, and climbed through the door.

Leigh searched the shadows for threats, for other vampires waiting to seize her.

Bartholomew and Elizaveta stood several feet away at the edge of the landing zone, with a hangar beyond them. Bartholomew checked his phone, and for a moment Leigh burned with the urge to do the same, but she didn't want to reveal its existence. They might take it away.

The night was silent save for the soft patter of a few raindrops and the rush of the wind.

"This way, please." Bartholomew gestured for Leigh to follow him. Elizaveta strode towards the hangar.

Following the somewhat known threat was better than running into the dark.

Not a soul greeted them when they passed through the empty hangar and its office and out onto the sidewalk. They walked along a well-lit street in a quiet neighborhood with none of the revelry she'd seen before they landed. Though Leigh saw a handful of figures a few blocks away, no one approached them.

Twice in Leigh's life, she'd been abducted by vampires. The first time, she'd been dragged kicking and screaming into the back of a box truck and chained to its walls. She still remembered how the metal felt, what the compartment smelled like, the desperation at being confined in the hopeless dark.

The second, a traitor to the Calvert coven had kidnapped her, taking her back to the place she'd sold her soul to escape.

Now, the vampires who might be her captors paid her no attention as they marched toward an unknown destination, expecting her to heel.

Was it good or bad that she hadn't put up a fight? And what good would it do her if she did?

Ten minutes later, the street ended at a park, and the sidewalk narrowed to a cobblestone path framed by knee-high hedges. The streetlights here were more golden than fluorescent, washing over an understated manor house and winter trees devoid of leaves.

Leigh had given no thought to where the aforementioned

interview might be. If she had, she wouldn't have imagined a small mansion on an otherwise unsophisticated city block.

Elizaveta climbed the few stairs to the back of the manor house first, and the door opened at her arrival. No light shone from inside the house.

Leigh stopped at the base of the stairs, the shadows of the house reminding her of past horrors, of chains and hunger and darkness.

"Good evening, Miss. Sir," a woman said as Elizaveta and Bartholomew crossed the threshold. She was a head shorter than Elizaveta, and wore a black dress shirt tucked into pressed black slacks. The way she greeted the vampires was positive and without fear, though she didn't smile.

The woman peered at Leigh with a questioning expression.

"Welcome," she said, extending an arm to beckon Leigh inside, as if she were here for a tour.

No guards had appeared to drag Leigh away. Maybe more vampires waited inside, but so far she hadn't been tossed around like a donor to be imprisoned and victimized.

When the woman's greeting went unanswered, she frowned in confusion at Leigh's inaction. She wore a band of leather around her neck, wide enough to cover her carotid arteries.

A donor, though a well-treated one judging by her demeanor.

Leigh drew a shaking breath. No matter what she was walking into, she'd come here to face the truth. Perhaps things were different because she—she wasn't human anymore.

She forced herself forward, past the woman who closed the door behind them. The sound of steps and rustling clothes guided Leigh down dark halls she could navigate with her bloodling vision.

Elizaveta waited in a kitchen, one spotless in its lack of human comforts or provisions, at least no visible ones. Bartholomew proceeded through another doorway, his focus once again on the phone in his hand.

"Vera," Elizaveta said to the other woman, who had followed Leigh and stood clasping her hands in front of herself. "Our guest will be resting in the blue suite."

Leigh had no intention of resting here, and something in her expression must have given her thoughts away. Elizaveta arched an eyebrow before turning toward another door.

"I've some business to attend to this night, and I urge you to rest in preparation for your interview. Vera will provide you with a meal and anything else you might need."

She paused as if measuring her words. "The library at the front of the manor may interest you until Bartholomew and I can join you again. Your interview will begin at twilight tomorrow."

A whole day in this place?

"I must prepare for your examination," Elizaveta said, answering Leigh's unspoken question, and disappeared into the dark of another corridor.

Why insist on a parley and bring her all this way if they weren't ready to test her now?

"This way, Miss," Vera said.

Leigh flinched at being addressed the same way as the vampires. Did that mean this woman thought she should be served like them? It made her want to cry, but she couldn't let that happen. No more vulnerability in front of strangers.

"Perhaps a short tour would be helpful?" The woman turned on several lights as they passed the switches. "Miss and Sir don't have much use for electric light. I can't see my own hand in some of these corridors after the sun sets."

Her manner was so casual Leigh chose to believe she was sincere. Why was this human treated so well? Elizaveta and Bartholomew might be kinder to their donors, but slaves were still slaves.

Maybe this woman, like Leigh, had made impossible choices to survive.

Vera led her around the main floor, pointing out the sitting room, a lounge with another small kitchen, and two different bathrooms. All Leigh noticed was that the rooms were empty of occupants.

"This is Miss Elizaveta's private office," Vera said as they arrived at a closed door. Leigh couldn't hear anything inside. "I'd leave her be if the door's closed."

When they got to the library, Leigh couldn't contain her gasp of surprise. Floor-to-ceiling shelves framed a viewing window onto the park across the street. Hundreds of books filled the shelves, and stacks of them lay on tables throughout the room, including one nestled between two wingback chairs before a fireplace. A cup of tea steamed on the small table.

"I was catching up on a novel when you arrived," Vera said. "I'll be here for the next few hours if you need me after I show you your rooms."

At the top of an open staircase, a door led to a sitting room with walls painted bright blue like a cloudless sky and trimmed in cream.

"This is the blue suite." Vera's tone turned sardonic. "Obvious, I'll admit, but still a lovely setting. There are two bedrooms with one adjoining bath. All the linens were changed a few days ago. If you get hungry, we're right above the smaller kitchen, just down the bottom of the stairs. Like I said, I'll be up for a while and would be happy to make you something if you don't feel up to cooking for yourself. I know bloodling appetites vary."

She spoke the word as if it wasn't something Leigh had been keeping secret for a year.

"Who—" Leigh's voice cracked. "Are there any others . . . like you . . . here?"

The tour hadn't included the basement, which was no doubt where the vampires stowed their donors.

"No," Vera said as she walked the periphery of the room, turning on lamps. Warm light spilled over a surprisingly welcoming space. "I'm the only staff. Miss doesn't like people underfoot. Keeping the house in working order takes up a lot of time. It does pay well, though, and I still have plenty of time left for my own work."

"Work?"

"I'm finishing up a history degree at the university here in Black Rose City."

A university. In vampire territory. And this woman . . . *worked* here. It was a job to her, at least on the surface.

"I'll let you get settled. Again, if you need anything, just let me know."

With the ghost of a smile on her lips, Vera left and closed the door behind her.

Alone for the first time in what felt like days, Leigh stood in the center of the room, searching every corner for threats and finding none.

Joan. She needed to call Joan.

Leigh crossed the room to the nearest window. The grounds below were still empty. She pulled her phone from her pocket—what could she tell Joan about where she was?—and found no signal.

Was it deliberately blocked, or was this why Bartholomew had been so focused on his phone earlier?

She'd have to try again later.

Now that the threat was in a different part of the building, Leigh took stock. So far, her every expectation had been thwarted. After discovering what Leigh was, Bartholomew could have dragged her from Mist. He had instead offered parley. Elizaveta and Bartholomew could have killed Joan and taken Leigh by force, but they hadn't. Upon arrival, they had been almost solicitous, as if trying to get a wounded animal to accept vaccination.

The woman, Vera, didn't act as if she was being held against her will, and claimed to be the only human in the entire residence.

One last suspicion led Leigh to check the door. Made

of solid wood, elaborately carved to match the motif on the wallpaper trim below the molding and, like everything else in the exquisitely decorated room, painted blue.

The door was unlocked.

The house was silent except for the distant crackling of the fire—a fire that now blazed. Vera must have added a log when she returned to the library.

Leigh clenched her fists at the reaffirmed knowledge that she could sense the fire downstairs.

Elizaveta and Bartholomew claimed to have answers, and if those gloves Elizaveta had been wearing were meant to suggest she had the same ... abilities ... as Leigh, then she was the best lead under the circumstances.

All the fight drained from Leigh's limbs and she collapsed into a nearby chair. Joan would be worried sick, and likely breaking things in response to how Leigh had left.

Would she ever see Joan again?

Leigh buried the thought as soon as it rose in her head. If she started crying now, she might never stop.

The vampires had promised no harm would come to her, that they wouldn't turn her. Maybe they'd meant it when they said she could learn to control her powers, and if so, she could go home.

Some of those answers might be in the library downstairs.

Leigh stood, and vowed to do whatever it took to get her powers under control, to get back to Joan where she belonged, which was not here.

With one more deep breath to center herself, Leigh opened the door and stepped into the unknown.

CHAPTER 13

ENDLESS FEBRUARY RAIN drenched the streets and muddied the roads, and the lines at the city gates were short.

Joan was grateful she wouldn't have to push her motorcycle for long.

Armed guards manned the wall and a few more languished near the gate, which was wide enough for three lanes of traffic. Barricades and two more guards blocked all but one lane, where a man with a clipboard stood beneath a pop-up tent beside a woman with a computer tablet.

Every vehicle was stopped, and the occupants were required to step outside for a complete search. Joan was in the pedestrian line, which moved a little faster. She couldn't recall whether this much security was normal.

"Please step out of the line."

The tense tone snapped Joan from her assessment. The woman with the tablet had one hand on her sidearm as she spoke to the group of people in front of Joan.

"Please," one of them said, a middle-aged Black man who sagged in exhaustion as if he'd walked miles on foot. "We just need a chance."

The man with the clipboard shook his head, though he

appeared sorry about it. "None of your skills meet the current criteria."

The lone woman in their group made a sucking sound with her teeth and raised her hands in disgust. "That's what they said in Eugene, and in Salem. How can we even get the skills you want if you won't let us in?"

"Kayla," the Black man said. "Let's just go."

"To where, Anders? We're starving out here."

The guard woman spoke again. "You could apply to the donor program—"

"We don't want to be monster food," Kayla said. "We're healthy and we can work."

"Then I urge you to try one of the refugee camps."

"They're all full." Kayla's anger faded into desperate pleading. "You can't throw people away like this. There's nowhere else for us to go."

The guard flicked open the strap holding her gun in its holster. "Please move along."

For a long moment, the tension was thicker than the rain. The guards by the barricades took a step closer to the tent, and in line no one else moved.

Anders put a supportive arm around Kayla's shoulder as he and the other man in their group stepped back into the deluge, the group huddling together as they walked back the way they'd come.

The tension broke. The guards returned to their post at the barricade, and the man with the clipboard scratched at his beard and didn't look up when it was Joan's turn. "ID."

"Don't have one." Not common in these parts, but not unheard of. A lot of people existed outside the larger cities where identification systems were reliable. Most other places didn't have the means or equipment to keep track and manually screened entry.

With limited resources, population management was

typical, and in a city the size of this one, the number of people rejected from the gates must be in the hundreds every month.

"You'll have to consent to an identification search and confirmation."

"I understand." Joan didn't plan on going to wherever they'd send her to have her identification corroborated. All she needed, though, was to get through the gate.

"Name."

"Kaia Wells." Joan had never given a fake name in her life. What was one more transgression if it got her closer to Leigh?

"Age."

"Twenty-eight." She'd stick to the truth where she could.

"City of origin." He yawned, bored and uninterested in her answers.

"San Francisco." Plausible—she could have traveled the distance alone, and far enough away no one would likely contest her story.

"Reason for visit."

Joan had considered her answer in advance, no matter how distasteful it was to say out loud. "Applying for donorship."

He took a long look at her, no doubt assessing her and the likelihood of her acceptance. "They don't take junkies."

"I'm clean," Joan said, playing her part of a desperate soul seeking salvation.

"You have forty-eight hours to get assessed for donorship. If you get rejected, you have seventy-two hours to find work. No viable employment, no city access. The city guard will arrest and deport you, at your expense if it requires towing your vehicle."

"Yes, sir." None of this mattered. She wouldn't be here that long.

A crow squawked nearby and Joan fought the urge to glare at it. She needed to get through these gates before a swarm showed up and gave her away.

He handed her a simple plastic band with a number on it.

"Here's your city ID. Wear this at all times and turn it in when you leave."

She nodded. He didn't appear to notice.

"Move along," he said.

Joan tried not to sigh in relief as she pushed her motorcycle toward the gates, gazing at the buildings ahead instead of the guards she was passing.

"Probably another crazy junkie," one of the guards said.

"Hopeless," said another.

Is this what Leigh had dealt with? The utter disdain of everyone she walked by, as if all she'd endured had meant nothing?

Joan stayed within the traffic-coned lanes to the city proper, pondering how fighting vampires was nowhere near as difficult as fighting human nature.

Over the next day Joan changed her disguise five different times. It couldn't be helped—the crows kept following her, and when the murders got too big, they attracted attention.

The third time, she ditched the bike since it was the one thing tying her previous glamoured personas together. Selling the bike yielded a little cash, which she hoped she could trade for information.

The fifth time she applied the glamour the burns were the worst, the skin now blistered and puffy from the ointment. If she kept this up, she'd have new scars to add to her personal collection.

Joan didn't have as much luck as she'd had at Loufield's, not even in the dark underground clubs where her money should have gained her a few secrets. No one spoke to strangers like her, which gave her no opportunity to bring up the vampires, or to find an unofficial way into their territory.

In the end, the path from Portland to Black Rose City was as simple as it was undesirable.

Joan walked into the donor center on the main avenue at

sunset on the second day. Humans manned the staff in a plain, two-story office building open twenty-four hours a day. One bloodling sat at an observational desk, implying he was some kind of manager. He had his head propped on one hand, eyes half-closed and jaw slack.

A dozen tables, each staffed by a human with an intake station, were arranged in rows of three and four across. Most of them were filled.

Joan picked a table with an empty chair, and offered her arm for a blood test.

The man at the station had the appearance of an old librarian, his hair and beard thin and white, his skin pale. Startling blue eyes regarded her.

"On-site or on location?"

Joan had never been inside a donor station. His questions didn't mean anything to her.

"Sorry, force of habit," he said with a smile. "I get a lot of repeat customers here. Do you want to donate blood on-site for a cash reward, or would you like to apply for a position in Black Rose City?"

She took too long to answer, and his tone changed from jovial to encouraging. "There are temporary positions if you'd like one of those. Seven, fourteen, or twenty-one-day stints in one of the donor centers. You can try it and see if you like it."

Like she was picking out an outfit or a car.

To her chagrin, her teeth chattered in nervousness. "S-seven days."

"Okay, great! That'll take a little more work, but we can get it sorted. Blood and urine samples are required. The blood results come back pretty quickly. The urine sample may take up to two hours. Still, we won't keep you waiting too long."

He sent her to a nearby restroom to collect a urine sample. When Joan returned, he'd donned a set of nitrile gloves and arranged his implements on a sterile tray.

While he assembled his materials, Joan eyed the vial that would contain her blood and mentally cast a small spell.

Nota sanguinem meum. Mark my blood.

Originally designed to use as breadcrumbs in hostile territory, the spell would instill a sliver of her personal energy to a location outside her body. She'd use it later to track down the vial.

No way was she leaving a sample of her blood here. Even if she had no intention of becoming a donor, blood magic was rare, though not out of the question, and a war witch's blood would be valuable to someone who understood its power.

The needle hurt more than usual. Joan hadn't eaten or slept, and pushing herself this hard was a drain on her reserves. Casting the spell was going to cost her.

Joan's blood was typed and the sample deemed viable. Her urine was clean, with no signs of any drug use, though her iron levels were high.

She pretended she had no idea why.

"Alright," the man said after he'd logged her latest fake name in his system. "Here's a badge to get you through the gate. Report to the Leonard Street Center for your donations."

Joan nodded in understanding, not trusting herself to speak as he handed her a plastic badge on a lanyard covered in the donor center logo. The whole thing was so benign, and he was acting so normal, like this was a library or something. It was creepy.

Once outside, she ducked around the corner. The shadows were long enough to hide her as she flattened herself against the outside wall of the building. She closed her eyes, visualized the vial of blood in the rack where the donor worker had stacked it, and cast her senses toward the marker of her spell.

In the dark behind her eyelids, she saw nothing. She felt the marker as if she could reach out and touch it.

Purgato fervere. Cleansing boil.

She funneled her power into boiling her blood in the vial to ash. It had probably also broken the vial, which would get someone's attention—with any luck, long after she'd gone.

All roads in this part of town led to the bridge between Portland and Black Rose City. A natural gully separated the two sectors, and at the bottom lay an old rail line, rusted and unpassable from disuse.

The bridge was narrow though sturdy enough for a loaded semi to pass over it one-way. No cars were queued to drive over now. A dozen or so pedestrians walked in the designated lane, passing the guard at the other end.

The Portland guards ignored her as she passed. She guessed they were more concerned with the people coming back, and all the foot traffic was headed into Black Rose City.

As Joan walked over the bridge, she peered over the railing at the gully below. A few cars, old and long rusted over, lay where they'd crashed. Towing them out might have been more trouble than those cars were worth. Another innocuous commonplace occurrence.

What else was she expecting? Piles of corpses?

A crow's cry reminded her to keep moving.

At the other end of the bridge, a male bloodling about twenty years old, with dark, lank hair falling to his shoulders, sat reading a book on a bench with his feet propped up against a water fountain.

The urge to shoot him made Joan's teeth itch.

He raised his head only long enough to see the lanyard and waved Joan forward. "Stick to the green streets and stay out of the parlors if you don't want to get munched on."

Green streets? She hadn't noticed any color coding the last time she'd been here.

He licked his thumb and flipped a page in his book. Gross. "Report to your assigned donor center by first light."

Anticlimactic, and Joan still twitched with the need to stab him in the chest. Then she felt guilty about it. How was this boy any different from Leigh? And who knew what Leigh was enduring right now?

All this was Joan's fault. If she hadn't dragged Leigh to Mist . . .

Joan forced herself to focus on the mission.

Dusk fell on the main road into Black Rose City as Joan walked with a guarded stance, anticipating an attack. None came. The "green" streets were ones where the curbs had been painted a bright Kelly green. Green fluorescent streetlights kept the street as bright as day, and vendors sold food and other wares as if it were high noon on a Saturday.

Was it a front, or had Black Rose City created a space safe for humans, a civilized society for vampire sickness? Was this better or worse than the ones who hunted out in the open?

She passed a "red" street, with similarly marked curbs and lights, and down the lane she saw several establishments where vampires and bloodlings lurked. Some young vampires, their nails still short by human standards and their fangs barely canine, yelled some bullshit from the shadows but kept to their zone.

Otherwise, no one gave her a second glance. This glamour would hold for only another few hours. She had to find Fiona or reapply the glamour, and she was required to report to a donor center sooner rather than later. After that, someone would likely come looking for her, despite how relaxed her admittance had been.

She hadn't expected corpses in the gutters, but she did think the vampires and bloodlings would have been partying in the streets. If this was the kind of ship Elizaveta ran, it wasn't the nightmare Joan had envisioned.

Joan passed a building with a donor center sign over the door. A vampire walked out holding a shopping bag as if he'd picked up a six pack and a loaf of bread from a convenience store. Through the wide tinted windows lay an otherwise uninteresting interior with a counter run by bored retail staff, like every other shop she'd ever seen.

Her unease morphed into dismay. In a place like this, Leigh would never have to hide.

CHAPTER 14

"I'M TURNING IN."

Leigh's neck cracked as she snapped her head from the book she was reading to look in the housekeeper's direction.

Vera stood in the doorway to the library, covering a yawn with the back of one wrist. "My apologies. I can't keep my eyes open a moment longer."

Leigh had lost track of time. She'd joined Vera in the library soon after her arrival, though they'd exchanged only a few words. Now, the first rays of sunlight shone on the empty garden and street outside the library's picture window.

"If you find your appetite in the next few hours, I've left a few snacks in the smaller kitchen refrigerator. Please help yourself."

Leigh nodded, still reluctant to say much to this baffling woman who said she was in this vampire's den by choice. She had been hesitant to ask Vera more about her experience here in Elizaveta's residence, concerned that asking those kinds of questions would cross the vampires.

She had been reading for hours, and had declined three offers of a meal or a beverage, and hadn't volunteered any details when Vera asked what brought her to the city or how long she was planning to stay.

Vera's footsteps faded as she ventured deeper into the house, somewhere upstairs. The silence brought Leigh some relief. Here in the library she could embrace the illusion of solitude.

Her phone still had no signal, so calling Joan was still out of the question, and leaving was in no way a good idea. Neither was wandering the manor, since she wasn't sure what she'd find, or what the penalty might be for discovering anything.

Better to take advantage of the trove of vampire literature and historical references at her disposal.

Much of the history Leigh had previously learned had been chronicled by humans. Here, she'd found one tome by a vampire, the text at least three hundred years old, detailing the "reappropriation" of the stretch of valley including Calvert.

The vampires hadn't cared those areas were already populated, instead concerned with how they could be appropriated since it was their responsibility to steward both the land and the people.

Such details were terrifying and fascinating all at once. She was distracted from that line of thought when she found an entire shelf of books dedicated to bloodlings alone—all scientific journals, archived research, and obscure academic papers from universities or institutions she'd never heard of.

Leigh knew how she'd become a bloodling—an unwanted sexual encounter with a vampire. She hadn't seen the woman before or since, and hadn't known at the time what the consequences would be of their interaction. The vampire, Sylvia, had been kind and gentle, but Leigh had been an unwilling participant. Still, the powers she'd gained had helped her escape.

The concept of bloodling experimentation hadn't occurred to her. Was that part of the interview? She didn't want to read the journals, but she did so she could understand what might be expected when the vampires came for her.

The older volumes were horrid—as archaic and violent as one might expect considering they predated most scientific and medical advancements. The more recent ones were somewhat better—not one so far had included any mention of powers like hers. They did mention those who had been witches before they'd been turned, and how some of them had held on to their skill.

This was no surprise to Leigh. Victor had created a coven of such vampires, and when he couldn't find enough, he kidnapped and turned several witches to see if their powers persisted after their change.

What happened to bloodlings who weren't turned into vampires? Did they live human lifespans with their new powers and abilities? Leigh had never talked to another bloodling. She didn't know what she might ask of one if she did.

And secretly she wondered if somewhere in all these books was the means of turning her back into something closer to human—to get rid of her powers altogether, to never put another person at risk.

The long daylight hours passed, and Leigh found herself less tense than she'd been with the vampires and the housekeeper around. This room in particular was calming. The scent of the books combined with the faint wood smoke from the fire's embers was comforting, along with a faint scent she couldn't place—something earthy and musky though not unpleasant.

An hour after sunset she stood next to the window, riveted by a book about a witch who'd become a bloodling and how the transformation had affected his powers. She couldn't read fast enough to satisfy herself, once tearing a page in her haste despite the gloves slowing her down.

"Good evening," Bartholomew said from the archway to the hall.

Leigh dropped the book. She hadn't sensed him coming, though she could now sense Elizaveta nearby. Frozen, she tried to control her rapid breathing. Her racing heartbeat would have to take care of itself.

"If you would join us, please," he said, and raised one long-taloned hand to place his aviator sunglasses on his face. Once again, he wore an immaculate black suit and white dress shirt with no tie.

He didn't come any closer, seeming content to stand as long as she might take to collect herself. Leigh remembered the interview was what she'd come for, no matter how informative the library might be.

She retrieved the book and set it on a side table before walking toward the door. Her fear was less about what Bartholomew might do to her now and more about whatever this interview would involve.

Elizaveta waited for them outside the back door they'd come in the night before. Once she saw Leigh, she turned without a word and marched to the street.

Leigh couldn't bring herself to ask where they were going, so scared was she of the answer, though it seemed they were headed back in the direction of the hangar. The streets were empty again, the houses all dark, and distant sounds of the only activity were blocks away.

Was the quiet typical of this neighborhood?

Pondering the puzzle was better for Leigh's mental state than thinking about where she was going and what might happen when she got there.

Would they ask her about the man she'd killed? What would they do if they found out about the vampire she'd killed to protect herself? Murder was a crime everywhere. She had no idea what kind of justice vampires would demand once they knew what she'd done to one of their own.

Their destination turned out to be a warehouse near the hangar, and during the walk not one person crossed their path. Was it because Elizaveta wanted to keep Leigh a secret, or was it a tactic to set Leigh at ease?

Either way, Leigh was not relaxed, and would never feel safe in their presence.

At the edge of a commercial sector, judging by the business

signage on single- and two-story buildings and warehouses along both sides of the street, one windowless warehouse was bordered by an eight-foot fence topped by razor wire.

Bartholomew unlocked the gate to allow their passage, and locked it behind them.

An ache in Leigh's shoulders and heat in her palms reminded her to deepen her breathing, to calm herself in the face of the unknown. What would happen if she lost control now?

Inside the building the air was musty and stale in spite of the ventilation system Leigh could hear humming from within. Bartholomew flipped on a few light switches as they passed, and much of the space was empty. He didn't slow until they came to a locked, fortified door in the heart of the building.

When he opened the door, the odor of wet, stale earth filled Leigh's senses and she faltered.

They were going underground, and though the memories didn't come to mind, the sensations slammed into her of being held captive in the dark, in the muck and mud.

Basement? Or dungeon?

The edges of her vision darkened, and she drew a sharp breath.

"No harm will come to you here," Bartholomew said, joining his hands in front of himself. With his suit and placid demeanor, he acted like he was en route to a business meeting.

Maybe that's all this was to him. By contrast, Elizaveta grimaced in impatience.

After a few deep breaths, Leigh's rational thought returned, and she convinced herself she wasn't about to be locked away in an underground cell, that this time was different.

When Leigh nodded, Elizaveta once again took the lead.

Plain wooden stairs led to an expansive lower level, one with twenty-foot ceilings and industrial-sized fans. One wall was covered in shelves stretching eight feet high, and Leigh didn't look closer at the contents because she was too distracted by two of the room's other features.

One wall was open earth, with several metal beams at even intervals supporting the overhead structure. Before that wall were three freestanding concrete barriers, six feet tall and four feet wide. From where Leigh stood, the barriers appeared to be a few feet thick, and their bases were set into the ground where some of the flooring had been removed.

A long, black metal trough stretched the length of the room along one wall. A foot-long lever was mounted at one end above the trough, which was empty and sizable enough to hold a lot of fluid. Leigh pictured it filled with blood, and bit her lip to keep from crying out.

Bartholomew lowered the lever. A deep grinding noise drove Leigh back a step as portions of the wall above the trough—each no more than a square foot—opened outward and flows of dirt fed into the trough. When the trough was ankle-deep full of dirt, he turned off the source, appearing satisfied with the results.

Leigh was only incrementally relieved, and now confused.

On the other side of the room by the shelves Elizaveta retrieved several objects and tucked them under her arm with the casual negligence of someone shopping for ingredients to a familiar recipe. The image was incongruous, since she was dressed in matching slacks and waistcoat as she stacked wood blocks in one arm of her crisp white dress shirt.

In the trough, Elizaveta made several small piles of different materials on top of the dirt. She said nothing, explained nothing as she worked, and did not look at Leigh as she did so.

One pile was made of scraps of shredded newspaper. The next was of wood kindling, no more than the size of the vampire's fist. Next were scraps of fabric followed by a block of wood, then a pile of metal shavings, and several shards of glass. The final item Elizaveta set down was the most confusing—a chunk of cement.

Bartholomew pulled one last item from a refrigerator in the corner Leigh hadn't noticed until now. While Leigh couldn't see through the black plastic as he set it in the trough, the smell made her uncomfortable.

Raw meat. Without understanding how she knew, Leigh was certain it was beef. She suppressed her horror at its appetizing scent. She'd been a vegetarian since she'd left the vineyard based on the unspoken fear that eating meat might lead to other . . . appetites.

Leigh closed her eyes to send a loving thought to Joan. When she opened them again, the vampires stood awaiting her attention.

She willed herself for the thousandth time not to flee.

The nature of the interview became clearer when Elizaveta removed her own gloves. She stepped to one side of the trough, leaving some distance for Leigh to approach.

"Do you need any instructions?"

Leigh shook her head. "I don't think so."

Her hands trembled so much, it took a few attempts to pull her gloves free. She tucked them in the back pockets of her jeans as she approached the pile of paper.

She summoned the spell Joan had taught her, her heart twinging at the thought. Joan couldn't help her now.

"Lux cordis mei, candens et sine fine." Light of my heart, incandescent and endless.

The pile of paper flamed and burned to ash.

"Must you always speak the spell?" Bartholomew asked, not unkindly.

Leigh was about to answer yes since she'd only called the spell once before, but she hadn't called the spell when she'd burned Joan, or killed the man in Mist.

"I—I'm not sure." She glanced at Elizaveta, who nodded for her to proceed.

This time, Leigh didn't cast the spell. She channeled her fear and frustration instead, casting all her uncertainty into her hands.

It worked, though she didn't know how she felt about that.

The kindling, the fabric, and the wood all caught fire without difficulty. Leigh assessed the shavings for a moment, trying to figure out how to get the flame on her fingers to transfer to something not easily burnt. This was different from touching clothes—or worse, skin—but if the vampires thought it was possible, there had to be a way to do it.

In the end, the solution was simple. She pressed her fingers against the metal, like she had done to Nathaniel's clothes, to the thrall in Mist, and visualized what she wanted.

She leapt back in surprise when the metal turned black, then red and finally yellow, melting to slag and sinking into the dirt until the molten sludge was covered.

Her breath quickened and her heart raced. In rapid succession, she melted the glass using the same method, and the chunk of concrete.

Without being asked she stomped to the last object, refusing to pull the meat from the bag before she pressed her fingertips to the plastic, and watched the whole thing warp and smoke as it burned down to a pile of ash.

This was so much worse than she'd feared. With this kind of power, she could burn down her home, kill Joan, kill anyone who came near her ...

Leigh rested her hand on the trough, and fire flared from her hand. The metal blackened and in the space of seconds dripped molten yellow to the floor.

She cried out as she stepped back, hands outstretched before her, and didn't stop walking backward until she hit the wall, her breathing now a pained whimpering in her ears.

"Press your hands together, palm to palm," Elizaveta said, demonstrating the movement.

To her shock Elizaveta knelt before her. Leigh had slunk down the wall into a sitting position.

Driven by the urge to *not* touch anything else, Leigh

followed her directions.

"Now breathe," Elizaveta said, and took a deep breath herself. For the first time she was gentle, placating, and for a moment Leigh was too panicked to be afraid.

Against her will she emulated Elizaveta's breathing until she could see through her tears.

"This is what you do when it's too much," Elizaveta said, her voice low and melodic, even-tempered if not soothing. "Pull back, press your hands together until you can center yourself, until the flames recede."

Recede? Wasn't this power constant?

A squeaking noise pulled Leigh's attention to the far side of the room. Bartholomew had lifted the lever again, and streams of dirt poured from the walls. The room was warm and clouded with smoke and steam, but Leigh could see the trough beyond Elizaveta's shoulders.

One end, near the place where Leigh had placed her hand, had melted enough for the trough's contents to leak out. A pile of dirt steamed, slagged metal smoking in clumps.

"I didn't—I don't . . ." What could she say? Her lack of control was self-evident.

Would this be considered a failed interview, or a success? What was it these vampires wanted from her? They didn't give the impression of being angry. Bartholomew had removed his jacket and rolled up his sleeves. He'd retrieved a shovel from somewhere and was using it to organize the mess, as if this were something he'd done before.

Elizaveta tilted her head to one side as if considering her words, her gaze measuring. "This is a rare power. One not easily mastered."

She stood and returned to the shelves. "It can be shaped into a skill, one you can command."

Leigh hastened to her feet, wiping the tears from her face with the sleeve of her shirt, embarrassed at the emotional display.

Maybe they wouldn't see it as weakness, but there was so little she could control about her circumstances. She wanted to keep her thoughts and feelings to herself.

At the end of the trough that was still functional, Elizaveta placed four blocks of wood at spaced intervals. After one glance to make sure Leigh was paying attention, Elizaveta rolled up one sleeve. She touched one fingertip to the first block, and didn't flinch as it flamed.

Though Leigh had surmised as much, here was proof she and Elizaveta had a similar power.

Elizaveta pulled her hand free, holding Leigh's gaze as she put the same hand back into the fire.

Leigh gasped. Before she could exhale, her breathing stopped altogether as the flame *moved*, sliding across the blackened wood until it flowed onto—no, *into* Elizaveta's hand.

Elizaveta's flesh glowed red, orange, and gold, like embers as the flames got smaller, until there was only the plasma of heat on the wood, and then that, too, was gone. By some miracle, her hand was whole and without injury.

She had pulled the flame back into herself. Not a hair was out of place as if this spectacle had required little if any effort, and not a blemish remained on her skin. Her clothes were still unsullied. She didn't even look out of breath.

Elizaveta did it several more times—conjuring flame and setting the wood alight, siphoning the flame back into her hand. The wood blackened with the exercise yet never burned enough to fall apart or collapse into ash.

Her control was as mesmerizing as it was enviable.

Leigh didn't ask out loud, but she wanted to learn how to do this one thing more than she had ever wanted anything since Joan.

If she could learn to control herself, to call fire back into her body when her control slipped, maybe she wouldn't hurt anyone again.

Leigh stepped closer to the trough, hoping Elizaveta would demonstrate again.

Though Elizaveta didn't smile, her eyes brightened with something like delight.

CHAPTER 15

OF ALL THE places Joan might have searched to find an informant, this wouldn't have made the list.

The clues she'd gotten at Loufield's led her to a small office building on the outskirts of town, in clear view of the St. Johns Bridge. Most of the gray building was hidden behind trees with thick branches bare of leaves. Several of the ground-floor windows were boarded up.

Low clouds hovered above streets still wet with the rain from the night before. Nine in the morning wasn't early in Calvert, but in Black Rose City only a coffee shop was open down the block. Everything else was locked up tight.

On the corner of a cross street in a run-down residential neighborhood, Joan stood in the inset-covered entrance of the office building. Only one button on the building's intercom board had a label, and she pressed it until a buzzer sounded.

"IA Inc.," said a tired female voice, low and scratchy with sleep or a rough night.

"Here to discuss some universal life for my uncle. Missed my appointment last Tuesday." Joan delivered the odd key phrase as she'd been directed by the witch back at Loufield's.

Instead of an answer the door buzzed. Inside, the two office doors on the main floor were boarded shut. Joan climbed the carpeted stairs to a landing with only one door.

"Independent Actuaries Incorporated," was painted on the door in thin gold lettering six inches high.

Insurance. The spying war witch deep in the heart of vampire territory was an insurance agent.

The door was unlocked.

The windowless waiting area reeked of cigarette smoke, wood polish and bleach, and had two cushioned thirty-year-old chairs at right angles around a chest-high potted plant of surprising health in the corner.

As Joan closed the door behind her, muffled footsteps approached the open inner office door, and a tall, red-haired woman emerged next to the empty receptionist's desk. She was lean and masculine presenting, wearing a white T-shirt under a black leather jacket, black jeans, and black combat boots. By contrast, her cropped red hair and blue eyes stood out against the monochromatic attire.

"My apologies," the woman said, wiping sleep from her eyes behind her black, block-framed glasses. "My assistant works the night shift."

Most likely a bloodling or maybe even a vampire. Working as an assistant to a war witch. This city was . . . extraordinary wasn't the right word. Weird was closer.

In the blink of an eye the woman sized Joan up and offered her hand.

"Fiona Gunnarsdottir," she said, squeezing once before releasing Joan's hand. They were about the same height. She held up her palm to stop Joan from speaking. "No need to share yours. Follow me."

She led Joan into her office and took a seat behind her desk, leaving Joan to decide whether to open or close the door.

Joan left it open.

Fiona lifted a pack of cigarettes in the air, wordlessly asking

Joan for permission. Joan waved her away.

After lighting a cigarette and taking a deep drag, Fiona leaned back in her chair and propped her scuffed combat boots on her scratched desk.

"Let me save you the trouble of crafting a bullshit story," she said, skipping the pleasantries. "You reek of magic, and you walk like a fighter, so I'm guessing you're a war witch."

She blew out her smoke, and gestured at the chair, offering Joan a seat. "You've got balls of steel sneaking into Black Rose City, and I'd also bet good money you're glamoured, so I don't want to know who you are."

Fiona left her cigarette between her lips while she scratched at her trim belly through her threadbare T-shirt. "So why don't you tell me what you want, I'll tell you whether I can help you or not, and we can both go about our business."

Joan's curiosity got the better of her. "How'd you end up in this gig?"

"Lost a bet," Fiona said without blinking behind her smudged lenses, though also with no sarcasm.

"No, seriously."

"I am serious. Someone needed eyes in here, and I gambled when I couldn't afford to lose. Ended up with this shit job." She spread her arms wide to include the office and grimaced at Joan, suggesting she get on with it. "Not much information to share on the sly when most of it's all out in the open anyway."

A lot to unpack, and no time to do it. Joan took a deep breath, and ignored the tight pull on the parts of her body aching from the latest application of the glamour spell.

"I need to find out what Elizaveta has been up to for the last two days, and where she's expected to be for the next forty-eight hours."

Fiona's expression turned from bland interest to surprise, her eyebrows rising.

"Well, you don't ask for much, do you?" She stared back at

Joan long enough for cigarette ash to fall onto her chest.

"Your death sentence, just sayin'." Fiona took another drag from her cigarette, then exhaled as she tipped more ash into an over-full ashtray on her paperwork-covered desk. "Word is, she took a rare trip out of town and has been more scarce than usual since she returned. She's blocked off a bunch of streets near the manor house. No access, no trespassing, with threats of harsh penalties for anyone breaking the rules. She has been seen out and about on those same routes with Bartholomew and some bloodling."

Leigh. Leigh was still alive and not a vampire. Good news, but for how long?

"For what it's worth," Fiona said. "I don't think Elizaveta's got anything to do with the attacks."

Joan frowned since she hadn't mentioned that mess. "Didn't think she did. Not since she sent her right hand to handle the clusterfuck in Mist."

"Bartholomew was there?" Fiona's jaw dropped in shock. "In person, to deal with a bunch of thralls? Interesting. Hadn't heard that. The relays between here and there are down, and it's been screwing up my comms."

She muffled a yawn. "Packs of thralls hit more than Mist. There was another attack a couple nights ago out toward Astoria in one of the unincorporated territories, one of those usually off the vampire lord radar since it's so close to here."

Joan's trip to Arock passed across her mind. Though the tiny town fit the description, they'd escaped vampire attention, and the oddity of it distracted her for a minute before she snapped back to the conversation at hand.

"You think they're related," Joan said.

"I know they are, and I'm surprised the High Coven hasn't spoken more directly about it to the new regional power with claims to the land."

Subtle. As in, not at all.

Fiona blinked smoke from her eyes as she frowned. "More communication is better for everyone instead of arguing about who's got which turf outside Black Rose City. It's all moot if we end up ceding it to the monsters."

Joan ignored that word, though she'd previously used it often. Since finding out about Leigh, it sat sour in her mouth, as if speaking it pushed Leigh to a side Joan herself stood against.

Not if Joan could help it.

In any case, the attacks and their resolution were problems for future Joan. Right now, she needed to retrieve Leigh and get out of town.

"What's the security like at Elizaveta's manor house?"

Fiona scoffed.

"What security? She's a *First*. Nobody fucks with her, and nobody is stupid enough to cross her by trying to invade her house. It's suicide." She shook her head in disbelief. "Maybe you're not who I thought you were. Hoping you'd be a helluva lot smarter than that. Ah—"

She raised a hand to cut off Joan's response when Joan opened her mouth to speak. "No need to dignify that with an answer."

Fiona ran her hands through her short hair in what might have been an attempt to neaten it. She only succeeded in making it messier.

"Whatever you're trying to do, be smart. You want to get eyes on her, the park is the closest vantage point that's not shut down. Make damned sure your glamour holds fast. If they catch you, you'll be lucky if they turn you. Worst case isn't death, mate. It's being bounced around among the exalted elite in here, all bragging they've got a war witch as a donor. Elizaveta doesn't condone it, and she's pretty harsh with those she finds, but she doesn't catch everyone, and you could go missing for a long time in this city. Feel me?"

So far, Fiona seemed to think Joan was only interested in

Elizaveta, not in the bloodling holding her attention. Time was short and Joan was on the right track, though her supplies were shrinking. She had enough of the glamor spell to get them out of the city, assuming she could find Leigh.

Fiona exhaled a stream of smoke. All those carcinogens would kill her, given time. Considering the double agent job she had and the effect it might have on her lifespan, maybe the cigarettes were a small price to pay for a little relaxation.

Joan kept those thoughts to herself.

"Do what you've gotta do and get the hell out of town," Fiona said. "And if that's all you need from me, I suggest you leave the building before street traffic picks up."

She stood and walked toward the door. "Take the back stairwell. It leads to a basement exit covered by the hedges. Stick to the scrub until you're a block or two away. I don't want anyone to see you, even in daylight. A lot of prying eyes around here."

Joan nodded in thanks, though she was somewhat uneasy with the one-sidedness of the trade. Conducting business in the exchange of information was common and Joan hadn't brought much of anything to the table.

She did think of something she could offer. Something about the way Fiona carried herself made her think it might be received well, if not acted upon in the immediate future. A war witch shouldn't work in a place like this—hiding behind enemy lines, trading in spycraft. Not when they were trained for standup fights instead of political machinations.

Sure, any war needed spies, but Fiona seemed more trapped by the job than satisfied. And she hadn't asked for anything in return, which was rare. She was smart, though, something that would be useful in Calvert.

Joan stopped at the outer door. "You ever get out of here, and want to land somewhere less . . . less whatever this place is, give me a call."

"Can't look you up if I don't know who you are." Fiona

saluted, adding a wry arch of one eyebrow. "And I'd appreciate a warning when any serious shit is about to go down. Otherwise, please leave before you get me killed."

The polite dismissal almost made Joan smile.

CHAPTER 16

LEIGH HAD DREADED coming to this place. Now, she didn't want to leave the warehouse, so driven was she to achieve what she now knew was possible.

Touching fire didn't hurt at first, a surprising miracle within itself. Like the twinge of bumping an elbow on a doorjamb or biting into tinfoil, the initial feeling was uncomfortable but not painful.

At some point, though, as quickly as a few seconds or as long as a full minute, the sensation would change to a pain that made her see white, and she would push the flame *away* from herself before she could attempt to draw it into her hands.

They had left the basement since the trough was now irreparably damaged. Bartholomew chose another part of the warehouse where a truckload of dirt had been dumped onto the floor for her continued practice. Burnt-out stacks of wood lay atop the dirt at irregular intervals, wherever Leigh made space for another attempt to control her powers.

She persisted. She would learn how to do this. If this is what it took to get back to Joan, she'd keep trying.

Until she couldn't anymore, and the pain swallowed her up before she could cry out.

When she opened her eyes again, terror froze her before she could take another breath.

Elizaveta's face loomed above her own, her lean, muscular arms holding Leigh. "You fainted," she said, her voice tinged with disapproval.

Instead of standing near the dirt pile, Leigh now lay on the floor in a vampire's embrace. She flinched, repelled by Elizaveta's proximity though not her scent.

Elizaveta pulled away once Leigh sat up. Should Leigh apologize for her reaction? Had she insulted her ... captor?

Was she a captive? She'd been given free rein at the manor, though she hadn't explored anything beyond the library. What was her role as far as these vampires were concerned?

Lightheaded, Leigh caught herself before she collapsed again.

"You can barely hold yourself upright," Elizaveta said. "Your strength is too far depleted. You need a real meal, and not those paltry bites Vera left for you."

Since Leigh hadn't answered Vera's questions, Vera had taken to leaving random foods on the kitchen counter. Only some of her choices had been appealing enough for Leigh to eat.

Leigh had to remember Elizaveta would know about anything that happened in the manor house.

"Maybe you need some inspiration to take better care of yourself." Elizaveta glanced at Bartholomew.

Some silent conversation must have been exchanged because he stacked a few pieces of wood on a pile of dirt and took several steps back.

With no ceremony or warning, Elizaveta cast an arm out from herself in the direction of the wood. A fist-sized ball of fire materialized, ejecting from her outstretched hand and exploding against the stack. Shards of flaming kindling arced in the air from the point of contact before landing and burning out in the dirt.

Elizaveta grinned, her canine fangs pronounced against her thin, pale lips. "With a little practice, bloodling, you might actually be dangerous."

A wave of nausea passed through Leigh. She didn't want to be dangerous. She didn't want to use this power she had at all.

Across the room Bartholomew shifted the shovel to one hand and paused to glance at his cell phone. Elizaveta watched him while speaking to Leigh.

"We have other business to tend to. I'm sure you can find your way back to the manor on your own, though since we don't have anything that meets your requirements, you'll have to visit one of the establishments on the Avenue for your breakfast."

Breakfast? How long had they been here?

"Dawn approaches," Elizaveta said, answering the unspoken question.

How could she wander around Black Rose City *alone?* What monsters might lurk in the shadows here?

Elizaveta once again answered before Leigh could speak out loud.

"My protection extends across the city, particularly on the Avenue and doubly so as a guest of my home."

Her observations were uncanny, and not for the first time Leigh wondered if some vampires could hear human thought. As if they needed any more advantages.

"I have an account at most places," Elizaveta continued. "Charge whatever you require to the manor as Vera does."

Was Leigh in service to them now? No, Elizaveta had called her *a guest*. How could that be true if Leigh had not been given a choice about coming here?

Elizaveta collected herself and nodded to Bartholomew who tucked his phone back into a pocket. What an odd conversation he must have had since Leigh hadn't once heard him speak.

"We can do no more until you're replenished," Elizaveta said. "We'll start again at sunset after you've eaten and rested.

Though you may not believe me, you're doing well."

A moment later, the only noise was the fans overhead. The vampires were gone, and Leigh was alone.

Could she run?

Another thought followed in an instant. Where would she go? If she managed to escape, the answers she needed were still here.

Memory of the burns on Joan's skin in the shape of Leigh's hands flashed across her mind.

No, she'd stay until she'd mastered holding in her powers—until she'd determined whether being a bloodling could be reversed. For now, she'd focus only on the next thing in front of her, which was easy to decide because suddenly she was beyond hungry. She was *starving*.

Leigh made her way back to the main entry. Outside, morning was nearly as silent. A bird sang from a hedge down the street, a car engine raced and faded blocks away, and the few remaining shadows revealed no threats.

Free from the warehouse, free for the moment from the vampires, Leigh dug out her phone to call Joan. Once again—or better yet, *still*—there was no signal. All her texts to Joan displayed "not sent" notifications.

If Leigh's phone wasn't working, how had Bartholomew taken a call? Were they on different systems or something? Then again, he hadn't spoken to anyone. Maybe his phone was malfunctioning, too.

Leigh's stomach growled like it was twisting in on itself. She stashed her phone. Nothing could be done about it now.

The only direction she was sure of was toward the manor house. The streets were no longer empty, and a few people glanced her way. She was otherwise ignored.

The scent of cooking oil drew her toward a parallel street and she found herself standing at the edge of a cluster of food stalls.

In the summer months, Calvert had a similar outdoor food court with a few stalls tucked into a corner of the main square park. This one was larger, taking up the whole block and lining both sides of the street. Each stall was a small single structure on a raised platform with a window or door open to do business. One was the back end of a small panel truck. Most of the stalls were open, though with only a few customers.

None of them paid Leigh any attention.

Tantalizing smells overpowered her reluctance. The nearest stall was empty of customers, and a young woman stood behind the raised counter organizing utensils and beverages. She glanced up at Leigh's arrival and set down the items in her hand.

In that instant, Leigh remembered her glamour had faded.

This woman could *see* her—her scars and her bloodling eyes yet all she did was smile at Leigh.

"Get you something?"

While Leigh's heartbeat slowed from its panicked pounding, Leigh read the menu on a mounted board on the stall's door. Everything smelled amazing, but as was her habit, she resisted any meat.

"The vegetarian stew, please."

"Just a moment," the woman said, turning to prepare the order.

Leigh glanced up and down the block to make sure nothing had changed, that no one had noticed her. No one was looking her way. Instead of feeling exposed, Leigh felt invisible.

"Here you go." The woman extended a covered pint-sized container over the counter in Leigh's direction.

She'd ask for payment next, but Leigh had no money on her, and . . . Elizaveta hadn't suggested Leigh would have to pay her back. If Leigh weren't so hungry, she'd worry about it more. That was a problem for later.

"I'm supposed to . . ." The words tripped on Leigh's tongue. "Charge this to—to the manor."

"Okay, sure. Never seen a bloodling at the house, but there's a first time for everything, right?" The woman grabbed a notepad and made a note. "Enjoy the stew and have a nice day."

With that, she returned to her work, as if this had been a regular transaction.

Was this a regular transaction?

So far, Black Rose City had not been as terrifying as Leigh had feared.

She popped the lid to dip a spoon in the hot and hearty stew with beans, grains, and winter vegetables. It should have been filling, but Leigh was even hungrier after finishing it.

She ordered a hulking roasted vegetable sandwich. Like floodgates she couldn't hold back, her appetite swelled and she ordered more food. Another serving of the stew. A double order of pasta teeming with cheese. Deep fried potatoes. A second sandwich.

Once she finally—*finally*—felt full, she noticed more about the neighborhood. The block of stalls was a break in the longer street that extended in both directions. Two different businesses had signs with names ending in "on the avenue" so this must be what Elizaveta had described.

Though caution and awareness were reawakened after the distraction of food, the thought of going back to the warehouse, to being in the steamy room of burning things, sounded less appealing than lengthening her walk outside.

With no visible threats and the fresh air in her lungs, Leigh ventured beyond the food stalls to learn more about her surroundings. Side streets fed into the Avenue, some marked green, others red. Now mid-morning, the day was cold and the rain was sporadic as more people arrived, most of them human.

Twice she saw other bloodlings, one closing a shop before walking in the opposite direction, and another running one of the food stalls.

A pause in the rain and a thinning of the clouds allowed

watery sunlight to cast her shadow.

No one stopped her or initiated conversation beyond a morning greeting. She wondered whether Elizaveta had told everyone who she was or if the people here did not care.

Or was it because she was a bloodling? She had thought she'd be in more danger and kept under lock and key. Yet, here in vampire territory, Leigh felt more freedom to be herself than she did in Calvert.

Without Joan by her side, though, this supposed freedom didn't matter.

A burst of curiosity drove her to adventure a bit more before returning to the manor house for a brief rest. Leigh gathered the courage to visit a few shops on the Avenue—the tea store, an herbalist, a bookstore, a shop filled with houseplants.

When she stepped inside the last one, the smell of the greenery settled knots in her shoulders she hadn't been aware of, much like working in the garden did for her back home.

She wanted to be surrounded by more than the potted plants this store offered.

Back near the manor Leigh crossed the sidewalk and strode toward a grove of towering cedars, oaks, pines, and firs. Dark clouds rolled in and a cold winter wind blew through the park as the rain returned and the first few splatters fell on her exposed skin. The cold still didn't bother her—an oddity she was adapting to—and she meandered among the trees, brushing herself against their bark, careful to keep her hands tucked in her pockets.

Reminded of the threat her hands posed, Leigh decided she didn't need more rest now that she'd been refueled by so much food. Time to get back to work.

A familiar squawking nearby caught her attention. Rufus jumped from branch to branch, getting a little closer to her each time.

Leigh stared at the crow, wondering if she was losing her

mind. Maybe it was a different bird, but it had the same ruffled chest feathers, same twist of its head as if inquiring where his snacks were.

Was he a messenger, or was Joan nearby?

Joan couldn't have figured out how to communicate with the crows in so short a time, could she? It'd only been, what, two or three days, depending on how you counted when vampires stayed up half the night.

Leigh thought of the fireball Elizaveta had thrown like an afterthought, how it had exploded through the blocks of wood, the flying fire faster than anything Leigh had ever seen.

What would happen if Joan were discovered so close to Elizaveta's home? If they faced off against each other . . . Joan was an exceptional war witch, yes, but she might not have a chance against that kind of destructive power.

Joan shouldn't be here. She shouldn't be anywhere *near* here.

More squawking nearby made Leigh look across the park where a tall, lean figure leaned against a tree. The person was not familiar. She was a taller woman with wide shoulders and a trim physique under her form-fitting outdoor gear.

A dozen crows swirled around as the woman waved at Leigh. The murder grew, now some thirty birds swarming into position, and the puzzle made sense.

Joan. It must be Joan, and she was using a glamour.

Leigh glanced around to make sure no one else was nearby and traversed the distance between them on her next breath.

She had to get Joan away from here.

"What are you doing?" Leigh tugged Joan's arm, pulling her behind a tree to hide them from the house. The vampires were most likely asleep, or whatever they did during the day, but Vera might see them and reveal Joan's presence.

The confused, angry expression was one Leigh had seen countless times, though odd on this foreign face. Joan was so pale she appeared Caucasian, and her eyes were a lighter brown.

Her hair was short, cut close to the scalp. A nasty scar marred the skin between one eyebrow and an ear.

"You escaped?" Joan asked, and her voice hadn't changed at all. "Makes things easier."

The worry and love in her eyes was all Joan.

"No, I . . . no, I didn't escape." Leigh would have hugged her, glamour or no, if the threat of discovery didn't petrify her where she stood. "You can't be here."

She didn't have time to explain how none of what she'd experienced in the last few days had been what she'd feared.

"Yeah, getting here was . . . something," Joan said. "I'll tell you about it later 'cause we don't have much time. I've got enough of the glamour spell for both of us, and then I can find a way out of the city before dark."

"Who else is with you?" Would Dayton have come?

"Just me," Joan said.

Leigh's jaw dropped. "You could have been caught. You could have been *killed*, and for what?"

Of course Joan had come to get Leigh. Doing so without a plan or backup was insane.

Confusion furrowed Joan's brows. "I had to get you out of here."

She reached for Leigh's arm, and the press of her skin against Leigh's triggered her memories. Those burns on Joan's hips were hard to forget, and remembering was enough to inspire the stiffening of Leigh's spine.

Leigh couldn't leave Black Rose City.

"You need to go, Joan. Get out of the city, but I . . . I'm not coming with you."

Not yet.

Joan's mouth gaped, her expression incredulous. "Not coming . . ."

"I have to stay here."

Joan's lips tightened to a thin, pink line, a warning that

whatever she said next would not be kind.

"So you're one of them now?"

Though the words were mean and spiteful, Leigh could see the hurt behind them. They still cut her like a knife. Anger, deep and righteous, swelled in Leigh's body and burst across her lips.

"How can you say that to me?" Heat flared in her trembling hands and she shoved them into her pockets. "After everything I've been through, that's what you think?"

Joan's strange face twisted in pain. "Okay, I'm sorry. I didn't . . . I didn't mean it."

"I don't *want* to be here. I have to. I have to *fix* this."

Leigh held her hands up, careful even in her anger to keep them from touching Joan. "I was going crazy looking for answers. Do you understand? What it was like for me to have burned you like that?"

"I know, baby, but—"

"You don't know," Leigh said. "Elizaveta is . . ."

She's just like me.

Horror at the truth sent a tremor through her. No, she couldn't think about what similarities she shared with a vampire. She'd shatter apart.

"Leigh, trust me, we don't need them to figure this out."

"You're not listening," Leigh said. "This isn't about them. This is about what *I* want."

She needed to stay, to learn what she could, and she needed to know Joan was somewhere safe, not in this mess. At least as a bloodling, Leigh wouldn't be treated as a donor. What would they do with a war witch like Joan?

Leigh wiped angry tears from her eyes. They didn't do her any good and were in the way. "I have learned more in the last two days here than I have in the last year at home. I don't mind hiding behind a glamour, no matter how much it hurts, but I can't go back without . . . I have to see this through. But you, you've got to get out of the city before you're caught. I'll be okay."

And as she said those words, she realized they were true. She had to trust that the treatment she'd received since her arrival would last.

"I love you, Joan." Leigh wanted to kiss Joan despite her strangeness, yet she didn't believe Joan was hidden well enough to escape attention. "You can't fix this for me. Go home."

Joan recoiled as if she'd been slapped.

Leigh turned her back and walked away before she did something stupid like leaping into Joan's glamoured arms.

CHAPTER 17

FOR ONCE, EVEN THE damned crows were quiet.

Joan's current problem, though, as she pondered the dusty overhead beams from her sprawled position on her living room couch, was that the silence was no better.

After Leigh had left her alone in the park, Joan had worked through several emotional states, none of them good, and made her way out of Black Rose City, out of Portland, and back on the road home.

Anger. Frustration. Grief. The worst, by far, had been the guilt.

If Joan hadn't taken Leigh to Mist . . .if she hadn't insisted she could find the answers Leigh needed . . .

She could fight vampires and would have fought like hell to get Leigh out of their territory, but Leigh wanted to stay, and . . . well, Joan didn't have anything to combat Leigh's free will.

When the guilt gave way to despair, Joan decided not to think at all lest she lose her goddamned mind, which brought her back to the silence.

The early morning rain had stopped, though something somewhere was still dripping. The gutters above the porch, maybe, with big plopping drops echoing through the open front door and the dim living room.

Why close the door? Nobody here but her, and she wanted to taste the air without having to go outside. The cold wasn't enough to dissuade her, either, since she wanted—no, needed—to feel some connection to the elements though it meant she was still wearing her winter jacket and boots in the house.

Her stomach rumbled. She ignored it though she couldn't remember when she last ate anything, or which of the abandoned coffee mugs covering the living room table was the one she'd used most recently over the last few days.

No plates, though. Food sounded more nauseating than appealing.

The silence resumed, as empty as the homestead.

Leigh's presence had been a thick, comforting warmth filling the house. Now it was dark and cold no matter how big Joan built the fire.

Oh. The fire was out again. She had stoked it the moment she woke at dawn. Now it was black and quiet, not even smoking, and the sky outside suggested the noon hour was approaching. The passing time hadn't registered.

"*Ignis.*" She pointed at the hearth.

A line of flame slid across one of the blackened logs, sparking the fire once more. The crackling broke the silence for a time, but the logs were too burnt to feed the flames, and it died again.

Shadows shifted as the day passed.

Two crows landed on the front porch. One was brave enough to walk through the doorway.

The birds were another indication of her inability to affect those things she should be able to handle. The crows. The vampires. The revelation of Leigh's secret. All of it was too much to hold inside her chest anymore.

The silence was unbearable.

Joan screamed, a long, sustained cry bordering on mania and made more powerful and resonant by the power coursing in her veins. The crows scattered. The floorboards rumbled and one of the dining room windows shattered. She stopped when the ringing in her ears grew painful.

The quiet that followed was heavier than the one before. A glass in the kitchen tipped over and broke, maybe already in the sink. Something thumped in the cellar—one of the furnace pipes since the damned thing kept acting up—before it settled.

She couldn't keep sitting here, yet she didn't move, not even when a strange shiver brushed across her skin.

Clicking noises encroached upon the silence, growing louder until they stopped at the same time Willy appeared in the doorway, blocking the pale light of sunset.

Hadn't it just been noon? And how could the dog get in here?

Right. The front door was still open. The niggling sensation had been the wards. Willy posed no threat so he'd passed through them without consequence.

The next slight to the uncomfortable peace was the sound of boots and their vibration through the porch stairs.

Guess Dayton wasn't a threat either, though his presence pissed her off. She'd managed to keep him at bay for a few—several?—days. Her time was up.

"I don't want to talk about it," Joan said.

His bulk blocked most of the light from outside, and he wore his usual working and fighting outfit of thick canvas pants and work boots with a buttoned-up flannel under his rust-colored hunting jacket.

"Think it's long past time." He leaned against the door frame, not daring to cross this threshold the way he'd bypassed the wards.

Smart man.

She sat up, pissed though glad for the distraction. "You don't get to tell me—"

"Joan," he interrupted, one hand held up between them. "We all know you can kick my ass. You wanted space and I gave it. You wanted me to vouch for you, and for—for her, and I did. Can't I get five minutes?"

Joan huffed. She didn't want to hear any of it, not now, but he wasn't asking for the moon.

"Hiding a bloodling within town limits is a crime."

Oh, that was rich.

"Who's going to arrest me? You?" No one in Calvert was a match for her unless they drugged her first.

"I'm here to talk some sense into you. You're a goddamned binder. You know as well as I do—probably better—why we don't let bloodlings in here. They bait the people who love them and sacrifice them to their masters."

"Not Leigh."

"Not yet." He wasn't arguing the point. He stated it as fact. She wished she could hate him for it.

"No, you don't understand. Not her. She's nothing like . . . the others."

Leigh's behavior was downright docile compared to any bloodlings Joan had come across in her years of fighting. How could Joan explain Leigh's differences without sounding like she was some kind of lovesick idiot oblivious to the risks?

Dayton scratched his beard, his eyes darting back and forth as he thought.

"How long has she . . ." He paused. "Wait, last year, when that vampire came looking for her. Did you know then?"

"No, I didn't know until later." Leigh had hidden behind her glamour when Joan had returned to Calvert. Nathaniel, the prick, had come knocking and demanded the town turn Leigh over to him. Something about how she'd "taken something" from him. Turned out he meant Leigh herself.

Leigh had let the glamour lapse the next day and told Joan everything.

What would Dayton say if he knew Joan had been hiding Leigh ever since?

"I'm not blind, Joan. I know you love her, and I can't imagine how hard this must be, but you're risking the town's safety. The town whose land you claimed and pledged to protect."

He had some nerve.

"Don't tell me how to do my job."

"I have to," he said. "You're compromised, and keeping her here is a betrayal to everyone who's lost someone to the monsters."

Don't call her that.

"How is that her fault?" She was on her feet now, pacing behind the couch.

"It's not, but living in Trevon's house with—"

Too far.

She whirled to face him, and he took a step back in response. "Dayton, look around. This place is more hers than mine. And Trevon left it to her when he died."

Well, that little tidbit got through and rendered him speechless.

"Leigh came to him for help," Joan said. "So the glamour, keeping her secret—all of that is thanks to dear old Dad."

Trevon had meant for Leigh to keep the place safe until Joan came to claim it. He hadn't known how long it would take Joan to come back to Calvert.

Dayton frowned in thought, his shifting gaze on the floor, before he spoke again. "People still deserve to know she's here. She's dangerous."

"She's not a danger to any of them."

The lie stuck on her tongue, because Leigh *was* dangerous. Just not the way Dayton thought she was. She wasn't going to drag anyone off to some vampire lord. She might, however, burn something down by accident.

Unless she learned to control herself. Isn't that what she'd said?

"I have learned more in the last two days here than I have in the

last year at home."

The anger and despair were back, twisting Joan's insides to knots.

"So where is she?" Dayton crossed his thick arms over his broad chest. "Since, obviously, she ain't here judging by the mess."

His commentary was unwelcome, and the snide tone was too much. None of his damned business.

"That everything you need to say?" Joan matched his tone.

"No, not by a long shot."

"Let's skip to the end. You've got two choices: take a swing or fuck off. Either way . . ."

She shrugged to make it clear nothing was about to change as far as she was concerned.

The wind rose again, matching the disquiet between them.

"Those aren't my only options," Dayton said. "And you shouldn't have kept this to yourself. We've been here before, and I got the impression you understood me."

Shit. He was right—back when Nathaniel had come hunting for Leigh, Dayton had told her not to keep anything from him again.

"Wasn't my secret to tell." Leigh was her own person, bloodling or no, and she'd asked to keep the glamour. "And it's not yours either. I mean it. Don't push me."

He scoffed, reminding Joan of a petulant child. "You mean you don't trust me."

"Dayton, it's not about trusting you." Protecting Leigh, that's what mattered.

"After all the times we've fought together, you didn't think I'd listen—"

"Are you?" Joan paced closer to the front door, a boundary he'd yet to cross. "Listening? Because I don't think you get it. She stays."

Joan didn't go so far as to say *or we'll go*, because she didn't want to leave Calvert. How rich—all those years ago, she'd done everything she could to escape this town, and now she couldn't bear the thought of leaving.

Dayton shifted his weight, fisted hands in his jacket pockets. "You keeping anything else from me that's gonna bite me in the ass?"

The radio at his shoulder squawked before she could respond in kind.

"Call for Dayton." A woman's voice, though not urgent.

Dayton kept his gaze on Joan as he thumbed the mic. "Go."

The voice on the other end gave the hourly report and mentioned some other local business. None of it sounded important enough for Joan to listen. How could she persuade Dayton to leave this situation in her hands?

"I'm going on a run," he said. "Repeater station on Saddle Mountain is out. Some thralls were seen in the area. Might be nothing, but a few folks up there asked for backup."

Joan ignored the words and stared at him, willing him to—to do anything other than reveal what needed to be hidden.

She didn't want to fight him, and she didn't want to beg.

Maybe he understood because he looked away for a long moment before he caught her gaze again.

"Joan, you've saved my ass more than once, and I owe you."

Were they keeping score?

He took a step down the stairs. "I hear where you're coming from, but . . . she could get it right ninety-nine times. It'll only take one."

"Won't come to that."

"That's on you."

Wasn't everything these days?

Willy sneezed and followed Dayton as they walked through the wards and left the homestead, headed back the way they'd come.

And Joan was alone once again.

Leigh's parting words sliced through her head.

"*You can't fix this for me.*"

Joan looked at the room—*really* looked—at the disarray and desolation on display.

Another minute here sounded like a prison sentence.

She slammed the door shut behind her as she escaped the house to follow Dayton.

CHAPTER 18

"IF YOU WANT to master the skill of absorption," Bartholomew said by way of greeting, "you need to be at full strength."

Leigh jumped at his arrival, whirling from where she stood in the library.

He ignored the start he'd given her and walked to the window with a view of the light late-season snow falling outside. His customary aviators were missing, and his milky eyes followed the path of the snow.

Leigh had stood there earlier herself, watching the wind blow lanes in the snowfall, pushing it into piles at the curbs.

"You need more carbohydrates considering the caloric expenditure of the pace you're keeping. You are, however, adapting quickly."

Leigh thought her progress was slow, too slow to satisfy her.

The last few attempts to absorb fire into herself had been more successful. She'd stopped repelling the flames, and could now draw them toward her hands. Instead of absorbing them, however, she only succeeded in burning herself. The healing took hours instead of days or weeks, which was impressive, but she was starting to question her ability to achieve the skill at all, much less master it.

Not that there was a single chance she'd quit. Every day Leigh missed Joan more, and the fastest way back to Joan was through this odd tutelage she was receiving from the vampires.

"You might also consider getting more rest," he said.

"It's hard to sleep . . . here," Leigh said.

He made a noise that might have been mistaken for humor in someone else. "I can hear you locking the door. You have no need to block it with the chair."

A hot blush flooded Leigh's cheeks. Sometimes she forgot their hearing was better than hers. The chair had been a compromise of a sort. She hated the idea of sleeping in a vampire's house more than she detested locked doors.

She also wouldn't apologize for her precaution.

"You've said I'm in no danger, but in my experience, that's difficult to believe."

A rare smile graced Bartholomew's pale lips, though he kept his mouth closed so his fangs didn't protrude. "Fair enough. I can only imagine what you endured from those feral children. It's understandable that you might not trust us."

Bartholomew clasped his hands behind his back, smile fading. "Your lessons will teach you what you need to know, yet you keep returning to the library. You've made it clear you're not interested in being fully turned, so what are you hoping to find in those tomes?"

"I want to know more about what I am." A partial truth, since she also wanted to know if vampire lore would tell her how to be a regular human again. Not a good idea to share, but knowing more about what it meant to be a bloodling, about this power she was trying so hard to control—

"Incendiant."

Elizaveta strolled into the room, surprising Leigh so much she took a full step back before she processed what she'd heard.

Incendiant.

The word had a weight all its own, dropped like an anvil in the room, and the vibration of it rattled through Leigh's bones. A name, a label for what she was, what she could do.

"That's what you are," Elizaveta said. "What *we* are."

Leigh swallowed the lump in her throat. That she had anything in common with this woman was unfathomable, yet the truth was evident. Elizaveta stood unmoving, her gloved hands clasped in front of her, another reminder of what they shared.

A low buzzing split the silence. Bartholomew reached into his suit jacket pocket for his phone. Leigh frowned. She hadn't been able to send a message or make a call since she'd arrived. Were the vampires on an isolated network? She was no communications specialist, so it was a troubling puzzle.

Most of all, she wanted to talk to Joan and explain she'd only been trying to keep Joan from getting hurt.

After a glance at his phone screen, Bartholomew left the library.

Leaving Leigh alone with Elizaveta, something she'd managed to avoid so far. Here was a First, a leader of a vampire guild, one who oversaw the governance of hundreds—thousands?—of vampires, and all the citizens of Black Rose City.

In short, not only a dangerous vampire, but a powerful one. Though Elizaveta had kept her word and no harm had come to Leigh—not a single instance of menace or intimidation—that didn't make her trustworthy.

"Many witches," Elizaveta said, "have mastered the element of fire, but few vampires have demonstrated even a minor degree of this power without incinerating themselves in the process. Fewer still—perhaps one in a hundred thousand—have conquered it."

Now Elizaveta's interest made sense. Leigh felt like a mouse staring down a lion, so direct and commanding was Elizaveta's gaze.

"If you ... transition ... to your full capability, you would be quite formidable in time."

Her obvious phrasing was the least tactful way to convince

Leigh to join her. Leigh would never choose the vampire's path, no matter how powerful she might become.

"Not to mention the fact that a blood diet would help you recover more quickly."

The bookcase behind Leigh pressed into her back. She hadn't realized she'd moved, though she wanted to be anywhere else.

The horror on Leigh's face must have been obvious because Elizaveta rolled her eyes in exasperation.

"Have I not been a gracious host? I will not change you without your consent. This resistance is tedious. You fight so hard against your true nature. You cannot remain a bloodling forever."

"It's not my true nature, and I will never choose to become what you are," Leigh said, voice trembling but clear. "If that's my only option, kill me now."

Once the words were out, Leigh couldn't take them back. She held her breath.

Elizaveta's gaze was hard though her words were soft. "So dramatic."

Bartholomew reappeared in another doorway. When he took a seat next to the fire, Elizaveta glanced away first. The taut moment snapped, though Leigh didn't feel like she'd won anything. The tension in her body eased with Bartholomew in the room, though he wasn't any less threatening. Perhaps his presence would keep Elizaveta from killing her in frustration.

Leigh vowed to consider this more when she was alone—why she found Bartholomew less of a threat than Elizaveta. She took a deep breath to calm herself when something occurred to her that stole her breath.

The difference in Bartholomew, and in Elizaveta as well though Leigh had only now noticed, was his scent. The earthiness about them had changed somehow, more like fertile soil than the musty dirt she'd sensed soon after her arrival.

Their scent attracted her, and the thought that they weren't repulsive to her, that she could be seduced into their orbit and part of her yearned to get closer to them, was awful and terrible.

Was it her proximity, the time she'd spent in their presence, that had changed how she sensed them?

Leigh pledged to keep her distance—an impossible task.

Elizaveta strode towards one of the doors. "No training today. Do your best to heal yourself before you resume tomorrow."

And then she was gone.

Bartholomew's clouded gaze was a measured one until—in the space of a blink—he too stood.

"Come with me," he said.

Leigh followed him out of the library without question, a dangerous action in itself.

He said nothing as he led her out the back door and down the stone path through the garden gate. The snow had stopped, leaving a translucent layer of white over everything in sight.

They walked in a direction Leigh hadn't been taken before, into a thriving residential neighborhood beyond the park's trees.

Another difference from her life in Calvert—though it was hours past midnight, most of the windows were bright with the lights from inside the houses. A city for the nocturnal.

The pang for home, for holding Joan in the quiet dark of the small hours, ached in her chest.

Bartholomew meandered through a dozen more blocks as the street sloped downward. They were headed toward the river, and the sounds of the city faded as the whisper of the water grew louder.

The curbs in this neighborhood weren't painted. She wondered why, and why she was following him without question.

"Where are we going?" she asked, concerned as she was about being too docile.

"Not much farther."

He guided Leigh toward a three-story building more

recently constructed than the homes nearby. Inside the double-glass door entryway was an empty lobby with no staff, no chairs or tables. Modern art graced the walls, subtly illuminated by recessed lighting, giving the room the ambience of a museum.

Bartholomew chose to take the stairs instead of the elevator—a far better choice in Leigh's opinion. After her mental pledge not to get to close to him, her stomach turned at the thought of being alone with him in such tight quarters.

On the third floor, he opened the only door along the hallway. Nothing so far had been locked. Not at the entrance of the building, and not this apartment.

Who would dare to steal from Bartholomew?

The apartment was unlit. Leigh could see anyway.

As Bartholomew walked into the main room, he took off his suit jacket, folded and laid it over the back of a settee. He didn't stop until he reached the windows looking out at the river.

Leigh didn't want to sit down. She didn't want to be disrespectful either. The open plan of the room meant the room was exposed, with nowhere for anyone to hide. She chose to perch at the end of the immaculate kitchen counter separating the unnecessary cooking area from the living room.

"I understand your fears," he said without preamble. "And your reluctance to join us. This is not a life I would have chosen for myself, though truth be told the monotony is more horrible to me than the bloodshed. I've lived through the eons you would consider history, and the passing of time has become tedious."

He turned toward her. "Yet there are still things—people—I find fascinating."

It wasn't the compliment he might think it to be. Leigh would much rather she'd never attracted his or Elizaveta's attention.

"You are . . . repelled by what you've seen of our kind, even though it is only a matter of nature. This is who we are, and who you might become."

"I don't want that."

Bartholomew smiled, revealing fangs long enough to protrude past his lips. Leigh gasped, and his smile faded though it did not disappear.

"Yes, Leigh, you've made that quite clear. The horror you seem to feel behind your emphatic refusal—be careful you don't turn such disgust onto yourself for something not your fault. You cannot change who you are."

It burned when he said it out in the open where she couldn't hide from the truth.

She clenched her fists until the burns screamed. "You don't know—"

"I do." He crossed his arms over his chest, his back still to her. "Over the centuries, I've watched hundreds—yes, hundreds—of bloodlings deny their fate and resist turning, some even searching for a means to reverse the process and become human once more. It is not possible."

She didn't want to believe him, but he said he'd been alive for a long time, longer than she could fathom. If she could become human again, he would know, wouldn't he?

"You could be lying to me," she said, then wondered if she'd gone too far.

"I could, but I'm not. It is simple biology—you have evolved into something beyond what you were, and there is no going back. Most bloodlings who try to resist succumb instead to madness."

A sound burst from her, not a sob or a cough. Something in between.

He turned to lean against the frame of the window. "A minuscule few who have chosen to remain bloodlings lived a long time, never answering blood's call while somehow maintaining their mental faculties. I cannot stress to you how rare this is. The odds are not in your favor, and it would be easier for you if you surrendered to your nature. If this, however, is your preferred path, I will not attempt to convince you otherwise."

"Elizaveta doesn't agree with you." Leigh hoped Elizaveta never pressed her case.

"She may believe she can sway you to her point of view," Bartholomew said, his phrasing communicating his disagreement. "I have seen you with your beloved, though, and I don't think you'll do anything you think might disappoint her, no matter what it might cost you."

"It's not about that." She didn't want to say Joan's name in his company. It felt disrespectful to Joan. "Not everyone is as—"

She couldn't say compassionate, because that wasn't the right word.

"Reserved in their . . ." She struggled for a way to say what she wanted without offending him.

Bartholomew tilted his head in understanding. "Ah. Well, not all of us are like Victor."

Leigh hadn't seen Victor until the day Joan killed him. His Legate, Nathaniel, however, had been sadistic, arrogant, and egotistical, and had ruled the human thralls and donors under his control like a despot.

"Maybe." She swallowed against the fearful lump in her throat. "But are you like Nathaniel?"

"I didn't know him well enough to say, though I doubt it."

Memories of her captivity and Nathaniel's cruelty flashed in rapid sequence.

"He treated us like animals, kept in cells and cages, fed to his subordinates like . . ." She couldn't think of a word to describe what it had felt like.

"I see," Bartholomew said. "I'd imagine you can see for yourself how humans are treated much differently in Black Rose City."

He stepped away from the window as if ending the conversation. Leigh peered out the windows at the lights along the river, the glimmer of dark water revealing its expanse.

Bartholomew laid a set of keys on the kitchen counter.

"The locks do function," he said with dry humor. "The guest rooms are fully furnished. I'll be staying at the manor for the foreseeable future. Please consider this residence exclusively yours for the time being."

He walked to the door without turning back as he spoke in parting. "We'll resume our work tomorrow evening."

She sensed him moving down the hall and heard him enter the elevator. The farther away he got, the more the tension in her shoulders eased.

Leigh locked the door behind him and, for the first time in what felt like weeks, allowed herself to exhale.

CHAPTER 19

JOAN CHOSE TO avoid another extended lecture and drove Luther, letting Dayton take the lead in his truck with Willy and another member of the watch. For two hours she distracted herself with the scenery of the drive, losing her thoughts in the dense evergreen woods. This part of the state was devoid of travelers or campers, and the light rain forced her to focus on the winding roads up the mountains.

The road narrowed from two lanes to one and changed from asphalt to gravel the last few miles. The rain had stopped by the time they reached the plateau at the summit.

The relay station near the summit of Saddle Mountain had a small parking lot with room for six or eight vehicles. Three towers, all covered in multiple antennas and several signal dishes, were erected over two squat cement buildings. One structure was only large enough to house the telecommunications equipment and had no visual damage though its double doors were wide open. The other smaller building was a power station, half burned out and still smoking.

Joan joined Dayton at the edge of the lot. He surveyed the sprawl of dead bodies across the path to the station.

A woman stood next to him, along with a few others who'd been waiting when the Calvert group arrived. Though the woman's hair was so blonde as to be nearly white, she had the ruddy complexion of someone who spent a lot of time outdoors, and she was as tall as Joan. Her eyes were blue like the deep ice of a glacier.

"Our shift keeping watch here starts three days from now." Astrid was the leader of the Cannon Beach watch, a town smaller than Calvert on the coast. She had a no-nonsense manner Joan appreciated. "Showed up as soon as we could when the call came out from the crew on deck."

Astrid sighed as she studied the remains of the melee. "Never spoke to the folks from Clatskanie again."

Another tiny town, this one north of the mountain range. Several local towns participated in the security rotation. Now four of the Clatskanie watch lay dead, along with three times as many thralls. The larger force had been armed with only clubs and knives, but their number had overwhelmed their better armed opponents.

"We'll clear out the ones we know," Astrid said, pointing to the watch people. "The rest ... those are the thralls who attacked. One made it over the wire. That genius did the most damage."

She pointed to a body inside the fence line. One of the attackers had broken into the building housing the telecom's power equipment. Whatever he'd done had been successful in severing the connections and had killed him in the process.

Electricity had knocked him out of the building, hitting him high on the right side of his chest, burning his clothes and charring his skin. Arcing paths of scorch marks covered his body where his clothes had burned off, exposing him to the elements. His face was blackened beyond recognition. One hand had been so damaged only a tendon and a thick, uneven strand of flesh connected it to the man's arm.

The gruesome corpse made Joan grateful for her lack of appetite the last several days. A handful of crows landed inside the fence right next to the body. One hopped closer and started pecking at the severed hand.

Joan couldn't stomach watching this idiot's eyes getting pecked out. Everyone deserved to be laid to rest. Even this guy.

"Need to get him to a pyre," Joan said. "Or bury him."

"Yeah, well, no one wants to get in there," said a paunchy Caucasian man with a few days of beard growth on his rounded jaw. His jacket was too big despite his bulky frame, and his oversized T-shirt was covered in unidentifiable stains.

He didn't look fit enough for a town watch. Some places didn't have the resources to be choosy.

"Go on and help yourself," he continued, grumbling.

Joan ignored his bitterness considering the body count. Maybe one of the dead folks was a friend of his.

Astrid cut in. "We think the lines are dead, but we need to get a crew up here to be sure. With the station down and poor simplex or CB signals thanks to the sketchy terrain, we're going to have to drive down to one of the nearby towns and get somebody up here who knows what they're doing. Probably won't get anyone up here until tomorrow at the earliest. I know I don't want to take the chance of ending up like that guy. You?"

Astrid looked at Joan like she expected agreement; then her gaze turned more measuring. Perhaps Joan could do something no one else here could.

Some other day Joan might have waited. She didn't need to prove anything to anyone, except Leigh. Then again, Leigh's last words kept ringing in Joan's head. Leigh hadn't come right out and said it, but the whole conversation suggested something else to Joan: Leigh didn't think Joan could protect her.

She considered the body within the electrified fence, as well as the bodies strewn across the plateau. Moving them all would take a lot of energy. True, Joan was tired and hadn't eaten much lately, but she still had some juice left.

Time to see how far she could push her reserves.

As Astrid and the others discussed who would head down the mountain for help, Joan assessed the surrounding terrain.

Centering herself physically and mentally was as easy and familiar as exhaling. Joan closed her eyes and cleared her mind of all thought, focusing on her own heartbeat and on the tendrils of power she sensed in the earth beneath her feet. Though the ley lines near the homestead were thicker, the strands here were strong enough for her to grasp them with her own power.

Sometimes, the connection between her magic and the ley lines was cold, like snow melt. Other times, the sensation was like sinking into a hot spring.

This was the latter—reaching into a heat almost too hot to bear.

The connection's resonance, the loop of energy passing from the ley line to Joan and back, settled into place with a low hum only she could hear. She opened her eyes, maintaining the connection.

First, she needed to move the bodies, and the first one would be the toughest.

Joan stretched out her hands toward the corpse, palms raised and away from her. She didn't need to raise her hands. The action helped direct her magic on its target.

For the space of two deep breaths, nothing happened. A moment later, to several cries of surprise from the people around her, the body twitched as if alive.

In the next moment, the body rose from the ground as if levitating, all parts—including the nearly severed hand—aligned on the same plane of air as if a sheet of plywood had been placed beneath the corpse. Rain splashed in mid-air and ran to the sides of the invisible plank.

The whole spelled apparatus ascended until it was higher than the fence. With a horizontal wave of her arm, Joan moved the body from the compound, past the limits of the parking lot, and over to a sloped hill before the tree line.

Lowering was easier than lifting. Moments later, the corpse lay on the wet grass.

She did the same with the other thralls, setting them as close together as possible while not piling them onto each other.

The next part was less of a spectacle, though it took more effort. Joan pointed toward the land beneath the bodies.

"*Liquefaciet terram.*" *Liquefy the earth.*

Solid ground quickened to mud, and the corpses sank into the soil. The mud consumed them, inch by inch, pulling them into a makeshift grave.

The trick was to move the earth without causing a landslide. When the thralls were no longer visible from where Joan stood, she turned her inner vision to the space where the bodies were now buried. She liquefied the earth under the corpses, and converted the mud above them back to dry, solid soil.

"*Firmant terram.*" *Solidify the earth.*

She didn't stop until they were fifteen feet below the surface of the ground, safe from any scavengers and too deep for any predators to disturb.

By the time Joan finished and released the connection with a soundless groan, sweat lined her temples despite the chill. She bent over at the waist to catch her breath, rubbing at an ache in her chest from the exertion. She hadn't driven herself this hard in a long time.

Man, she needed some food and a good ten hours of sleep.

She pushed herself upright and rolled her shoulders to ease some stiffness. That's when she noticed the quiet.

No one had spoken a word during her feat, and a couple of people had stepped away from her. Giving her room or a wide berth, she didn't know.

Would this display of her powers be good or bad for her already notorious reputation?

A whisper on the wind interrupted her thoughts and turned into the hiss of tires on dirt and gravel, alerting her to an incoming presence. Bright headlights pierced the afternoon dim, and two black SUVs appeared.

The seal of the Portland High Coven, a green pentagram surrounding a tree with sprawling roots, was painted on the doors.

"Well, this ought to be good." Joan wiped her clammy hands on the backside of her jeans.

They parked on the grass beside the full lot and opened their doors in sync, three from the first vehicle and two from the second. They each wore matching hunter green jackets with the same seal on a chest patch. Yet none of them looked like the people Joan had seen last year when she'd gone to the High Coven for help and been sent away.

Messengers or grunts. Possibly both.

"You missed the party," Joan said in wry greeting to the one in the lead. "Hope one of you is an electrician."

The woman in the lead was a head shorter than Joan and had a pissy demeanor. Her skin was a warm umber, and her straight, black hair was parted in the middle and fell past her ears.

She tipped her chin up, her disapproval plain. "I've come to deliver an official edict on behalf of the High Coven. Joan Matthews, binder of Calvert, you are no longer welcome, nor are you allowed, within the Portland city gates. This is non-negotiable."

So they hadn't heard about the relay station?

"Since when are war witches banned from Portland?"

"Only you are banned. Before you decide to plead your case—not that we'll listen—this is beyond appeal. You entered Portland without permission."

Shit.

Somehow, they'd found out who'd been behind the glamour. Had Fiona snitched? She didn't seem the type, not after she'd made such a big deal about disavowing Joan's true identity.

So the cat was out of the bag, at least about her venture in the city. The real question was whether they knew what she'd done while she was there, and if they knew anything about Leigh.

Still, banning her from the entire city was overkill.

"So I entered without telling you." Joan said, affecting nonchalance she didn't feel. "Since when do travelers need to receive sanction?"

"By using a glamour, you passed through the gates under false pretenses. Invaders have been executed for less."

Joan laughed, though it held no humor. "Invader? I wasn't even in town a day and barely spoke to anyone. I broke no laws." Unless they were going to come after her for stealing her own bike, a minor offense that should have been beneath the attention of authorities like the High Coven.

"But you don't deny the charge of glamour or subterfuge," the woman said, shaking her head. "Is this kind of quibbling normal for you? I'd have thought it beneath the binder of the open territories, a role we do not recognize, by the way, no matter what you've claimed by ritual."

Open territories. The old High Coven name for all the lands outside the gates, as if it were all free for the taking.

The woman stepped closer. "Furthermore, you will not extend your spellcraft beyond Calvert's boundaries. You will be penalized and stand trial if you use ley-line powers within sensory distance of the Portland High Coven."

Good thing this witch had missed the demonstration Joan had given moments before. No one else mentioned it, either. Everyone in the vicinity seemed like they were staying out of this conversation.

"No one tells me where I can go," Joan said. Not since the day she'd left her father's house. "You have no right."

She stepped forward, and the woman bared her teeth and flexed her hands at her sides, eyes bright at the opportunity of a fight. Even these foot soldiers appeared to be witches.

"*You* have no right. You've consulted no one, warned no one, negotiated with no one to change the terms of any of the terrain agreements. You just claimed the land and now you venture around the region whenever it suits you, with no regard for the rights of others. You're like a dog pissing on trees. You are no one and nothing."

What petty words. They might have made Joan laugh if she hadn't been so angry.

"You sure took a long time to bring it up," she said, her voice little more than a growl. "Why? What the hell have you been waiting for?"

All those fights Joan had been dragged into over the last few months. Since they were so damned interested in keeping the peace, they should have stepped in sooner. If they had, she wouldn't have had to leave Calvert, and could have stayed home with—

No. Too late to change any of it now.

"For that matter, what are you doing about all this bullshit?" Joan waved at the battleground behind her, at the aftermath where the bodies of fallen watch members still lay in grisly repose. "Unless you're blind as well as an asshole, you can see people need help, but you're turning them away at the gates. The towns are at maximum capacity. Portland's the only place they can go, and they're not getting any help from you judging by how much thrall numbers are increasing. So how are you protecting these people you seem to think are within range of your territory since it means so goddamned much to you?"

Somehow, the woman frowned deeper. "If you had stayed where you're supposed to be, we'd have found you sooner. And High Coven business is none of your concern."

"Guess we agree it's coven business then, not that you're doing anything."

"Stay in your lane, Matthews," the coven witch sneered.

"What lane? There's no fucking road, and people are dying."

Her frustration must have attracted the crows. A dozen launched from the nearby trees, squawking as they darted overhead, circling each other and making more noise than normal.

The woman's expression was shuttered closed, the emotions leaking away as she pulled herself to her full height.

"Back off. Or face the consequences." She glared once more at Joan before sparing a glance at the others. "I'll report the station's condition. They'll send technicians as soon as possible."

With a gesture, she rallied her companions who climbed back in their vehicles.

"You sure do know how to make friends." Dayton spoke in a mumble barely heard over the engines as the SUVs drove away.

The words fell flat, sounding like something Leigh might have said, and the thought made Joan's heart ache.

Astrid cursed. "It'll be weeks before they get someone up here."

"You're the big shot now," the paunchy man said, staring Joan down. "Why don't you throw some weight around and get this fixed?"

His tone suggested something other than grief.

"What's your problem?" Joan asked. "Since you're not bright enough to be subtle."

He flushed and squared up his shoulders. "You're a hypocrite."

Astrid groaned. "Jesus, Grant. Just let it be."

An insult meant to incite her, but Joan didn't think it was a good time to kick anyone's ass. Besides her shriveling resource levels, this man, Grant, and the others had seen enough death to make anyone cranky.

Still, his words cut into her. "What are you talking about?" she asked.

"You make a big fuss at those coven witches about taking people in even though you're throwing them to the wolves the same as they are."

Joan glanced at Dayton, who raised his eyebrows and let them fall in a way suggesting he had no idea, either. Calvert got its share of refugees and homeless folks, and did its best to feed people and give them what they needed to help themselves. Several businesses had job placement programs, a few of the churches had rotating beds, and most of the farms contributed to a common food assistance organization.

No one was wealthy by any stretch of the imagination or had a ton to spare, but everyone helped a little.

"We haven't turned anyone away."

"That's a lie," Grant said, spittle on his lips.

The short hairs rose on the back of Joan's neck as the wave of hot anger passed through her. This was more than a wild accusation, and unless he started making some kind of sense, she was going to correct him with a punch in the face.

Grant didn't acknowledge her anger or didn't care. "Some of your rejects came begging just this morning, asking for supplies. They said their people were starving and they weren't going to make it through the winter."

He sneered and stomped close enough for Joan to get a whiff of his stale body odor. "They said you turned them away, threatened violence, and told them their kind wasn't welcome in your precious town. Didn't even offer rations for the kid with them."

Alarm bells clanged in Joan's head as she exchanged a heavy glance with Dayton.

"Where'd these folks say they were from?" Joan asked, but she knew what he was going to say.

"Arock," Grant said. "Came over two mountain ranges in a big old van on its last legs, if you can believe it. Somehow, they've avoided the vampires, and they were skinny enough to lend some credence to their starvation story. We gave them what we could, not that we could spare it. Bet you don't do anything about that either. What good are you then?"

Dayton's eyes widened, no doubt thinking the same things as Joan, and it wasn't about what a waste of space Grant was.

This must have been the same group that had come knocking asking for Joan's help—which she had given once she got past their rough demeanor. And now they were all the way on the other side of the state telling lies and begging for assistance they shouldn't have needed.

Maybe the whole thing had been a front and there'd been another reason they'd come to town besides needing the binder witch to remove their blight.

And maybe Calvert and Cannon Beach weren't the only places they'd visited under the guise of asking for handouts.

CHAPTER 20

WITH A SAFER place to rest, Leigh's sleep improved. She locked the doors, a symbolic precaution since they would do nothing to stop Bartholomew. A newborn vampire could have demolished the door without difficulty.

Every day, she rose in the early afternoon and went to the warehouse to practice. Leigh lost count of how many times she set objects on fire and attempted to absorb the flame back into her own body without damage. So far, she had managed only partial success. She could now pull small flames back into her hands, at the cost of significant burns.

Frustrated by the hours it took her to heal, she began alternating hands, using whichever was in better—or perhaps *least* worst—condition.

When the tests of her skills yielded diminishing returns, she would visit the food carts on the Avenue and eat until she couldn't take a deep breath. Afterward, she walked around the city until her hands healed enough to resume practice, or she gave up and returned to Bartholomew's penthouse.

Often exhausted, she would fall asleep the moment she closed her eyes. After a few nights, she slept without nightmares.

Train, eat, walk, sleep. The sooner Leigh got better at controlling her fire, the sooner she could return to Joan's side.

The days ran together as if they'd become one long revolution on rinse and repeat, until one evening. Bartholomew was waiting at the warehouse door when she arrived.

He glanced at her hands. She'd stopped wrapping the burns since she healed so quickly. Yesterday's practice had been grueling. One hand was a blistered mess, and it hurt too much for her to tuck it back into gloves, or into a pocket to avoid his attention. Then she wondered why she cared what he thought. Wasn't this why they'd brought her here? Hadn't she proven she wasn't the danger they had implied?

"You're pushing too hard." Bartholomew gestured for her to join him as he turned away from the door. "And tonight presents other opportunities for education."

As usual, he offered no other commentary. At first, Leigh had assumed he was withholding information as some kind of security measure. Now, she thought he was reticent by nature.

They walked the late evening streets of Black Rose City, and though many noticed their passing, no one spoke to them. He strode beside her, and instead of turning on the street that led to the manor house, he continued to the next block.

They reached a four-story building of brick and stone, set back from the street and surrounded by a rose garden. The roses were all trimmed back for the winter, though a few leaf buds showed signs of life. A plaque mounted near the double-door entrance cited 19th-century construction.

There were no windows, and a wave of uneasiness passed through Leigh. Night had fallen, adding to her apprehension.

"What is this place?" she asked.

Bartholomew opened one of the doors and walked inside first. "Somewhere we will find answers, though the next steps require a discussion in a venue that may make you . . . uncomfortable."

He meant where more than he and Elizaveta would be in attendance. More vampires.

"The Ruby Court meets this night, and you may be interested

in the discussion."

The idea of being around more of them, or in the room while they drank from their donors brought back too many memories.

Yet her time so far in this city had been different from what she'd expected, what she'd feared.

Would this, too, be different?

"You may choose to decline my invitation," Bartholomew said, "though you will lose the opportunity to learn about events possibly affecting those you care about."

Leigh shuddered, embarrassed her discomfort was so visible.

He'd given her the option to avoid the situation, and she craved the relief she'd feel if she took advantage of that choice.

Could she trust Bartholomew and Elizaveta to tell her everything they discovered? What if, as he suggested, she could learn something that would help Joan?

In some ways there was no choice at all. With equal parts pride in the effort and dismay at what she might see and hear, Leigh chose Joan.

"I want to know for myself," Leigh said.

The interior beyond the doors was bright with warm light and a modern decor. The entrance hall was empty except for a woman at the far end next to a sign designating a coat check. She didn't look up, focused on her task of tagging a pile of coats.

Up two flights of wide, red carpeted stairs, halfway down a long hall adorned with ostentatious portraits and ornate lighting fixtures—all of which Leigh barely noticed—Bartholomew paused at another set of double doors.

"You are in no danger here."

Leigh couldn't help it. She peered into his eyes, searching for subterfuge. He met her gaze.

She had to take him at his word. Otherwise, this had all been an elaborate pretense, and she prayed that wasn't true.

Bartholomew didn't knock and pushed open the oak door without announcing himself.

Leigh's eyes found Elizaveta first, since she was the one speaking.

"Let's carry on with order business before we proceed with individual concerns, Istvan."

When Leigh noticed who else was in attendance, she nearly fled.

So many vampires... dozens of them, standing or in chairs around the room. More than she had ever seen in one place before, and though the sight of them was scary, the scent of them was worse.

They smelled well-fed, the fragrance of fresh blood evident in the closed room. She could almost taste it, and horror rose like bile because she wanted to. The hunger was different than the one she had for food, baser and urgent.

When she'd been thrown to the floor before Victor and his court, they'd taunted her, threatened her with violence, with the specter of becoming just like them.

Tonight, if these vampires offered her a taste, would she be able to resist?

Was this why Bartholomew had brought her here?

The door behind her closed with an emphatic thud as the corners of the room faded, darkness seeping in from the edges of her vision until she remembered how to breathe.

Bartholomew had not moved, and stood still in front of her, blocking her from view to some degree. She didn't want this, to be trapped in here though no one was looking at them and—

No one was looking at them.

Nor were they taunting her, or offering to change her. Everyone in the room was focused on one vampire reading something aloud though she couldn't concentrate on his words.

Yes. She could resist them because she did not want to be like them. No matter how enticing some parts of her nature might be, she would not succumb to becoming something she abhorred.

And Bartholomew had said she'd be safe here. No, he'd only said she wouldn't be in danger. Was anywhere safe?

Leigh ached for Joan, for the familiarity of their homestead. She clenched her fists, and the pain of her burns snapped her back into the moment.

She could do this, especially if it might help Joan and the people of Calvert. She had to.

The door opened behind them to admit another late arrival. This vampire, a pale woman in a crisp blazer and matching skirt, glanced at Leigh in passing but didn't acknowledge her presence. Instead, she crossed the room to claim an empty chair. Her dark hair was pulled back so tightly her forehead was smooth as a ball, and after nodding in greeting to Elizaveta, she too focused on the vampire who was still reading aloud. She didn't look at Leigh again.

Leigh had been dismissed, as if she were just another bloodling. A sobering thought, that Leigh was nothing of note. As if she belonged here.

Leigh didn't, but that wasn't the point, was it? This, too, was who she was now. She wasn't one of them. She wasn't *not* one of them, either.

Was this why Bartholomew had invited her?

And if she took him at his word again, wasn't that a sign of trust? Was he still one of the—was he still an enemy?

Leigh squared her shoulders in an attempt to settle her nerves and quiet her breathing.

After she had taken a few shaky breaths, only then did Bartholomew step aside, as if he'd been waiting for her to pull herself together.

He tilted his head toward a nearby empty bench before taking a stance not far from the door. Not far from Leigh as well.

She claimed the end closest to the door. The bench beside hers was occupied. A stout black man who didn't appear a day over twenty-five and an elderly woman dressed in century-old clothes gave her inquisitive glances before looking away.

Leigh did the same, once again surprised—this time at the diversity in the room. The vampires varied in age, race, attire, and bearing. Some were riveted by the droning reading, others bored. Several took notes on pads or in journals.

With no perceived immediate threats, Leigh directed her attention where everyone else's seemed to be, on the vampire near the middle far wall. His dry voice matched his boring, decades-old clothes. Thick brows covered deep-set eyes focused on sheets of paper in his hands matching another stack on the table.

"The witches confirmed the contract renewal discussions will resume after the full moon. As usual, they want concessions regarding the number of volunteers for the donor program, and for us to revisit the security rotations at the dam. They're also claiming the trade yields are down from the unincorporated territories."

"Never mind that, Andreyev." One of the vampires looked younger than the others, incongruous with his 17th-century attire. "Yet another mass of someone's toys tried to burn down one of my stables last week. I demand reinforcements."

"Which leaves the rest of our lands vulnerable as well, Istvan," another vampire said, speaking in clipped consonants and elongated vowels. He appeared middle-aged, with sepia skin and black eyes.

Someone hidden from Leigh's view spoke up. "We could move some of the staff from the dam temporarily. Might prompt the witches to reconsider their donor position if their water and food supplies are threatened."

"I doubt that will play out the way you think," Elizaveta said. "Those water rights affect us as well. We've still much to do to secure the city."

"Let the witches handle these upstarts for once," a woman said, her skin black and her eyes a piercing green. "Isn't that the point of their damned coven? Must the guild resolve everything?"

A few others muttered in response.

"According to the surveillance, they're closing up the borders. They're reluctantly allowing donors through but rejecting the petitions for new residents."

One vampire, portly and dressed in flamboyant and flattering robes, set his notes on a side table. "They're not the only ones. Most of the locations under observation are doing the same, which is clogging the open roads with people scrambling for somewhere that will take them in. I suppose these towns can't be blamed for protecting their interests."

"And we won't have a guild if we don't protect *our* interests, which is why I'm calling for reinforcements." Istvan directed his request at Elizaveta, though his tone wasn't as harsh as his words. "I don't need them forever. Only until I can improve fortifications."

Elizaveta frowned, though she nodded.

"In other news," the vampire Andreyev continued, "several masses of human capital have been seen throughout the territory. On more than one occasion, they have defied the terms of parley or neutral ground. Of more interest is the fact they are not openly claimed by any faction we're familiar with."

"Someone's kicking over castles in your sandbox, Elizaveta," Istvan muttered, and the humans behind him tittered at his jokes, acting more like courtesans than thralls. They were all dressed much the same as he was.

This was nothing like Victor's court, full of those who kept their opinions to themselves. The Ruby Court guild's discussion by contrast was boring, like any other council meeting though on a grander scale.

"*Our* sandbox, Istvan," Elizaveta said. "They have to be compelled by someone, who remains to be seen. And stop pretending you bow to me in any fashion. You're here because this city brings you more coin and land than you could acquire elsewhere."

Several of the attendees spoke over each other in their haste to make their points.

Leigh tried to push down her terror enough to absorb all the information flying around the room—that vampires owned territories throughout the region, existing near humans in ways she'd never heard about before.

"Elizaveta, perhaps the time has come for you to face facts." Andreyev continued perusing his papers as he spoke, as if his attention couldn't be spared for anything else. "Your grand experiment in democracy has always been precariously balanced on a blade's edge, susceptible to outside agents from other guilds and the whims of the populace here."

"Populace, he says." Istvan continued to perform, as if all in attendance were his adoring audience. "Less than ten thousand souls. Hardly merits the name 'city.'"

"And now that you've all made your fortunes in this experiment," Elizaveta said, ridicule dripping from her words, "you'd just as soon surrender to archaic traditions, whether or not you agree with them."

She crossed one leg over the other, resting her clasped hands at the end of her knee. "The positions you each hold on this council would have taken you decades, if not centuries, to acquire under the older guilds. What you've accumulated here won't buy you favor elsewhere, so don't act as if you have nothing to lose."

"Oh," Istvan said with what must be his characteristic dry humor. "Are we saying the quiet parts out loud in front of children?"

He waved in the general direction of a clustered group of half a dozen vampires, all appearing younger by comparison to Bartholomew, Istvan, and some of the others. They all laughed at the joke.

Istvan turned a piercing gaze on Elizaveta. "You must realize one of the guilds has decided to move against us." He was serious now, no longer teasing.

Another vampire, who looked twenty-five years old though his clothes had a century-old style, raised an eyebrow, its dark arch suggesting his displeasure. "The treaties have stood for years, and none of the other guilds would gain anything by assimilating our territory except the possibility of defeat. Our forces are better trained than any of the others on this side of the continent."

"I agree with Sridhar," Elizaveta said. "It must be a vampire lord, and this one is smart—a tactician hiding behind guerrilla tactics. Any word on new players in the area?"

"No," Bartholomew said. "I have, however, reviewed the data and confirmed these thralls have avoided most of the larger cities—Portland, Salem, Eugene—though they've attacked dozens of the cell towers and at least two radio substations."

He paused while he scrutinized Leigh, his milky eyes thoughtful.

"And they've stayed away from Calvert."

"Can't blame them for avoiding a wild card," Istvan muttered. "I've heard even the Coven's witches are giving that one a wide berth."

A few others mumbled in response. Leigh couldn't make out anything distinct. Whatever they might say couldn't be as bad as the fact that these vampires knew of Joan, and perhaps of the land she'd claimed.

What would they do about it?

Leigh must have made some sound because Elizaveta glanced at her. The others took note of her as well.

"Bartholomew," Istvan said. "A new pet? Have you finally given into your baser impulses?"

His voice was teasing, though his gaze was fixed on Leigh's hands and he wasn't smiling.

Leigh felt like she was staring at a predator with no defense.

Elizaveta ignored his comment even though it hadn't been directed at her. "The wilds do not interest me, but whoever it is will be called to task before they grow any delusions of grandeur."

Istvan's focus returned to the conversation in progress, which carried on for some time as the vampires discussed farms and their yield, industry and trade, shipping and contract negotiations.

Leigh couldn't process all the information and filed it away, hoping some of it would make sense when she had a chance to think.

A clock somewhere signaled the midnight hour, and the voices died down from contentious debate to a more sedate murmur. Moments later, a messenger arrived via a side door, a tall, tanned genderqueer in bland, earth-toned attire who approached Bartholomew.

They exchanged a few words, and Bartholomew's brows lowered in a rare frown. Once the message had been delivered, its carrier left without further acknowledgment.

"A brief recess," Elizaveta said, calling everyone's attention back to herself. "Please enjoy the refreshments I've provided in the downstairs lounge."

Refreshments. She meant donors. Leigh trembled as indecisiveness and fear warred inside her—the urge to stay and get more information, the urge to escape.

Elizaveta was staring at Leigh as the room emptied, though she was speaking with Bartholomew.

"Your invitation seems..." Elizaveta arched one pronounced eyebrow in admonishment at him. "Premature."

"Perhaps it is overdue," Bartholomew countered.

Elizaveta did not contradict him or negate his invitation. Instead, she sighed, acquiescing without a word. In Leigh's experience, vampires did not surrender anything, and those in power did not give in to their subordinates.

Elizaveta and Bartholomew acted more like colleagues than First and Legate. Was that part of what was different about this guild?

"The messenger?" Elizaveta asked.

Bartholomew crossed his arms over his chest. "A sizable human force has amassed to the south."

"Another horde?" Elizaveta scoffed in irritation. "Which worthless backwater are they attacking now?"

"Mount Angel." Bartholomew was speaking to Elizaveta, but his cloudy gaze turned to Leigh. "Perhaps fifty or so. This time a vampire leads them."

That captured Elizaveta's attention, and Leigh's as well for a different reason. Mount Angel was less than thirty miles from Calvert. Joan would be in the thick of whatever was happening.

The vampires shared a wordless exchange. Elizaveta nodded though Bartholomew had said nothing more.

"We should leave at once," he said.

"I'm coming with you," Leigh said, surprising herself both by both speaking aloud and by how close she'd gotten to them without thought.

"Of course," Bartholomew said.

She had to trust she had learned enough to keep from hurting anyone, but if Joan was in danger, Leigh couldn't stay here.

CHAPTER 21

THE HUNT PUSHED Joan's fatigue into the background as she drove Luther's engine to its limits. Dayton's truck had taken the lead again as they pursued the people from Arock in the hopes of catching up to them.

These speeds on country back roads required her attention.

The citizen's band radio mounted on her dash squawked before Dayton's voice filled Luther's confines. "Charlie Victor Tango-4 to CVT-1."

Startled by the noise, Joan cursed as she turned the volume down and detached the corded mic.

"CVT-1. Trying to drive here."

"Heard, but I just got a call from the Canby watch. They got hit by thralls last night and asked for volunteers to fill the slack since some of their folks are injured."

Such calls were common, and they'd been happening with rising frequency. This was the third in a month.

"Can't believe how brave these groups are getting." Halsey, the other member of the watch riding with Dayton, spoke clearly enough to be heard via Dayton's open connection.

"Nobody seems to know who sent 'em." Dayton said, then clicked off his mic.

Joan pressed the button of her radio mic back on. "No, and it's weird they don't have any stronger support. If they really wanted to press an advantage, they'd send a bloodling or two, or even some younger vampires."

The cost of human life was staggering, and for no reason anyone could fathom.

"I don't understand how there's so many," Dayton said.

Joan did. Not everyone qualified for citizenship in the smaller townships, which wouldn't let you past the checkpoints if you were on drugs or had no prospects for employment. That left a lot of people with limited choices—and if they couldn't meet the donor requirements in Black Rose City, they chose to serve a vampire who would at least make sure to feed their humans.

"It's almost like . . ." Dayton faded out, and Joan followed the thought.

"Like they're testing defenses." The hairs on the back of her neck raised up as she performed the mental calculus of reassessing the months of attacks.

She put herself in the shoes of a mastermind attacker and pondered how she would test fortifications, response times, and communication. With an endless supply of potential cannon fodder, if she didn't care how the battles played out, how would she use those pawns to her advantage?

She'd throw them at her target from every possible angle and search for weaknesses. All she'd need would be a list of locations and a timeline. Sending out small parties of human thralls, though, was a crap tactic. They were often in bad enough condition most places wouldn't let them anywhere near crucial information sources. Who would reveal security details to recovering drug addicts and visible donors?

Now the Arock visits made sense, and the invitation to their town—though it had been more of a taunting summons—must have been about assessing Joan herself.

Might be time to update their assessment.

They hadn't made a move on her, so who was the ultimate

target—the Ruby Court or the High Coven? Neither of those groups cared about the backwater towns the thralls had attacked.

Joan drove over the rise in the road, which was high enough for her to see the long straightaway ahead. The white van was easy to spot, though it was still a couple of miles away.

Dayton floored it, racing faster than Luther could match.

By the time the road twisted into a series of switchbacks, Joan had lost sight of both the van and Dayton's truck.

"Luther, don't get me wrong—you're the best, but this is a bad look."

Luther didn't comment.

The two-lane highway curved into town, which meant the locals had no warning before Joan and the others showed up. Mount Angel had a watch, but the wooden barricades on the road weren't sturdy enough to block a full-sized van that didn't bother to slow down.

The van and Dayton were several blocks ahead, with no sign of stopping. A lone man stood on the side of the road, staring at the busted-up barricade while holding a rifle in one hand and a radio held to his mouth with the other.

He whirled in surprise at her arrival and dropped the radio.

Shit. This could go badly, and she didn't have time.

Joan activated her mic. "I'll check in with these guys and catch up."

"Roger." Dayton's voice was tight.

Joan rolled down the window as she slowed, waving at the watchman who was just now raising his rifle.

"Hold and parley!" Joan yelled. "I'm Joan Matthews, from Calvert."

Heavy brows frowned in recognition, and though he lowered the barrel, it was only a few inches.

"What the hell are you doing here?" His face was flushed, and Joan would bet it was more from blushing at someone getting the drop on him than any effort on his part.

"That van is full of folks who probably won't do your town any good."

"Oh, shit!" He looked around wildly, as if something were going to attack him any moment. "Bloodlings?"

Joan's grip on the steering wheel tightened. Too close to what—*who*—she didn't want to think about right now.

"No, but they might be connected to all the thrall attacks—"

The watchman's handset screamed to life with panicked voices at the same time as Joan's radio squawked.

"Caught up to the Arock van a mile up on the main road," Dayton said, his words rushed together. "They've got backup. A lot of it."

"Already on my way," Joan said. She called through her window to the local as she took her foot off the brake. "You've got company. The bad kind."

The watchman sputtering into his radio while trying to keep his rifle half-trained on her could fend for himself.

She floored the accelerator and raced through town at double the posted speed limit on the town's main street. Blind luck no one was in her way. She honked her horn a few times to encourage the pedestrians on the sidewalks to stay where they were.

The buildings thinned out, as did the houses. Mount Angel didn't have an established border like Calvert. Around another blind curve, the last building on the road marked the edge of town. Sprawling farmland took over the landscape.

Several cracks and booms made her duck in her seat before her brain caught up and identified the noise.

Gunfire.

Well, Luther was enchanted against bullets, which hadn't been cheap and came in handy in moments like these. Joan sat up to assess the conflict.

Dayton's truck was parked in the middle of the opposing lane. Both side windows were shot out, and the windshield was shattered though it hadn't yet caved in. One tire was flat and the engine smoked.

The passenger side door was open, and Dayton and Halsey hid behind the vehicle's bulk. Halsey was sitting. Maybe he was reloading.

Another round of fire took out the truck's windshield, and Dayton pressed himself flat against the side of the truck bed, head tucked low.

Beyond them, at least a dozen thralls had fanned across the road, blocking escape. Most were armed with axes, hammers, bats—the usual implements to cause hurt and destruction. They hadn't moved closer, no doubt because of the guns, and they were eyeing Dayton and Halsey like they'd beat their corpses once the shooting was done.

The shots were coming from the van near the wall of thralls.

Joan's people were pinned down, with no path to retreat. If Joan could get them into Luther, they'd be clear, but they might get shot before they got inside.

She pulled Luther to a screeching halt, opened her door and reached for the gun usually holstered in the mount by the gear shift.

It was empty. She'd left the homestead in such a hurry, she'd forgotten it.

Of all the times to pull a rookie maneuver. Damn it. Guess it was time to show them what a war witch could do.

She leapt from her seat and, once she was past the door, cast a cantrip air spell across the distance between her and the van.

"*Crasso aere.*" Thicken the air.

The spell wouldn't repel or stop the bullets, but it would slow them down enough for her to move from their path.

Bullets whistled by her as she crouched and rushed to Dayton's position. Dayton lifted his gun to shoot back at his attackers, raising his head to peer through the busted windows of his truck. Beside him, Halsey sat facing the other direction, eyes blank. Blood stained his chest and one of his legs where he'd been shot. The dark pools on the ground suggested he'd bled out in minutes.

Dayton shook his head, calm but not with his usual confidence as the enemy's guns peppered what was left of his truck. "This is not good."

"Been through worse," Joan said, and winced. She shouldn't have said something so casual while Halsey cooled beside them.

And then, so suddenly Joan thought she was imagining it, all was quiet except for their heavy breathing. Someone shouted. She couldn't make out the words, and a door slammed.

"I'm out!" A second person yelled. "Let's go!"

They were out of ammo.

The van's engine started, and Joan reacted without thought. She rushed from her cover, drawing her sword and her knife. Whoever was driving shifted the van into gear and hit the accelerator so hard the engine sounded like it might explode in protest.

Nope. No way were they getting out of here.

"*Tumescant aerem.*" *Swell the air.*

Her vision blurred for a moment as she concentrated on aiming the energy in the right place. The van's back two tires exploded, the air inside them expanding enough to pop the rubber.

She shouted in victory as she raced toward the van.

Two men and a woman jumped from the van's side door, and the first to turn Joan's way was a lanky man with murder in his eyes.

There were fewer of them than she'd expected. Maybe this party had been smaller than the one that had come to Calvert. Didn't matter since the other thralls had arrived, but Dayton was picking them off as they tried to rush forward.

"Shouldn't start what you can't finish," Joan called out to the folks from the van. The thralls were too far away to help this first guy, who didn't have the build—and judging by the way he was holding his hatchet, the experience—of Dayton or Halsey.

They'd killed Halsey. Joan let the anger and bitterness fire her up.

"Trying to do the world a favor," the man said, and swung wide at her with his hatchet. "You think you run everything around here, don't you?"

Why did people keep asking her that?

He swung again. "People like you are why we have to deal with the devils."

He must mean vampires, which answered some questions about Arock. Joan had thought they'd somehow escaped a worse fate. Maybe they hadn't.

No time to get into that now. He made a few feints, telegraphing his every intention, and then swung again at her midsection without much grace.

She severed the hand holding the hatchet, though it turned her stomach. He sank to his knees, screaming until Joan slit his throat.

The other man and the woman closed in. Joan whirled to face them as Dayton roared his arrival, his axe already moving to cut the man down.

Joan kicked out the woman's knee before backhanding her unconscious. She winced—she hadn't meant to hit her that hard.

A child's head peered out from the door of the van.

Joan wanted to scream. She didn't have time for this, but she couldn't let the kid get hurt.

"Lock the doors and hide," Joan said. "And don't come out until I come back for you."

She slammed the van door shut.

"Behind you!" Dayton yelled.

More thralls closed in, and Joan sank into instinct beyond thought. No time to plan or assess the incursion until she cleared some space for herself. Spells cast without speech required more power than she could pull right now—the lack of sleep, of recuperation, of sustenance pushing her back to the quicker cantrips and rote spells from her younger days.

"*Sphaera aquae.*" *Sphere of water*, aimed at a man so underfed and gamy she didn't want him anywhere near her. The ball of muck water, pulled from a gutter puddle along the side of the road, was larger than his head and hit him square in the face. He fell on his back, choking on the water until he stopped moving.

"*Obstructionum aeris.*" *Block of air*, pushed at a woman twice Joan's size with wild, almost rabid black eyes. Joan uttered the spell a second time, taking no chances against the possibility of a close-in fight with this opponent. Knocked off her feet, the woman smacked into the asphalt so hard she cracked her skull. Blood poured from the wound.

They kept coming, each wave of thralls struck down by her, Dayton, and the Mount Angel watch who'd joined the fray. Once defeated, the thralls were replaced by another group. Golden hour faded as the sun went down, and on they fought.

Battles with thralls were always worse when regular people were pitted against people just like them, but down on their luck. The attackers never fell back, forcing those on Joan's side to stop them by any means necessary. The body count was alarming.

Where had these people come from? And who was driving them to attack on so many fronts?

"*Comae flammae.*" *Hair aflame*, at a woman who looked terrified but nevertheless swung a two-by-four at Joan's knees. Sparks snapped around the woman's head, lighting the unkempt strands of dirty blond hair. She screamed as the shoulder-length waves caught fire, blinding her in the process.

"*Excutere terram.*" *Shake the earth*, beneath a cluster of three men who had no weapons, yet whose hands were already covered in mud and blood. The ground below them trembled and quaked, slowing them down enough for some of the Mount Angel watch to handle them.

One slipped past, roaring at Joan as he escaped another man trying to subdue him. Joan's arms were so heavy her shoulders screamed in protest at raising her tanto one more time. Two of the town's defenders rushed forward, taking up positions in front of her to block her attacker.

She had seconds to catch her breath before some other idiot no doubt tried to take her out. The fight had spread wider than the road and onto the farmland on both sides. Dozens of thralls lay dead, yet they kept coming.

Joan's reserves were shot. Her knees threatened to fold, and she widened her stance to stabilize them. Her legs trembled with the effort. Sweat had cooled and flared and cooled again. She wanted a shower *and* a bath.

She thumbed the blood splatter from the face of her wristwatch.

Twilight had come and gone, and a new moon thickened the darkness. Flashes of fire, of flashlights on gun muzzles, highlighted the size of the horde. Someone's dog was growling and attacking one of the thralls. Dayton was somewhere else, lost in this mess, and she hoped he was still alive despite their current disagreements.

From the north several fist-sized balls of lightning sizzled and crackled as they flew through the air into the melee. Screams pierced the night as they hit, spreading over clothes and skin like liquid.

Someone with new powers had joined the fight on the same side as Joan. More war witches?

The wind shifted, bringing a different yet familiar stench.

Vampire. One who stank of decay and burning flesh.

Joan recentered herself, using some of her waning energy to call the spell to push back the darkness, revealing the scale of the battle. She focused her senses, following the scent to the east, where a figure stood motionless.

More thralls followed him, which was awful, but at least

now she had a parasite to blame for all this bloodshed.

Joan recognized who it was, though he looked different. Half his face was now twisted with burn scars, and he still had the same smarmy arrogance about him. He wore a suit, and despite the fact he was too far away for Joan to gauge its quality, she was sure it was expensive and overstated.

Nathaniel. Joan and Leigh had believed him dead, yet here he was.

Victor's Legate, his second-in-command, though Joan had considered them an unlikely pairing. Joan had killed Victor that night. Nathaniel must have escaped the fire at the vineyard, and not unscathed judging by his face.

What was he doing here? He'd never struck Joan as an idiot, which he'd have to be if he was proclaiming himself a lord in Ruby Court guild territory. Elizaveta would wipe him out if Joan didn't kill him here.

She hoped she had the strength left to do it because he'd recognized her in return. The scowl on what was left of his face meant they'd be facing off sooner rather than later.

Joan took a deep breath. She pulled more power into herself from the ley lines, and for the first time the sensation burned like a sharp pain along her nerves.

All or nothing because she wasn't giving up.

His lips moved, as if he were speaking to someone nearby though no one stood next to him, and his eyes remained on her.

In a pocket of air that floated about her head, his voice was as clear as if he'd been standing beside her.

"I will succeed where Victor failed and kill you, Joan Matthews."

No chance she'd let him, but she didn't have the strength to spell back a reply.

A reverberating blasting followed by a crackling sound like a storm's lightning strike pulled Nathaniel's gaze elsewhere, and the anger on his face morphed to rage.

Beyond the skirmish of bodies, two figures stood to the north. Joan lost track of the ground between them as she struggled to believe what her eyes were showing her.

One was Leigh, staring at Joan, with her eyes wide and her mouth open. She looked terrified enough to bolt.

Bartholomew was in front of her, his hands casting the lightning Joan had noticed earlier.

The shock of Bartholomew's power was nothing compared to the horror of seeing Leigh in a battle with a magic-wielding vampire. Leigh took a step forward, but Bartholomew said something to her over his shoulder and Leigh stopped.

Leigh was taking orders from vampires now?

Acid roiled in Joan's stomach. Tears and helplessness swelled before she swallowed them down. Joan hadn't protected Leigh, and now—

An ocean of bodies and combatants and dogs and the damned crows lay between them. Joan hated this fight, and she hated being separated from Leigh.

Enough.

One stomp on the ground, one chest-rumbling growl, and as if summoned by Joan's fury the power of the ley line once again rose through the earth and into her body.

If the High Coven didn't like it, they could go fuck themselves.

"*Sola mea voluntus.*" *My will alone.*

Her will was that everything between her and Leigh would *move*. Joan didn't call for anything specific so much as her powers decided on their own what would accomplish the goal.

A thunderous boom, like that of an explosion without fire, split the night. The entire field quaked, disengaging every fight in progress. Crows blew back, scattered by the percussive force of Joan's spell.

The backlash was immense, slamming Joan in the chest and knocking her on her ass.

For a moment she couldn't breathe.

Her vision flashed white for so long she feared she'd gone blind. All sound was muffled in her ears, and when she could see again, her vision was blurry.

Joan pushed herself to her feet before her weariness drove her back to one knee, squelching in the mud.

Giving in to fatigue wasn't an option. Not when she needed to get to Leigh.

"*Restitue vires.*" *Restore my strength.*

The bolstering spell should have fed new energy from the ley lines into her limbs.

Nothing happened.

She couldn't feel the ley lines or the power of her own magic. Everything was completely dark, blown out, unavailable.

How was that possible? Panic swelled in her body as she tried to rise again, this time succeeding.

The blast from Joan's spell had knocked everyone to the ground, and only a few figures stirred, though she couldn't identify anyone yet.

"Joan!" Dayton called out to her, a burly blur several yards in front of her. "You all right?"

Her blurry vision cleared. A car was on fire, casting fiery light across the road and surrounding fields. She ignored Dayton, searching the far edges of the battleground.

Nathaniel had disappeared and Bartholomew was nowhere to be seen, but they weren't the one who mattered.

Leigh was gone.

CHAPTER 22

"KEEP UP." ELIZAVETA called back to Leigh as she ran with Bartholomew at her heels, weaving without effort through the dense trees. "Or we will lose him."

Elizaveta had not joined Leigh and Bartholomew at the battle, choosing instead to veer around it and surveil the vampire orchestrating the horde of thralls.

Leigh couldn't believe it. Nathaniel was alive. All this time, she'd believed him dead. After every nightmare, she'd convinced herself as she lay in Joan's arms that the boogeyman was gone and couldn't hurt her anymore.

She'd been wrong, and the way he'd been staring at Joan, he planned more violence. The only reason Leigh was here and not running to Joan's side was because the two vampires in front of her were certain they could stop Nathaniel for good.

"We cannot let him escape," Bartholomew had said. "We hunt him now."

Nathaniel had seen them all in return, and had fled. With a second to decide, Leigh had chosen to run with the hunters instead of staying behind.

Leigh ran close behind them both, wondering how they could keep up such a pace. She noticed she wasn't out of breath and pushed harder, amazed she could run faster.

Her brief enthusiasm ended when she remembered why.

Here was another instance proving she was no longer human.

She caught up to Elizaveta, who smirked in satisfaction. Her approval was unsettling, but soon enough Elizaveta's focus was back on their pursuit.

The distance between them and their quarry was closing. Good. The sooner they dealt with Nathaniel, the sooner Leigh could get back to Joan. Joan's display of power had been immense and impressive, but the cry she had let out at the end—

Joan was fine. She'd looked different with her shorter hair, and so tired. She had to be okay, else Leigh had left her to face an unknown threat alone.

Ahead of them Nathaniel crashed through the shin-high brush and adjusted his trajectory toward the forest. The more he ran, the harder Leigh pushed. Never mind Elizaveta and Bartholomew—*she* couldn't let him get away. She didn't want to see him, but she couldn't sit by while he escaped again.

Nathaniel was attached to the small army of thralls—was he their leader? The vampire lord and tactician Elizaveta had suggested at the guild meeting?

No matter what, he was a threat to Joan, and somehow Leigh was going to stop him. What had once been fear of him had become resolve.

Though she couldn't see him up ahead, she knew he had pivoted south. Elizaveta and Bartholomew changed course to follow him.

Could they sense Nathaniel the way she could? Not only could she hear him running, she could feel him, the energy of his essence darker than the rest of the forest with no less instinct to survive.

Nathaniel changed directions.

"How do we know this isn't a trap?" Leigh panted as she ran. She might be faster and stronger, but she was still running more than she had in months.

"Could be," Bartholomew said without strain.

Nathaniel altered course again. He must have been able to hear them as well, so it couldn't have been a false trail he was trying to leave.

"It is not," Elizaveta said with certainty.

Leigh understood when Nathaniel shifted once more. He didn't know the terrain—not like Leigh did after a lifetime in this country, and this section of woods ended in a bluff over river rapids swift and high with seasonal mountain runoff. On the other side of the river was a rocky crest that would be difficult to climb while escaping pursuit.

Leigh signed to Bartholomew to pursue, and mimed a forking gesture before running in a different direction. She ran faster, eager to reach the bluff first, parallel to him for a short time until she arrived at her destination. Seconds later, Nathaniel burst through the trees, followed by Bartholomew from the woods and Elizaveta alongside the rock wall.

The sight of him shook the tenuous resolve she'd had a few moments ago. Echoes of his laughter at his own cruelty, the way he'd tossed her into dark rooms with new vampires, ordering them not to kill her but to stave off their hunger with her as an appetizer.

Every healed bite on Leigh's skin itched with him so close, the vestigial terror releasing adrenaline in her bloodstream.

Surrounded, Nathaniel froze. He ignored the others as he sneered at her, the expression emphasizing his wounds. His face—the wreckage of his face . . . had she done that to him, or had it been the fire at the vineyard? Shocked, she realized through the lens of her most recent experiences that the whole blaze had been her fault.

This was what she'd wanted to prevent happening to Joan. If nothing else, she felt vindicated for taking the time to learn to control herself.

"You," he spat at Leigh. "You did this to me."

Against her will, Leigh took a step back.

He crouched, hands raised at his sides as the air around him thickened and swirled. "If it's the last thing I do, I'll rip your head off for what you've done. You *ruined* me."

Fog rose from the ground at his feet, like dry ice streaming over the earth.

Leigh's hands ached with swollen power, useless at this distance. If he came any closer...

Bartholomew waved his hand in a closed circle at his waist, and a burst of rough wind emanated from his fingers, dispelling Nathaniel's fog and knocking him back a step. The force of it reached where Leigh stood and pushed her to one knee before she could prepare herself.

By the time she regained her feet, Bartholomew was next to Nathaniel. Elizaveta stood beside Leigh as if she'd moved in a blink.

"You couldn't have enthralled so many," Elizaveta said. "Who are you working for?"

Nathaniel stared her down, brave though he was outmatched. "Any one of your enemies. And I'm not talking to you, traitor."

He scowled at Leigh. "I treated you too well before. I should have taken you for myself."

Revulsion washed through Leigh. She'd only heard what Nathaniel had done to some of the others he'd imprisoned, and the thought of such brutal treatment made her shiver.

Elizaveta snarled, her hands beginning to glow red. "You will tell me what I want to know."

"Your fate is already sealed," said Nathaniel to Elizaveta. "You deserve it for your betrayal of our entire—"

Bartholomew snatched Nathaniel forward as if he weighed nothing, gripped his head with one hand over the crown of Nathaniel's skull, and twisted.

With a wet, tearing squelch, he tore Nathaniel's head from his shoulders. He held the head at arm's length away from him, and black blood splattered in the dirt.

Leigh swallowed bile as Bartholomew let the body fall to the ground.

"A fitting end for such a loathsome creature." He turned his milky eyes on Leigh, his expression gentle. "Wouldn't you agree?"

Leigh closed her eyes, the horror and disgust and *relief* intertwining. Nathaniel was dead. Truly dead this time.

Bartholomew tossed the head over the cliff. The splash of its landing was lost in the rustling song of the rapids below.

Everything else was silent, except for Leigh's thundering heart.

Elizaveta scoffed. "You might have given him a chance to yield some information first."

Bartholomew exhaled, as close to a harumph as his nature allowed. "He would have revealed nothing. Not to us."

Leigh tried to pull herself together, swallowing against her rising gullet.

"Who do you think he was working for?" Her voice was too shaky, but at least she could speak.

"For," Bartholomew said. "More likely *with*."

"Balazs or Arnaldus." Elizaveta turned her back on the corpse and walked the way they'd come. "Both of them hold territory alongside our province, and each would take advantage of an unaligned loose end like this rubbish."

"We cannot accuse either of them without more proof." Bartholomew seemed like he was admonishing her. "And with their plausible deniability headless, their attacks will cease."

Elizaveta frowned, her displeasure plain. "We've been too long away from the city," she said, changing the subject. "We'll find out more there than we will in these wildlands."

Bartholomew turned to join her. Leigh didn't move.

"I'm not coming back with you."

Though two vampires of immeasurable power directed their focus at her, Leigh held her ground. She wasn't as afraid of them as she had been prior to her time in Black Rose City, though they might not respond well.

It didn't matter. She'd been away from Joan long enough.

"You would benefit from additional training," Elizaveta said, her words crisp but without anger.

Which wasn't an order, Leigh noticed.

"I probably would." No time to dissemble. She may not have done so before, but she had to speak up for herself. "I've learned to control my powers well enough for now and you know it."

Admitting she possessed inhuman power was still a difficult concept to say aloud. So was confronting the two of them.

She settled her shoulders and let the truth out with her next exhale. "Your world is not the place for me."

Bartholomew tilted his head to one side, a considering gesture. "You're a part of that world whether you want to be or not."

Leigh recognized the truth in his words. She would never again be human, but her need to live a human life had not changed.

"One day, sooner than you might think," Elizaveta said. "You'll have to make a choice."

Leigh took a deep breath. Whatever the consequences, she knew where she belonged.

"I already have."

Elizaveta frowned in displeasure. "You're a child with only an inkling of understanding. How can you choose when you don't know what is being offered?"

Leigh took offense but didn't respond. Elizaveta glanced at Nathaniel's headless remains, then toward the east before turning to Bartholomew. "Time grows short."

After another parting glance at Leigh, Elizaveta disappeared back the way she'd come.

"Leigh," Bartholomew began.

"Please don't try to stop me." She couldn't overtake him,

either, if he tried to restrain her.

He shook his head, his manner almost placating in the slow movement. "I won't, but listen to me. As you've no doubt surmised, Nathaniel may not be your only problem."

"I have to warn Joan." The need to get to Joan was overwhelming.

"There are other ways to get word to her."

"I'm not going back." The words rang true as she said them. She'd gotten what she needed, and Black Rose City would never be her home.

His expression was indecipherable. "If you require aid and call me, I will come."

Leigh nodded, not wanting to say any more. Perhaps he wasn't the kind of ally she'd prefer, but he was a powerful one nonetheless.

"Take care, Leigh Phan. I hope you're able to live the life you want."

He didn't sound like he believed it was possible.

Leigh didn't stay to persuade him.

Joan had left the battlefield by the time Leigh returned. A pyre's stink filled the air as the Mount Angel watch rounded up the few remaining thralls.

Leigh watched from the shadows of the woods. She didn't want to interact with any of those people who would prefer to shoot her, and didn't let herself think about how she'd receive the same welcome in Calvert.

She had already recovered from her earlier run, and for once she didn't begrudge her bloodling strength since it allowed her to jog most of the way from Mount Angel to Calvert.

A normal human in peak condition would have taken twelve hours to walk that distance. After using a few shortcuts, Leigh ran it in three, and didn't let herself think much further beyond the path ahead.

When the gnarled oak came into view, marking the last turn before the watch perimeter, Leigh pulled a white handkerchief from her pocket. The sky had lightened for the coming dawn, but to be on the safe side she held her hand high so there was no mistaking the gesture, and waved the cloth as she approached the checkpoint.

The watch was heavier than usual, six people lining the road instead of the standard trio.

Four of them took firmer hold of their weapons as she approached. They gaped in open horror or glared in disapproval as she got closer.

Without the glamour, Leigh felt naked, but the time for hiding was behind her now.

"You gotta be fuckin' kidding me." Piper gripped her rifle so hard her knuckles were white. "You're a goddamned bloodling?"

The others looked ready to shoot her, though no one had aimed a weapon at her yet.

Leigh didn't respond to the question since the answer was obvious. "I want to talk to—"

"We don't care," Piper said. "Is this new, or have you been like this the whole time?"

"Who's your master?" One of the others spoke now, a man she didn't know.

This was an easy question to answer, though she'd rather have slapped the man for suggesting the proposition.

"I have no master, and I don't serve anyone. I'm the same person I always was." Her knees trembled with the revelation—and what a truth it was, one she only now understood.

She was no different than she'd been before she'd left with the vampires, no different than she'd been with Joan before anyone knew about her changes, no different than she'd been all the years she'd lived in Calvert, except now she knew the truth.

Bloodling or no, the core of her hadn't changed at all.

"So you have been keeping it from us," he said.

This was tiresome, and not what she'd come here for. "Will you call Joan, please?"

"Why should we do anything for you, you lying monster?" Piper said as she stepped forward clutching her rifle.

Leigh had expected no less. It still hurt.

A bark and the rapid patter of paws were her only warning.

Dayton's dog, Willy, raced between watch members on a collision course for Leigh. He was big for a Siberian Husky, and Leigh had avoided him for months for this reason: once he saw her, a bloodling, he would strike.

Leigh dropped into a crouch, less to prepare for a fight and more to defend herself.

Willy stopped so quickly, she expected to hear squealing tires. To her shock, he sneezed and whined at her as he leaped up to plant his paws on her chest.

He licked her face.

Leigh wasn't the only one who didn't know what to do about this development. The nameless man's mouth was hanging open. Everyone knew how dangerous this dog was in a fight. Willy had killed vampires before, and had faced off against quite a few bloodlings.

She settled for pushing him down and scratching behind his ears.

"White flag of parley," Leigh said now that her heart had decided not to explode. "Either you're going to honor it or you're going to shoot me where I stand and then call Joan and explain who you killed and why. Good luck with that by the way. So which is it?"

The biggest man, a burly bearded guy Leigh knew by the name of Huck, tugged his radio from his belt and spoke into it.

Leigh waited in the anxious, unsettled silence of the impasse until she heard the approaching rumble of Luther's engine. She tried to contain her relief since the hard part wasn't over by a longshot.

Joan parked and leapt from the vehicle without closing the door. Dayton climbed from the passenger side, his mouth open in shock. Was it at Leigh's lack of a glamour, or the fact that she was petting his otherwise ferocious dog?

Joan hadn't changed yet, and her clothes were torn and dirty from the fight. Her expression was a mix of wariness, fear, and something like shame or embarrassment. Behind it all was pain and distrust.

The other members of the watch gave Joan a wide berth, leaving the situation to their leader. As usual, Joan didn't waste any time.

"What does this mean?" Her voice was rough with exhaustion and something else Leigh couldn't decipher.

Such a simple question with so many answers.

Leigh tucked the handkerchief back into her pocket and took a few steps closer while Willy pranced around her legs until Dayton whistled for him. The watch twitched at her approach, Piper going so far as to raise her rifle again.

Joan didn't move.

"We need to talk," Leigh said, glancing at the others before softening her voice for Joan. "Just the two of us."

When Joan's shoulders fell and sadness washed over her face, Leigh could have sworn her own heart cracked.

CHAPTER 23

NOTHING GOOD CAME from conversations starting with "we need to talk."

So it all came down to this. Her wife was gonna dump her in front of the goddamned town watch and make Joan look like a sucker in the process.

The power blowout had affected her worse than the fight. Everything was blanched out—faded though not quite black and white. She couldn't taste the air, or sense the currents of the earth beneath her. She couldn't feel the ley lines and their thrumming power.

What was one more stab in the chest?

Anger was easier to give into than more grief.

"Just say what you've got to say and leave if that's what you're going to do."

Someone behind her grunted in agreement, though it wasn't their place to speak. Hell, none of them needed to hear this conversation. Having Dayton and the others here, though, kept Joan from begging.

"I'm not leaving," Leigh said.

Joan swayed forward before catching herself, the exhaustion making it hard to focus. She wanted to lie down and die somewhere in peace.

Wait. Leigh's words finally got through. Not leaving?

No way was it that simple. Not after what she saw only hours ago—Leigh next to Bartholomew, Bartholomew protecting her.

"Maybe not now, but sooner or later, you'll go back to . . ." What were those vampires to Leigh now?

"I belong here, and you know it." Leigh took a step forward, and one of the watch stepped back in alarm.

Leigh scoffed.

"I don't know shit," Joan said. "I don't know what you think or-or feel about any of this anymore."

Someone twitched in discomfort. Who could blame them? This was the oddest, most uncomfortable breakup conversation in history.

"You know what I think," Leigh said. "And how I feel."

"I don't—"

Leigh's face was a perfect sculpture of beautiful anger. "I have never in my life, Joan Matthews, wanted anyone but you."

Her brown and golden eyes flashed, the yellow sclera setting Joan's instincts on edge, though the words made her heart start beating again.

"I don't want to *be* anywhere else," Leigh said. "I didn't choose this, I didn't want this, but I have always been and will always be yours, so you can put that bullshit out of your mind."

"Then why did you leave?" Joan hated how plaintive she sounded. "And why did . . ."

Why had Leigh sent her away? She didn't want to say it out loud, not in front of all these people.

"I didn't have a choice." Leigh's voice boomed, surprising Joan with its power. "I had to, until I was sure I was never going to hurt—hurt anyone."

Joan understood what Leigh hadn't said. Leigh didn't want to hurt *her* again. The force of holding in her tears tightened Joan's throat.

"You're not welcome here," Dayton said.

Oh, *fuck* this guy.

"I'm not talking to you," Leigh said before Joan could say a word.

Joan didn't know whether to be elated Leigh was showing some spine or disquieted because it was a new behavior—at least around other people. Leigh had never held back when alone with Joan. Here in front of the watch was another story.

She wondered what else had changed.

"I don't want to be anywhere," Leigh continued, "but in this glorious backwater of ours with these half-bigoted idiots who don't know how good they've got it with you here."

Someone else was talking, spewing bullshit at Leigh, and Leigh was glaring them down.

"Enough," Joan said, and grunted when tensing her gut triggered a new wave of aches across her beleaguered body.

The silence was as painful as her wounds. Joan stared at Leigh as if she had all the answers to every question in the known universe, as if Joan herself was begging Leigh to prove in the span of a breath that she wouldn't let Joan down.

Leigh never blinked.

Was there any other choice? Everything already hurt, and it hurt so much more without Leigh.

Joan closed her eyes against the tears she couldn't let fall. Maybe later, when the world gave her a fucking break.

"Leigh Phan," Joan said, fatigue weighting her words though they were no less clear. "If you come in light and in peace with an open heart, at my hearth and my table, alongside me and mine in peace and at war, you are welcome."

Leigh's shoulders dropped with the exhaled breath she must have been holding.

"In perfect love and perfect trust," Leigh said, "I am bound to you. I have returned to you in light and in peace with an open heart."

Joan wanted to collapse with the relief washing over her.

She bit her lip to keep from crying.

Hell of a way to announce their handfasting. Guess the whole town would know soon enough.

The watch lowered their weapons, though they didn't appear any less tense or on guard.

Dayton turned to face Joan, a challenge in stance if not in words. "You're not going to discuss this with the watch? With the coven?"

"Nothing to discuss," Joan said. "She stays, or I go."

Someone in the watch gasped. So? It was the truth.

Dayton voice dropped an octave. "You sure you wanna do this?"

She wanted to knock him over with a cantrip. Without power, all she could do was glare. Didn't stop her from reaching out with her senses to the ley lines beneath her.

The thick, cloying nothingness didn't change, and the cracks she imagined in her heart split deeper. What if it was permanent?

She couldn't deal with that right now, and she was tired of him trying to tell her what to do.

Powers or no, she was still Joan Matthews.

"I have given my blood for Calvert, and have pledged to defend it and the lands beyond until the land refuses me. I have bound myself to the earth on behalf of the people. That has not changed. I would not put this town in danger, and have stood before every threat since I came back, at some cost as you well know."

Dayton lowered his eyes.

"So don't stand here and tell me what I can or cannot do."

Truth be told, it wasn't a good look for either of them in front of the rest of the watch. One crisis at a time. At least now she knew her marriage was intact, though she and Leigh still had a lot to talk about.

Leigh ignored the way everyone gave her more space than needed when she stepped forward. When she was close enough, she claimed Joan's hand and squeezed.

Joan's heart seized with the touch, and she turned toward the SUV before she started bawling.

Muttering rose in their wake as she pulled Leigh alongside her. Leigh let go of her hand when they got to the car and walked around the vehicle to the passenger door.

"Joan." Dayton sounded resigned. He'd stepped closer as if he didn't want anyone else to hear him.

Joan's respect for Dayton made her pause one more time before she climbed into Luther. He was watching her with a wariness bordering on suspicion.

"Whatever happens," he said, "this is on you."

She held back a scream. Everything in this whole damned town seemed to be *on her*, the way he and the watch and the coven acted. It was infuriating, but she was too tired to hash anything else out now. Not with another conversation with Leigh looming.

Joan and Dayton had met for the first time right here at this checkpoint. She thought about all the times she'd saved his life, and he'd saved hers.

Joan didn't want to lose him as a friend, but given a choice between him or Leigh, he didn't stand a chance.

"Let's all get some sleep and then . . . I'll talk to the coven and all the watch. You have my word." She held his gaze with her own until he finally nodded. A tense truce, maybe, but a truce nonetheless.

She willed herself into the SUV, ignoring her protesting muscles.

Joan didn't speak as she drove Luther one-handed through the predawn streets. Leigh had reclaimed her other hand the moment after Joan had latched her seat belt, her grip secure yet gentle.

Leigh had said a lot just now, which meant it was Joan's turn. She wanted to say something, but she couldn't form thought much less words.

Rapid-fire images, muted in memory, passed through her mind. The thrall dead in the summit compound. Grant's judgment. Dayton's disapproval. Bartholomew's protective stance across the battlefield. The kid in the van, who was now fed and lodged at one of the churches for the night. Nathaniel.

Right. How could she have forgotten about him?

"What happened to Nathaniel?" Her voice sounded like a croak. If they had to hunt him down, it was going to have to wait.

"Dead," Leigh said, her tone matter of fact, though she exhaled a shaky breath. "For good this time."

Joan's mind blanked again. She slowed the SUV as they approached the last turn to the homestead and didn't remember half the drive so far.

The first rays of sunlight touched the tops of the trees as Joan drove down the driveway to the house. A stray observation pierced her brain fog: Leigh had planted the flowers lining the driveway and set the stones framing Luther's parking space. The boards in the porch had been replaced and stained by her hands. Leigh might have been raised by her grandmother in the house next door, but the Matthews house was her home and had been for a long time.

Joan released Leigh's hand to park Luther. Her hands were shaking so much it took three tries to unlatch her seat belt.

She had to lean on the door to climb out without falling on the ground. By the time she got to the porch, she was shaking.

The expression on Leigh's face, of care, of wariness and surprise, snapped Joan back into reality.

The wards hadn't been reset. The front door was unlocked.

Inside, Leigh flipped the living room light switch. Dirty mugs covered the coffee table. Bunched-up pillows and disordered blankets on the couch showed where Joan had been sleeping. Opened books and journals filled every space on the dining room table not covered in things left behind after their use: empty wine bottles and glasses, discarded clothes, and—surprising Joan with fresh perspective—a few knives and her forgotten pistol.

Leigh made no sound as she stepped closer and gave Joan every chance to stop her. Joan didn't put up a fight as Leigh reached for her jacket and pushed it from her shoulders.

By the time Joan managed to kick off her boots, Leigh had disarmed and half-undressed her. She led them to their bedroom, and tossed a spare blanket over the bed.

Half-dressed herself and still unspeaking, Leigh climbed onto the still made bed and pulled Joan into her arms before tugging the blanket over them both.

Still shivering, Joan couldn't relax, her muscles taut as she tried to hold something back inside her. It was like she was still fighting, still embroiled in a fierce battle.

Leigh kissed the top of her head and tightened her embrace. "I'm not going anywhere, Joan."

The dam in Joan's chest collapsed, and the wave of tears swallowed her whole.

CHAPTER 24

AFTER JOAN FELL asleep, Leigh shed a few tears of her own.

Leigh hadn't seen any injury or smelled any blood beyond the small cuts on Joan's hands and arms, but Joan had barely held herself up coming into the house and had limped up the stairs.

The rest of her appearance made Leigh squeeze her tighter. Joan had changed so much in such a short time, and not only the botched hair cut suggesting she'd used one of her knives. She'd lost weight, and the bags under her eyes spoke to her exhaustion.

Pale sunlight revealed the dust in the room, eddies passing motes back into the shadows. The air in the room smelled stale, like Joan hadn't been in here in days. She'd been sleeping downstairs, on the couch where Leigh had seen the untidy blankets and crumpled pillows.

Leigh should have known what effect her leaving would have on Joan. Now, it was clear Joan had taken horrible care of herself, and for someone who was as independent and self-sufficient as Joan was, that was saying a lot.

The slow, warm hours of morning passed in uninterrupted quiet. Leigh watched Joan sleep and contemplated the long list of their undiscussed concerns, from the watch and the vampires and the coven to the things Leigh had learned from

Bartholomew and Elizaveta, not to mention whatever Nathaniel had been up to before his death.

Was it all too much for them to find a path through together?

In her sleep, Joan squeezed Leigh back.

Leigh kissed Joan's forehead, breathing her in as if the scent of her was as necessary as oxygen.

No more questions for now. Leigh yielded to sleep's pull.

When she woke, Joan was no longer in her arms.

The fragrance of her homemade rosemary and mint soap was strong, and Joan was now under the covers on her side of the bed. She must have risen to shower and crawled back into bed without waking Leigh.

Leigh had been more tired than she'd thought since she hadn't noticed. Still foggy from sleep, she rose to do the same and was halfway through washing road grime from her skin before she felt awake.

The need to get back to Joan quickened her shower. Now clean, the thought of putting on clothes to climb into bed seemed ludicrous. She slid between the sheets, trying not to wake Joan, and pressed herself to Joan's naked back before she could think better of it.

Still asleep, Joan made a sound of approval and recognition, and Leigh's heart soared with the knowledge she was welcomed even when Joan was unconscious. She wrapped her arm around Joan's waist, nuzzled the back of her neck, and closed her eyes.

Leigh dozed as late afternoon shifted the shadows in the room, pushing any thoughts aside as she rested. Holding Joan was more healing than anything else might be, and her sense of belonging reestablished itself with each synchronous breath they took.

She noticed the exact moment Joan woke up—a split-second stiffness Joan immediately released.

Leigh started to pull away, but Joan wouldn't let her. She held Leigh's arm against her as she rolled over within its confines, resting her head on the pillow mere inches away, and intertwining their legs.

The silence between them stretched long. They had so much to talk about, yet Leigh couldn't speak.

For all that Joan had changed, she was the same. The same direct gaze, as if she already knew all Leigh's secrets. Even now, lying on her side, Joan compelled Leigh to warm the deepest parts of herself by the fire of Joan's strength and power and presence.

Leigh couldn't help reaching out to stroke Joan's brow. The softening of Joan's eyes, so dark brown they were almost black, was like a tangible switch on Leigh's arousal. She held it back, not wanting to push so soon after being reunited. It seemed too much to ask.

Joan didn't say anything either. She traced her hand over Leigh's arm, pausing to caress each scar—the bites and marks from needles and knives. She had never pushed Leigh to explain each token of horrible past experiences. She had never asked Leigh to cast the glamour spell that hid her scars and bloodling eyes. That had been Leigh's choice.

As Joan stroked down to her hand and pressed their palms together, her expression didn't change. Did Joan see her differently now because of her bloodling traits? Love her differently?

As if she'd heard Leigh's thoughts, Joan trailed a fingertip along her jaw, faint enough to tickle, before resting the pad of her thumb against Leigh's closed lips, like a pause before asking a question.

With a surrendering sigh, Leigh parted her lips. She sucked Joan's thumb, the question asked and answered, holding eye contact, and as if sparked by lightning, Joan sat up.

Joan tossed the covers aside as she straddled Leigh's thighs, and Leigh clasped her hips, pulling Joan against her as she spread her legs wider. The feel of Joan, the scent of her, was perfect and maddening and so, so welcome after what felt like an eternity.

This was the point of no return—no chance of slowing down or stopping—the familiar give and take they'd exchanged countless times before.

Beyond thought, Leigh was swept away by the slow, warm grind of Joan's hips, by the heat where Joan was pressed against her, by the strange, powerful, delightful magic they built between the two of them every time they touched like this.

She loved to draw it out—to palm and caress wherever she could reach of Joan's smooth brown skin, wanting to touch everywhere at once and make sure she didn't miss anything, to build Joan's pleasure and make it last as long as they could bear. She cupped Joan's breasts and couldn't resist pinching pebbled skin until—impatient—Joan pulled one of Leigh's hands away and pushed it between her thighs.

Leigh stroked, firm and persistent, directed by each breath, each moan, each movement, and glided inside, her own desire sinking into the undertow, into the confirmation of how much she was wanted.

Joan's magnificent beauty, vivid as she arched on the brink of orgasm, was too distracting for Leigh to focus on maintaining the driving rhythm. She closed her eyes, wanting only to propel Joan's pleasure ever higher, as if all the knots inside Leigh would only be unraveled when Joan cried out her release.

And when Joan did, when her orgasm stretched long and seemingly endless, she clung to Leigh as tightly as she'd always done. Leigh sagged against Joan's chest, hiding her relief.

Joan clutched Leigh's face, wiping the tears from her cheeks. She tilted Leigh's head up for a ravenous kiss. Leigh tasted salt.

"Shh, lover," Joan whispered, still catching her breath. She kissed Leigh again. "We're home now."

Hours later, and though Joan protested she didn't have much of an appetite, Leigh dragged her from the bed and insisted on making them dinner. She herself was hungry enough for three people, so she was sure nothing would go to waste.

They kept the conversation limited to ingredients and the weather while Leigh cooked and Joan set the table. After Joan rallied well enough to clean her plate, Leigh pushed the dishes aside and rose with a mission in mind. The next item on Leigh's list was restoring some order in the chaos.

The hunt was brief, and she returned to the dining room table with an electric hair clipper in one hand and a towel over her shoulder.

Joan scoffed. "This is what's important right now?"

"Yeah, it is," Leigh said, and pulled one of the chairs toward the mudroom. "You can't see the back of your head."

The faux gasp Joan let out made Leigh laugh. Everything seemed normal, though it wasn't.

Not with so much left to talk about.

Joan stripped off her T-shirt before she sat down, and Leigh covered her shoulders with the towel. The burr of the clipper complicated conversation, so Leigh focused on her task.

The touch of tilting Joan's head to and fro was as intimate as what they'd shared upstairs.

Task completed, Leigh blew the loose short hairs from Joan's nape, loving the effect when Joan shivered. When she was finished cleaning Joan's shoulders off, she kissed the join of Joan's shoulder and neck, resisting the urge to lick Joan's neck above her jugular vein.

The impulse sobered her, and she pulled away.

Joan hadn't noticed, but it reminded Leigh of what was at stake. Of what she hadn't yet told Joan about her time with the vampires.

Which also reminded her of what Joan hadn't told her.

"Why did you owe Elizaveta a favor?"

Joan frowned as she pulled the T-shirt back on. "Do we really need to get into this?"

Leigh let the question lie for a moment as she swept the floor around the chair and dumped the dustpan into a bin.

"We're getting into all of it. I . . . I've been too scared to talk about any of it—the vampires, about what was happening with me, because I didn't think you wanted to hear it."

The house wasn't the only thing that needed to be cleared out. Loving Joan had made Leigh bold. Time to get everything out in the open.

Joan met her gaze with sorrow but no shame. "I didn't bring it up because I thought you didn't want me to. I wanted to respect your—not privacy, I guess. I wanted to leave it up to you."

"And I thought you didn't want to talk about it."

They were idiots.

"So tell me," Leigh said in a softer voice as she claimed Joan's hand and led her through the kitchen and back into the dining room.

"When the High Coven wouldn't help me stop Victor . . ." Joan began as she reclaimed her earlier seat. Out came the tale of how Bartholomew had ended up at the vineyard, and how the favor had loomed over Joan's head all this time.

"I had no idea when she'd call it in, or how," Joan said. "I damned sure didn't think it'd have anything to do with you so I—I didn't bring it up."

Understandable, but they couldn't move forward like that. The things they knew were bad enough without hiding more on top.

"No more secrets," Leigh said. "Even the tame ones."

She swayed their arms between them with affection. "We face it all together."

"I like this," Joan said, her eyes bright. "Feeling you touch me again."

And then it was Leigh's turn to share—about Elizaveta's

power and the capabilities she'd demonstrated. About how Leigh had worked through failure attempting to learn how to control herself.

She told Joan the truth about how awful she'd felt sending her away.

"If I'd known then what I know now, maybe I would have handled it differently. I was terrified they'd hurt you."

"You don't think so now?"

"No, I don't." Leigh shook her head. "I think there would have been a conversation first and not an immediate bloodbath."

She wished she'd chosen a different word. "I mean, if they gave someone like Nathaniel a chance to speak up for himself . . ."

They had, hadn't they? They'd asked him who he'd been working for, and he hadn't revealed anything before Bartholomew had killed him.

"You're sure Nathaniel's dead?"

Leigh swallowed the lump in her throat at the thought of his demise. "Positive."

"That bad, huh?"

Squeezing Joan's hand was easier than answering.

"And they just let you go?" Joan sounded incredulous, and more than a little untrusting.

"Yeah." Leigh almost didn't believe it herself.

Well, she believed Bartholomew. She didn't think she'd ever trust Elizaveta.

"I think . . . they wanted to make sure I wasn't about to become some kind of loose cannon. I can control it better now." Not well, but if she kept up her practice, her control would improve.

At some point, Elizaveta would attempt to convince her again. With their similar powers, Elizaveta wouldn't leave her alone forever, though there was no telling how much time might pass.

Now she understood Joan's favor to Elizaveta, which was not at all comforting.

"I'll say," Joan said with a sly smile, pulling Leigh from her darker thoughts.

New confidence filled her, bolstered by Joan's proximity and their earlier closeness. "It's going to take some practice, which is not in the least bit pleasant, but I can do it."

A foreign pride planted itself in her chest until she remembered the root of it all. She was no longer human and would never be again.

Bartholomew's warning came to mind.

"There's more to the story, and I'll tell you all about that later, but there's also something else. Something Bartholomew said."

She took a deep breath. "Since there's no way in hell I'll ever turn, I, uh, might go crazy."

Joan stared, her expression blank.

The walls—like Leigh's encroaching loss of her faculties though she hadn't yet seen any sign of it—pressed in on her, and the room felt small.

"Grab some air with me?"

Joan rose without protest and followed Leigh to the porch. They sat side by side in the old swing, and Joan wrapped an arm around Leigh's shoulders.

She didn't push to speak, and Leigh was grateful as she gathered her thoughts.

"Bloodlings," Leigh continued, "who choose not to—to change . . . according to Bartholomew, they ultimately go mad. He said he'd seen it before."

Often enough to be certain, he'd said. Leigh hoped otherwise.

"And you believe him."

"Honestly, Joan, I don't know what to think. Of course I feel different—how could I not? But I'll die before I become one of them, so if insanity is my only other option, I'll take it."

She laughed without humor. "Naturally, I'm hoping to dodge that particular bullet."

Leigh couldn't imagine such a future.

Joan kissed the crown of Leigh's head.

"Well," she said, matter of fact. "Doesn't change anything as far as I'm concerned. I love you, crazy or not."

She made it seem simple. Maybe to her it was.

"While we're clearing the air," Joan began, pausing to swallow.

What could she be nervous about? What was more serious than Leigh's possible future insanity?

"I—" Joan's eyes clouded as she hesitated. "My powers are gone."

"I don't understand."

Joan pulled her arm back, steadying the swing with her legs as she moved.

"I can't feel anything. Sense anything. It's all . . ." She shrugged, the helplessness of the gesture doing the rest of the talking for her.

"What happened?"

"That last spell at Mount Angel. I—I think I drew too much power, and I was already pretty tapped out. I just reached for everything I could, and—"

She stared at her hands on her lap. "They're gone."

The hush of her voice meant she thought they were gone for good. Leigh had never heard of such a thing, but she wasn't an expert on all things magic.

She was, however, an expert on Joan, who looked lost. Well, Joan might doubt herself, but Leigh would never doubt her.

"You're worn out, Joan. After you get some rest, take a few days off. I'm sure it's temporary."

The encouragement couldn't hurt. She could use a little herself about the showdown the night before.

Leigh didn't want to bring it up, but she'd said they needed to clear the air. "Kinda like the reprieve we got last night. We gonna talk about the watch or the coven?"

Joan sighed, a mirror to how Leigh felt.

"I can't handle any more heavy stuff."

They rose together and went back in the house. The moment Joan closed the front door, a low metallic moan reverberated through the floorboards and vents.

"Furnace again?" Leigh asked.

"I swear it's cursed, and I would know." Joan groaned. "I tried a couple of times to adjust the lever. We might need to take the whole thing apart or replace it."

"My turn to take a peek at it," Leigh said. "You seem a little worn out."

She winked, only half joking. Joan still looked tired.

"Why don't you head upstairs? I'll come join you when I'm done."

When Joan offered no comment and headed for the stairs, Leigh knew she'd made the right suggestion.

In the half-finished cellar, the cooler air pebbled Leigh's skin as she adjusted the lever without difficulty. Not much was stored down here—crates of old jars, tools past their prime, old furniture stashed here for a short time that had turned into decades, and belongings from Joan's old room she'd cleared out last summer.

Leigh hadn't been down here since the previous winter, back when she was still applying the glamour spell every few days. To her muted senses this had been just another space in the house.

Now, the coolness of the earth was like a breeze against her skin, and its energy thrummed a beat in her body. A mouse skittered on the far end of the cellar open to the underground, too fast for her to see before it vanished.

Her senses were much sharper now, and she caught the scent of things that didn't belong.

Metal. Old wood. Leather. Aged paper. All those smells

were coming from the empty shelves along a wall where the light didn't reach.

With a grunt, Leigh shoved the old shelves aside. Set deep into the cellar's dirt walls was a narrow door covered in cobwebs, dirt, and old dust. The door's handle yielded to her grip, and a sharp tug was all it took to yank it open.

The old food cellar had metal walls and shelves, but instead of preserved jars and baskets, books and trunks and a few stacks of old loose paper had been stored here. The journals and reference volumes were much like the ones upstairs she and Joan had been searching through for months.

Leigh lifted one book from one of the shelves, careful not to brush it against the other objects. The dust was thick yet did not hide the careful slanted script burned into one corner of the leather cover and naming the most elusive witch in the Matthews family lineage.

Agnes Matthews
Summer 1823

CHAPTER 25

TWO DAYS LATER, the floor in the center of Joan's childhood room creaked beneath her every time she took a deep breath. When she sat anywhere else, though, the sound and feel were off, like she was leaning too far to one side, which was more of a distraction than the creaking.

She'd have to live with the trade-off.

Once this room had been filled with all the trappings of her younger life—bed, desk, bookshelves, walls lined with posters and Leigh's burgeoning art from their teen years. Now, all the furniture had been moved into the hall, the garage, and the cellar. What was left was an empty room perfect for her meditations.

Joan remembered one of the phrases from the journals Leigh had found—and how ridiculous was it that the answers she'd been searching for the last several months had been buried under the damned house. One passage had so captured her attention that she thought of it often.

The song of the crows reminds me of the sound of the corn in high summer, a dry whispering wind both unsettling and familiar.

Agnes had been a visual writer. Wading through some of the language had been like sifting sand, but this—this was clear.

Those who wage war with the craft use the crows as sentinels and fodder for battle. Those who bind spirit and earth to protect those under their care from others who would do harm, those witches commune with the crows and seek vision to aid in their craft, and call to them for guidance, for prophecy, for their sacred guardianship.

Caller of crows, the witch from the High Coven had called Joan. Time to find out.

Joan took another breath, ignored the resulting creak, and settled into her most relaxed meditation position.

Her mind was quieter than she was used to, an off feeling though not necessarily a bad one. The resonance of her powers and the spiritual energy of her ties to the land had been a constant in her mind and body for so long she hadn't paid much attention to it.

The absence of the sensation felt uneven. Like she was standing on one foot, or was only half dressed.

Not now. Focus.

The window was closed. The first time Joan had tried this yesterday, the crows had pecked their way through the screen. With her eyes closed, in the dark of no vision, she focused on the center of herself, the place she imagined housed the steady flame of a lone candle. As she relaxed, she settled into a centered sensation of wholeness, even without her power, the oneness of her own essence.

Her awareness shifted, and she fought to hold that center.

Now it felt like . . . like there were pieces of her *outside* her body, though she still felt whole within herself. Those pieces fluctuated and itched, and there were so many of them. When the craziness of it all pressed in on her, Joan breathed her way through it. It was a lot like being injured—she could endure it as long as she let herself sink into the discomfort and become one with it. All these sensations were tied to the feeling she got when the crows joined a fight, or swarmed to her when she was on the road.

The journals held extensive notes on the ways Agnes had learned to commune with the crows. Some steps of the instructions were missing, which was not helpful.

Joan had nothing but time to figure it all out, and the next step was to connect with one of those outside pieces.

It was like hearing voices at a concert, all blending into a low roar hinting at a future headache. She kept the visual in her imagination, like one of the amphitheaters she'd seen in her travels to the bigger cities, and narrowed her focus to those in her region, down to the land within the town boundary, the block, then ...

One piece felt nearby, closer than the others, as if—

She opened her eyes. One crow sat on the window ledge, tapping at the closed window.

How to communicate with one bird? She couldn't pat it on the head.

Unless ...

She closed her eyes and thought about patting it on the head. In her mind's eye, that piece seemed to glow, and a warmth rose in her, foreign yet not. She visualized a crow rising from her ledge, flying a circuit around the garden and landing on the tree closest to her window.

When she opened her eyes again, the crow jumped twice, squawked and launched into the air. By the time Joan rose and crossed the room to the window, the same crow was circling the yard. She opened the window as it—no, *he*—perched himself on a branch.

He preened under her gaze.

Joan grinned with pride since there was no one there to see it.

After she had tracked down an apple in the kitchen and inhaled it in three bites—Jesus, when was the last time she'd felt hungry?—she found Leigh in the backyard, on the far side of the garden.

Leigh had been busy.

She'd dug out the raised bed at the end and built up a knee-high mound of dirt stretching about ten feet long. On the near side of the mound, clusters of burnt wood still smoked.

Leigh knelt near one such pile, her fist clenched in the middle of a small fire.

Joan forced herself not to run to her side, not to save Leigh from the flames. Odd and difficult as it was to watch Leigh use her new powers, Joan was overcome with the feeling of, well, *rightness* at having Leigh back here in the garden.

Bloodling or no, power or no, politics with the coven and the watch aside—having Leigh home where she belonged felt more important than anything else.

When she was finished with whatever she was doing, Leigh stood. She offered a wan smile in greeting and picked up a nearby shovel. She covered the stacks with dirt, then dug new divots between them.

Guess this was their new normal—Joan courting birds and Leigh battling fire.

"What's with the dirt?"

"Stops the spread of the fire." Leigh replied as if they'd been conversing for a while. "Water won't put it out, and it'll burn anything else in its path."

Which meant Leigh's fire—the bloodling power she had—was dramatically different from the fire spells Joan cast, and proved Leigh wouldn't have found the answers she needed here at home.

"You said you'd—" Joan paused to keep her tone neutral, a feat of will. She still felt some bitterness about their exchange in the park by Elizaveta's manor. She wanted to get over that feeling, and not let it come between them. "You'd learned a lot while you were there."

Leigh offered a small smile at Joan in understanding, then looked serious again. "Well, as you've probably guessed, bloodlings are made when vampires have, um, sex with humans."

Leigh did not speak much of the night she became a bloodling. Only that the vampire had been kinder than expected and had promised Leigh her freedom, though Leigh hadn't known at the time what would happen.

"There's more consensual interaction in Elizaveta's territory than I... I guess I feared. And nothing like Victor's compound."

"Did you find out everything you needed?" Joan wouldn't let it bother her that she couldn't help Leigh with this. She *wouldn't*.

"No," Leigh said. "But I found out enough, and I couldn't stay away from you anymore."

She stacked three small piles of wood at intervals in the dirt as she shared with Joan what she'd seen and learned, the interactions she'd had with the locals, the way she'd been treated by Bartholomew and Elizaveta—even the conversations she'd had with different people in Black Rose City.

"You're saying the whole program is one hundred percent voluntary?" Joan asked.

Leigh paused to shrug as she shoveled more dirt onto the back of the pile. She made it look effortless.

Maybe it was, considering her bloodling strength.

"I didn't see any proof otherwise. And some of the bloodlings serve or work for the vampires in the guild. Others aren't affiliated with them and just live in the city. *I* felt safe out in the open, or at least safer than I did at Elizaveta's manor."

None of this sounded real, and the idea of Leigh spending any time with Elizaveta still made Joan's skin crawl.

"So what's the deal with you and them now?" Since Leigh had said she was staying, Joan meant. Joan was desperate to believe her, and just as desperate not to let it show.

"I told them I'm not coming back, and I don't want any part of their guild or anything else in Black Rose City. I believe them—well, Bartholomew—when they said I can make my own choice."

Joan hoped that was true.

"Anyway," Leigh said, propping the shovel against the side of the shed. "I found what I needed to find. I know how to—I won't hurt you again."

"That wasn't the only way you hurt me."

Joan wanted to take those words back, but they were real, and this time it wasn't bitterness speaking. Only pain, and the wounds still ached like fresh bruises. The house and homestead weren't so warm and bright with Leigh here that she could forget the cold dark of her previous absence.

"I am sorry." Leigh crossed her arms over her chest. "I meant what I said, Joan. I'm here for good. Time will be the only way to prove it to you. As for the rest, you don't know what it was like, to have a power you can't control."

Joan arched an eyebrow, and Leigh rolled her eyes in response.

"Okay, yes, you do, but it was different for me. I was afraid I was going to kill you because I didn't know how to handle what was happening to me."

What could Joan say to that?

Leigh was right. Only time would heal them both, and poking at the wounds wouldn't help.

Joan pledged to herself in that moment to give them a chance to move on.

"So you're here to stay," she said. "And they're not coming to drag you back. Nathaniel is dead, and his spying thralls have been put down. Sounds like we can get back to plain old everyday crises around here."

Leigh stared at nothing while she thought. "Yes, but . . ."

"But what?" Joan prompted. If it was bad news, best to get it all out in the open.

"The vampires," Leigh said, and Joan knew she meant Bartholomew and Elizaveta. "They were convinced someone else was backing Nathaniel. Someone from one of the other guilds.

Would they give up if Nathaniel isn't leading their thralls?"

A year ago, Nathaniel had been a second-rate Legate to a two-bit vampire lord in what most would consider a back-land nowhere. Made sense he must have been acting on someone else's behalf since he couldn't have raised so much manpower alone.

Would they find another puppet to do their bidding?

"Depends on how much they want the resources from around here. More farms under their control maybe."

Leigh shook her head. "No, I don't think that's it. The guild reports said the crop yields traded to them by Portland were down, but their own holdings were secured."

"Well, there's the power knoll." Joan began to pace along one of the garden's raised beds in response to the conversation, and also because she couldn't feel that knoll. "But it's not the only one in this region. There are others spread out across the whole northwest. This wouldn't give them a foothold to take over Black Rose City, if that's what they want."

In fact, taking over Calvert didn't offer much of a stronghold for that kind of defense. There was too much flank.

Something nagged at her. Something about the attacks so far.

"I don't think Calvert's the target." Joan said. "It would make more sense for them to claim territory upriver from Portland."

Leigh's eyes widened. "You mean the power plant at the dam."

Joan didn't understand the significance. "Maybe."

"The vampires in the guild suggested anyone with a brain would stay away from Calvert, and the treaty between Elizaveta and the High Coven is dependent upon the guild securing the plant. If the Ruby Court doesn't protect it, they have no leverage to gain support of their donor program. The rest of the treaty won't matter if an outside guild controls the power to the city. The treaty will fail and either Black Rose City or Portland will fall."

Or both.

"Well, I hope someone else has done the math, because the High Coven isn't going to listen to me," Joan admitted. "Not after what happened."

"Do you want me to call the vampires?" Leigh's lack of eagerness was reassuring. The vampires didn't appear to have any hold over Leigh. "I don't trust them, but you can count on Elizaveta and Bartholomew to fight on their own front."

How bizarre to hear those names roll off Leigh's tongue now. Names she'd once told Joan had terrified her.

Yet Joan didn't want to involve herself any further in the politics outside Calvert. Not for a while at least.

"They've already got all the pieces to the puzzle. We've got our own problems."

CHAPTER 26

JOAN HAD DREAMT of flight. This was different.

Instead of a single body floating high in the sky, she was broken into pieces, each soaring closer to the ground.

Hundreds of bodies, dozens of places, glimpses shifting so quickly, it might have given her nauseating vertigo if she'd been awake.

The last few images were more unsettling, and in every one she was a target.

A group of children throwing rocks at her. A dog leaping into the air, tail wagging and tongue lolling as it jumped, trying to catch her and pull her down. A black SUV almost running her over on an empty country road near a state highway marker.

Joan grabbed at wakefulness until she sat up in bed, covers falling to her waist, sweat at her temples and neck.

The dreams were weird, yes, but something more was off. The crow that had almost been killed by an SUV . . .

Something dangerous was in that car.

Without waking, Leigh tugged her back down and pulled her close. Joan settled her racing heart by closing her eyes and pairing her breaths with Leigh's.

She wondered if the more she connected with the crows during the day, the more they tried to do the same while she slept.

At last, she fell back asleep. The dreams persisted and repeated.

The black vehicle raced north, and the crows followed.

"I know it's crazy." Joan fastened her seat belt while Leigh closed Luther's passenger door.

"You don't have to explain, Joan. If something's off, let's go find out for certain."

After two nights of wild and vivid dreams, Joan couldn't sit still anymore. She didn't know what it was she thought she might find and it was maddening. She had, however, gambled on hunches before, and learned long ago to trust her instincts.

She guided Luther through town. A few people on the streets paused to stare as she drove past. It was more attention than normal, and she guessed the word was out about Leigh. So far, she hadn't heard much in the way of protest.

The itch to get on the road north persisted.

As they approached the checkpoint, Joan slowed.

Five people, men and women on foot with backpacks worn from a lot of time on the road, stood at the barricade. More petitioners asking to be let into the Calvert boundaries, like Joan had seen at the Portland city gates and elsewhere.

Dayton was on watch with a couple of other familiar faces, and he ambled over to Luther. Their most recent conversation had gone the same way as their previous ones—he didn't approve and Joan wouldn't budge.

He deferred to her instead of pushing the impasse. The watch had followed his lead, which as far as Joan was concerned was good enough for now.

The other watch people glared at Leigh. When they saw Joan glaring back, they looked away.

"These folks just showed up," Dayton said through Joan's

rolled-down window, glancing tersely at Leigh without offering a greeting.

Not disrespectful, but not warm either. Joan let it slide.

"Anything off?"

"No," he said, squinting over his shoulder at the petitioners. "Hungry and desperate, but not violent. Just about to send them on their way to the refugee camp up near Salem."

If they made it. These people were most likely going to end up dead or thralls if they didn't find some kind of cover. The memories of all the thralls Joan had killed in recent weeks made her wish she'd skipped breakfast.

For that matter, Joan's guts were screaming at her on multiple fronts, making it harder to think. The number of humans with no place to go, the pull to get on the road, the watch's response to Leigh.

One problem had a simple though controversial solution.

"Let 'em in," she said.

Dayton's head snapped back in her direction.

"We don't have any openings," he said, as if she needed reminding. Calvert had a habit of finding locals for various jobs so petitioners rarely found work here, but they did receive aid in some fashion before they were sent elsewhere.

She thought of Grant, the annoying man at the relay station.

"Doesn't matter." At least one sense of urgency in her belly eased. "We'll find something for them to do, and we'll have to trust they'll respond in kind and not tear the damned town apart."

He looked incredulous, and she leaned toward him and lowered her voice.

"We can't turn them away. We'd only be feeding them to any vampire lord who wants to claim them, and we can't ask other towns to do what we're not doing ourselves. These people need help. From now on, no one gets left out in the cold."

"Security will be a nightmare."

"Keeping an eye on humans is a lot easier than fighting off thralls."

Willy poked his head in the passenger side door, and Leigh busied herself with scratching behind his ears. Damned dog was going to scratch Luther's paint job. Joan might have been more irritated if Leigh wasn't so happy about the attention.

Dayton leaned closer to the driver's side door. "Guessing things went well at the meeting this morning?"

What was he talking about? "Meeting?"

"Heard the coven met at the library this morning." He frowned, confused. "You weren't there?"

"Nobody called me." Had she missed a call or message, or had they not invited her?

Dayton scrutinized her as if there was some meaning she was missing, and perhaps there was. As the town binder and head of the coven, Joan should have been the one to call the meeting. She should have at least been invited to attend. For them to meet without her was bad form, and a firm breach of protocol.

Could be the coven had met to talk about her, or her and Leigh. If they tried to oust her or in any way sanction Leigh, they weren't prepared for how Joan might respond.

Nothing felt as urgent as the itch in her spine screaming for attention.

"Gonna have to deal with that when I get back."

"Your funeral," he said, though without malice. "Where you headed?"

Telling him she was following a crow-directed hunch seemed like a bad idea. She wondered if it was any weirder than anything else she'd told him of late. There was always the chance it was only a dream.

"Recon," she said instead. "Might be nothing. Shouldn't take long."

She hoped.

"Need backup?" He sounded like every other time he'd offered in earnest. The normalcy of it felt good after their more recent interactions.

"Thanks, but . . ." Joan glanced at Leigh again, who had petted Willy one last time and was shooing him away from the window. "Leigh will have my back."

Leigh turned and smiled, eyes shining.

CHAPTER 27

LEIGH DROVE LUTHER five miles an hour over the speed limit and distracted herself from the uncertainty of their destination by appreciating the first teases of spring.

Daffodil buds not yet open added spots of yellow in the brown scrub and green grass lining the highway. The first small clusters of new leaves on deciduous trees hinted at winter's end though spring was still weeks away.

If she didn't think about it too much, the drive through the country might be relaxing.

In the backseat Joan growled. Leigh hit the brakes too hard in surprise and the back tires skidded.

"How's it going back there?" Leigh asked once she'd corrected the vehicle.

"Goddamned troublesome." A shuffling sound suggested Joan was changing positions. "Tough to get a read on them when I don't know where they are."

Joan had been trying for the better part of an hour to connect with the crows and their aerial perspective to find the car she'd seen in her . . . dreams? Visions? She'd been prickly about this power of hers, and Leigh wasn't sure which term would irritate Joan the least.

"Give yourself a little credit," Leigh said instead. "Remember when you couldn't connect with them at all?"

When no counterargument was added to the conversation, Leigh assumed Joan had taken her opinion into consideration. She did her best to keep the ride as smooth as possible. The tighter she gripped the steering wheel, the less her hands trembled from nervousness.

"Got 'em," Joan said, low and soft. "Now if I can just get a closer look..."

Leigh kept her attention on the road, eating up the miles as she drove in complete trust Joan would figure out where they needed to go.

"They're coming from the east," Joan said, proving Leigh right. "Four vampires headed toward us."

Leigh maintained control despite the shock and fear knotting in her belly.

"They don't look local." Joan's voice was flat, whether from concentration or her own assessment Leigh couldn't tell.

"How do you know they're vampires?"

"They rolled down a window to shoot at the crows. Bastards. Too formal for vampire lords. And since you said the guild is in charge of watching this place with the High Coven, and judging by the way these guys are driving, I don't think they're from Black Rose City."

"Driving during the day?" Weren't all vampires supposed to be afraid of UV damage to their mostly dead flesh?

"The windows are tinted, but I guess they don't care. Must be part of the mission to take someone by surprise. Who'd expect vampires before sundown? I haven't seen one out in broad daylight in years."

A story for another day, Leigh was sure.

"That's not enough for them to attack the city. Nothing else out here except for the power plant and—wait, it's under lighter guard." Leigh's excitement at having something to contribute pushed her nerves to the background. "One of the vampires asked Elizaveta for more protection against the thrall hordes.

She pulled guards from the plant."

"Sounds like someone's thinning out the herd, which makes it a prime target for infiltration. If someone takes over the plant, the High Coven and the guild are at their mercy. Portland would be easy pickings without power, and the Coven would have to wage war to defend it. Nasty business."

She looked at Leigh, though Leigh was too focused on the road to look back.

"We're the only thing between them and the plant," Joan said. "And we don't have time to get there first to warn them."

As sure as Leigh knew how to breathe she knew Joan would try to stop them, even without her powers.

"We could call for help," Leigh said. "The High Coven, or the guild." Either of those would be unpleasant choices, but Dayton and the Calvert watch were farther away.

"Well, I've got zip for signal, so I'd bet money these bastards stuck to their playbook and blacked out the comms." Joan climbed through the gap between the front and back compartments to claim the passenger seat. "That's how they've been keeping us all disjointed, knocking out the cell towers and relay stations."

She buckled herself in. "Not that anyone can get here in time. Someone's gotta take 'em out now."

Two against four. Those were not great odds.

"Give me a sec," Joan said, closing her eyes. "I'm going to try something."

Several minutes passed, full of Leigh worrying about how she could help Joan. She was a decent shot, though she didn't practice much.

Joan rolled her head over her neck in a tight circle. The cracking sound seemed loud to Leigh.

"Agnes said she sent messages with the crows," Joan said. "I don't have time to write notes and tie them to claws. Tried something different. I bet if a crow shows up acting weird, folks will figure out it's me."

"Which folks?"

"Dayton, Fiona, and . . ." She glowered and twisted her mouth like she wanted to spit. "Bartholomew."

Leigh couldn't help a smile of pride despite the tension. Joan was adapting no matter how much she didn't like it.

"How are they going to find us?"

"Haven't figured that out yet. Pull over. We don't have much time."

Leigh braked so hard they both had to reach for the dash to keep from smacking their heads against it. "Sorry."

Joan let out a laugh and leapt out the door. "Let's arm up."

Next to Luther's rear end, Leigh rocked on her heels in nervous anticipation as Joan lifted the back hatch and slipped the latch of the armor case open.

"Okay, here's what we've got." Joan started assembling armaments. "Pistol for me, pistol for you, two extra clips each. I've got my blades, but you've got nothing for close quarters."

"That's not true." Leigh did, she just had to touch them for it to work.

"Right." Joan squeezed her hand. "Hopefully we won't have to get that close."

Leigh hoped so. "You want to try to shoot 'em down from the car?"

"That's plan A." Joan paused to wipe her palms across her shirt over her belly, a nervous gesture Leigh didn't see often. "Without my powers, I . . ."

She cleared her throat. "Not sure how this is going to go. Sorry about dragging you into this kinda mess with me again so soon after all that happened in Mist."

"Joan, I'm with you. Period. Am I scared shitless? Absolutely. But I'm not going anywhere, and I'm not leaving you to face whatever this is alone."

She kissed Joan, though they had no time.

Joan spared a smile that went all the way to her eyes. "Come on."

This time, Joan took the wheel and guided Luther to a spot in the middle of the road. She blocked both lanes, parking Luther at an angle that gave her a line of sight up the road without giving the enemy a straight shot at their windshield.

"You think they'll stop."

"No," Joan said, resigned as she turned off the engine. "I really don't."

Leigh's stomach plummeted. "You're kidding, right?"

"Should be fine. I haven't tested the impact enchantment for something this strong." Joan handed Leigh a pistol, one Leigh had practiced with before. "I can't block the impact with air spells, though, if they keep coming. So this is gonna hurt."

Well, shit.

The black vehicle appeared on the horizon, speeding toward them sooner than Leigh thought possible.

Joan fired. Despite the distance, Leigh saw the shots hit the windshield, the driver side window, and the grille of the engine.

The suburban monster of a vehicle accelerated. Joan shot one of the tires.

"Yes!"

The vehicle didn't slow despite the warping rubber, the tire wobbling now on its path. The vehicle was too close to stop.

The impact overpowered Leigh's senses, sight and hearing muted as she was shaken like a rag doll in her seat, at one point weightless until gravity slammed into her. Leigh forgot how to breathe, and when she remembered, the pressure on her limbs suggested she'd feel the aftermath of the crash for awhile.

Luther had been knocked back twenty yards on the road. The passenger side windows were shattered, and the windshield was a spiderweb of cracked glass.

A groan broke the silence. "Well, that sucked."

"You okay?" Leigh didn't sense anything broken, but she

was physically stronger than Joan now, and Joan might not have fared so well.

"Good, or good enough." Joan aimed her gun out the window again. Her hands trembled. "Hope it was worse for the other guy."

Smoke streamed from the engine of the other vehicle in the middle of the road. Its front end was caved in by the force of the collision, the hood bent in on itself like paper, the grille pushed into the engine and the entire section compressed into the passenger compartment. Both front wheels were crumpled inward.

One of the doors opened as flames began to pour out of the engine. Three figures emerged from the heat haze and smoke.

"Here they come," Leigh said, gripping her gun.

Joan tried her door. "I can't get out on this side."

She fired through her window, four shots in rapid succession.

One of the vampires collapsed with a blown-out knee.

Leigh shoved her door open so hard, something mechanical broke. The door sank lower than designed with a creaking groan. Joan would be pissed about the damage later. They had to survive this first.

Using the door as cover, Leigh shot at one of the vampires. This one was a woman, features marred by blood streaming from a head wound. The first shot went wild but the second punctured her neck, and the third hit center in her forehead.

Shooting someone dead wasn't as terrifying as it had been to kill the man in Mist, but Leigh's stomach still lurched. Joan had trained for this, and Leigh didn't think any less of her for the times she'd killed someone. Leigh didn't think she'd ever get used to it.

The remaining vampire crawled toward them, cursing in some language Leigh didn't know. Joan shot it several more times before it collapsed, quiet and still.

Leigh didn't feel relieved.

"Crisis averted," Joan said, sounding as worn out as Leigh felt. "Don't know how we're going to get out of here though."

"You said there were four?" Leigh hadn't lowered her pistol.

Joan checked her clip. "Yeah. I better make sure the last one's dead."

Leigh walked with her to the wreck. From one side, as close as they dared with the fire and smoke still a threat, they peered inside one of the shattered doors.

The remaining vampire's neck had been broken in the crash. He stared, unseeing.

Joan shot him in the head. Leigh jumped, startled.

"Sorry," Joan said. "Can't be too sure."

Over her shoulder in the visible distance another vehicle appeared, identical to the one beside them. Then another.

"Joan," Leigh said in warning, and a new wave of dread passed through her as Joan turned her head to look.

"Shit!" Joan grabbed Leigh's arm and ran for Luther. "I didn't see—I thought it was only one car."

The back hatch still opened despite the crash, but the armored case had been knocked around. Leigh helped Joan right the case since it had flipped upside down in the crash.

Joan sifted through the remaining contents in a rush.

"Nothing big enough to take 'em all out. We're gonna have to shoot 'em down." Her eyes were wide.

Somehow, Joan's fear eased Leigh's own.

"Hey," she said, catching Joan's gaze. "We'll get through it."

Joan nodded, though she didn't look like she believed Leigh at all.

The new vehicle announced its arrival with a screeching application of brakes. Leigh took up the same position at Luther's front end, resting her extended arms across the hood as she took aim. And then it was shot after shot, from Joan, too, as they fired on the vampires.

One fired back, and the protective spell cast over Luther

that made the SUV bulletproof forced the bullet to ricochet somewhere unseen. Disgusted, the vampire tossed the gun aside, joining the others who had spread out to either side of the road.

The vampires rushed them.

Joan shot two vampires in the head, one right after the other. For every one of Joan's shots, Leigh squeezed out three, her aim nowhere as precise. When she finally hit any of the targets, she had to expend more ammunition to finish them.

More shots from the enemy—Leigh couldn't see who was firing—ricocheted off Luther's enchantments, so far missing Leigh and Joan.

"Last clip," Leigh said as she slammed the magazine home.

Nine or ten targets—her estimation of their number at the start—were down to three, and then she saw movement in her peripheral vision. She pivoted and got off only one shot before the vampire was upon her.

A gunshot deafened her. The vampire collapsed, dead from Joan's point-blank shot.

"See any more cars?"

"I—" Leigh tried to shake off her latest brush with mortality. She peered up the road. "No."

Leigh hoped with everything in her that was true.

"Give me some cover," Joan said, and closed her eyes.

"I'm almost empty." Leigh had lost count of the remaining bullets, but she had to be close.

"I know." Joan's brow was furrowed in concentration. "Take mine, too."

Leigh took the second pistol in confusion. Had Joan's powers come back?

She did as Joan asked, and shot with whatever aim she could manage to keep the vampires at bay.

A rising crescendo of a hundred caws drew her attention skyward where crows circled and collided with each other in an ever-growing flock in the afternoon sun. From over the horizon in both directions, from the trees in the woods dozens of yards from the highway—from every direction, more of the crows arrived until the swarm overhead was a shifting black mass of increasing volume.

The sound of running drew Leigh back to her task, and she fired at the moving target, too late to hit the vampire running for their flank. And then he disappeared. Where could he have gone?

Joan's breathing was labored from the exertion of her effort, and she let out a deep sob of a sigh as the cluster separated and the crows dived for the road.

In seconds, the area around the wrecked vehicles and the confrontation was swarming with crows. Leigh found it impossible to see anything but Joan, who sagged against Luther.

Leigh touched Joan's shoulder, thrilled she could control herself and wouldn't cause any pain.

"I'm okay," Joan answered the unspoken question, chest heaving, her face covered in sweat.

And then they were yanked apart.

Surprised, Leigh dropped Joan's gun. She smacked at her assailant with her pistol, useless now without bullets.

With strength belying his thin, gaunt build, the dark-haired vampire shook Leigh, raising her to the tips of her toes as he brought his pale face close to hers. Eyes so black their pupils were lost even in daylight glared at her in disgust.

"Whose little toy are you?" He hissed, his hands clenching tighter against her arms, the talons digging into her skin until she cried out. "No matter. They can't help you now."

Flashes of other faces filled her vision, of people who had treated her like this. As nothing but a donor, or a plaything, or an annoyance to be removed. The thrall in Mist.

Nathaniel.

She wasn't helpless anymore.

Leigh pressed her hand against his chest, and *pushed*. Flames erupted, and the shock of their appearance made him release her. She did it again, and he fell back, swatting at the flames. Now the flames spread to his hands, his arms, and by the time he hit the ground, screaming, the entire top half of his body was on fire.

She turned to Joan and her heart nearly stopped.

Two vampires had attacked Joan, who was armed with only a knife.

Joan was in constant motion, darting forward to strike or dancing to one side to avoid a blow. Leigh stood outside the circle of the fight, the slight chance of stopping one of the vampires not worth the greater possibility of getting in Joan's way.

The vampires ignored Leigh as they double-teamed Joan. When their brute strength couldn't overpower her, they switched to combat tactics with punches and kicks. These two had hand-to-hand skills similar to Joan's, and with the crows attacking from all sides, the fight was more like a brawl.

Without her powers—without her spells—Joan must be relying only on her martial skills, but against two larger opponents, how long could she last?

One of them clawed at Joan's face and neck, and bloody rivulets traced her cheeks. The other snarled, mouth stretched in a grim smile.

Leigh couldn't hold back. She had to do something.

Before she lost her nerve, she rushed to the closest vampire and snatched him backward. Releasing her fire was less difficult this time, and a cluster of flames erupted at the small of his back.

He whirled around and backhanded her across the face in one fluid move. Leigh staggered back, catching herself before she fell.

The distraction allowed Joan to stab the last vampire in the chest. She twisted her blade in his heart.

Leigh watched it all happen as if in slow motion.

The vampire pitched forward, his body lurching against

Joan, pushing her back several steps before knocking her to the ground. One of the dead vampire's legs landed on the fiery corpse of the one Leigh had killed, and caught fire.

With new fuel, the fire spread across the second body.

By the time Joan managed to shuffle out from under the dead weight, the fire had jumped to her clothes.

Leigh's heart thundered in her chest and in her ears. An explosion nearby barely captured her notice—one of the SUVs. The crows raged, some of them dying in the blast while the others swirled in the din.

"Leigh—" Joan cried out as the fabric of her clothes blackened and crisped. She scrambled to her feet, trying to pat out the flames with her hands, worsening the spread. "I can't stop it."

The crows' agitation increased, some of them pecking at Leigh as she rushed forward to clutch Joan's arms, but Joan didn't even notice her.

Joan grabbed at her clothes, screaming when the fire spread to her skin, the flames growing as she moved.

This was Leigh's nightmare. Joan was in pain, *Joan was burning,* and it was all Leigh's fault. Horror stole her voice, and Leigh shook with the need to do something.

Joan collapsed to the asphalt. Leigh knelt on all fours beside her as tears clouded her vision. "I'm so sorry."

Joan sobbed in Latin, repeating a phrase as the fire spread across her body. Was she casting a spell? Leigh hadn't studied Latin as much as Joan and couldn't translate all the words. Something about healing, but Joan didn't have any of her powers.

Joan screamed.

"I know," Leigh said, smacking the tears from her own cheeks. "I'll—I'm going to try."

She pushed aside her horror at Joan's suffering and thrust her hands into the flames.

Leigh cried out at the burn, and closed her eyes to

concentrate, ignoring Joan's screams. This wasn't like the fires in the warehouse or the garden at all, not like practice, not with Joan in agony and crows attacking them both, burning and dying, not with all of it being *Leigh's fault*.

Joan's screaming faded to a croak.

No. Leigh couldn't lose her, not like this. Not when she could do something about it. Joan wouldn't die like this. Leigh loved her too much to let her go.

That feeling, the warmth of loving Joan, swelled in Leigh's chest, and in an instant the power she'd tried so hard to summon in training flooded her senses.

It hurt—oh, how it hurt. How had Elizaveta endured such agony? Leigh's nerves howled at the pain as she persisted, drawing more of the fire's energy. Smoke assailed her lungs along with the odor of her burning clothes.

Leigh put all her will into the effort of enduring the suffering, the torment of pulling the fire into herself, until there were no flames left.

That wasn't enough. Leigh kept pulling, except now she was focused on Joan's burns. She closed her eyes, the challenge easier to face without her vision. In the darkness, she could somehow sense the areas of Joan's body that had been burned, and she stretched out that same power and *pulled* the burn to herself.

She could see everywhere Joan hurt, every place she wasn't whole, and Leigh extended herself further to pull every imperfection to her own body. She remembered a similar sensation from the garden back home, the feeling of coaxing the seedlings from the dirt and the blossoms from the vines.

When it was done, when no blemishes remained in her mind's eye, Leigh collapsed.

She rolled onto her side and opened her eyes.

Joan lay beside her, staring at the sky. The crows still swarmed, but they weren't attacking Leigh anymore.

Beyond Joan, the fire had spread to the grass next to the road.

The flames were knee-high now. Soon, the fire would reach the woods and consume them. Who knew how far it would burn?

Tears streamed down her cheeks, stinging burned flesh. What had she done?

The ground quaked, jarring her from her misery, the tremors rumpling the road and tearing it apart. More Latin reached her ears, and Leigh wiped the tears from her face so she could see.

Beside her, Joan was on her knees, most of her shirt and jacket in burned tatters, her jeans black with carbon. One of her hands was submerged into the dirt under the split asphalt.

"I don't know how you did it, but . . ." Joan shook her head, incredulous, and extended one hand toward the wildfire.

The earth beneath the fire palpitated as it pulled the fire within itself. Yard by yard, the ground agitated and folded, churning and twisting until all the flames had been consumed.

Where the green had been burned black by Leigh's fire, Joan's mastery of the earth had smothered its impact.

Relief hit Leigh so hard she fell back to the ground face down, despite the pain in her limbs.

"Thank you," Leigh said.

Joan gifted her with a tired smile.

"Vampires?" Leigh's throat was so dry, and everything hurt so much.

"They're all dead."

Leigh managed to roll onto her back. The crows soared overhead, quieter now—perhaps because Joan was unharmed.

"Leigh, your hair . . ." Joan's voice cracked and tears trickled down her cheeks. "You know, if you wanted so badly to match my new cut, I think this was a pretty drastic way to do it."

Leigh raised her hand to one side of her head, shocked to discover coarse naked skin instead.

"It burned off," Joan said. "How did you do that? Healing me, I mean."

They both helped each other upright.

"I'll tell you later." Maybe she'd have to think of an answer since she had no idea.

"Your hand—your arm." Joan reached toward her gingerly, not touching her. "Those burns look awful. Will they heal?"

The skin was gnarled and pebbled, red and wet in places. The pain was muted somehow—perhaps the nerves were too damaged to process how much the burns must hurt.

Leigh was too focused on the fact that Joan was whole, and she herself hadn't burned the forest down.

Elizaveta's voice echoed in her head. *Incendiant.*

Now Leigh knew what she was capable of, and how dangerous she was in more ways than one.

A thumping sound from the west became the steady chopping of a helicopter's blades. A sleek black craft with tinted windows circled overhead before landing several car lengths beyond Luther. The crows kept their distance.

The engine spun down to silence as an umbrella poked out the open boarding door. Bartholomew emerged and jumped to the ground. His suit was charcoal gray this time, and his customary aviators hid his eyes.

He strolled toward them as if he were on his way to a luncheon.

"The timing is either impeccable or deliberately unpunctual." Joan's words didn't have any heat to them.

"It could be both, Joan Matthews." Bartholomew greeted her with surprising humor.

Joan snickered in response, shocking Leigh. Leigh took her hand, clutching it tightly despite the pain of her burns.

"You okay?" Leigh whispered, though she knew Bartholomew would hear.

After a deep stabilizing breath, Joan nodded. "You got here fast," she said to Bartholomew.

The crow she'd sent couldn't have traveled that distance in so short a time.

"I was already on my way."

"How'd you know?" Leigh asked.

"Istvan." Bartholomew spoke to Leigh and didn't elaborate for Joan's understanding. "He owns this land, from the river to the base of the mountains."

"So he's been hiding Nathaniel and his thralls all this time?" Joan frowned and coughed at the smoke in the air. "Was he working with these guys?"

Bartholomew's silence might have been answer enough, but Leigh remembered him mentioning those outside forces—other guilds who didn't agree with Elizaveta's management of Black Rose City.

"Will Elizaveta censure him?" Joan asked.

Bartholomew shrugged, an odd gesture on an ancient vampire.

"Not likely. Istvan admitted to harboring a space for thralls to converge, and he has some plausible deniability in terms of the guild agreements."

"He bet and lost," Leigh said.

Bartholomew nodded as if he approved. She wasn't as nervous around him now as she'd been when they'd met.

Joan watched them both, and her uneasiness at their exchange was palpable. Leigh squeezed her hand to reassure her, though it hurt.

"Considering the severity of your wounds," Bartholomew said, "you may need some extended healing time. You might also reevaluate the importance of more formal training."

The implication was far from subtle. Joan froze, but she had nothing to worry about. Bartholomew had sworn to leave the choice up to Leigh.

She tugged Joan closer to her and didn't let go of her hand. Thinking about the homestead made her ache to be back in her garden, tending to the plants and to the life she'd rebuilt with Joan.

"I can take care of myself," Leigh said, though what she meant was that she and Joan would take care of each other. "And I know where I belong."

EPILOGUE

THREE DAYS LATER the slam of a door caught Joan's attention as she added silverware to the place settings on the dining room table. Through the window, the approaching sunset backlit the new arrival, but Dayton's bulk was easy enough to identify.

"He's here," she called to Leigh, who emerged from the kitchen with a tray of bell peppers stuffed with rice and cheese.

Dayton had accepted their invitation to dinner—what would most likely be an uncomfortable get-to-know-you meal.

Leigh's idea. Seemed optimistic, but Joan could be wrong.

"Tell him to hurry up," Leigh said, then licked some spilled sauce from a fingertip. "These get cold quickly."

Bandages still covered her arm where the burns hadn't healed, and she'd shaved the other side of her head to match the evened-out patch where she was now bald, leaving a wide strip from front to back where her hair hung long. The damage from healing Joan—and Leigh claimed she had no idea how she'd removed whatever had blocked Joan's powers—might be permanent.

Leigh also said she'd bear it since Joan was whole in the bargain.

Still, a confident Leigh was a sexy Leigh. In the wake of the battle on the road near the power plant, Joan noticed something different about her—as if something had centered and settled within her.

Joan's greater appreciation would have to wait until there wasn't company around.

By the time Joan got to the door, Dayton was grumbling as he climbed up the stairs, as if the effort taxed him.

"Pablo respectfully declined," he said in greeting, referring to the other person Joan had invited—once again at Leigh's suggestion.

Joan's olive branches to the coven weren't having the desired effect. People would speak to her, but didn't want to be in the same space as Leigh.

Leigh said it would take time and claimed it didn't bother her. Joan didn't care if those folks ever came around to her way of thinking. She'd made her choice.

"I brought a different mouth to feed," Dayton said as he passed her, aiming his thumb over his shoulder. "Didn't think you'd mind since she said you sent a crow her way. And here I thought I was special."

Ballsy chat from him. Joan was getting used to it. He deferred to her less than he'd done when she'd first returned to Calvert. Maybe all the time they'd fought alongside one another—and all the things they'd argued about—had worn enough of the shine off her for him to treat her like another human being instead of a warbinder.

That one word kept crossing her thoughts unbidden.

Willy nosed at the scattered birdseed on the walk below the stairs of the front porch and sneezed. The crows and the dog ignored one another as he strolled past them and through the open door.

Dayton might still be a little prickly around Leigh, but the dog was not. Over the last few days Willy had come by the house no less than half a dozen times as if satisfying his curiosity about Leigh, who had adapted to his repeated presence.

Leigh carried in another tray and set it down in one of the remaining bare spots. "You'd better not be tracking mud in here, dog. Go lie down until dessert."

The dog circled in place on a folded blanket Leigh had designated as "Willy's spot" by the fireplace. After three complete rotations, he curled up in a bundle and peered longingly at the dinner table.

Dayton scratched at his beard. "He listens to you better than he listens to me."

Probably wasn't true, but Joan appreciated the effort.

"Only because I feed him," Leigh said, and turned back toward the kitchen. "Dinner's in five minutes. You get caught up, Joan, I'm starting without you. These sprouts are better hot."

The corner of Dayton's mouth twitched in a brief grin when Joan glared at him on her way outside. Guess his prickliness was easing in the face of all this domestic bliss.

At the bottom of the porch stairs, Fiona stood poking one booted toe at a weed in the walkway.

"Waiting on an invitation?" Joan asked.

Fiona's gaze was piercing behind her glasses. "Yes."

She pushed her shoulders back, as if she was about to make a presentation, and held her hands away from her sides to show she carried no weapons.

Damnit, Joan was hungry.

"Fiona Gunnarsdottir." Joan growled as she spoke, irritated at having to observe the formalities on her own land. "If you come in light with an open heart, at my hearth and my table, alongside me and mine in peace and at war, you are welcome."

Fiona's shoulders were less tense, but she was still frowning.

"There's, uh, some things I need to tell you—"

"Tell me all the bad news after dinner. Last time I was late Leigh left me only cabbage."

"It's not all bad," Fiona muttered, adjusting her glasses and following Joan to the porch.

Joan leaned on one post, rubbing her over-full belly while Fiona perched against another.

"Mind?" Fiona held a pack of smokes in one hand and raised it in question.

"Not out here," Joan said. "Help yourself."

After the ritual of lighting a cigarette and blowing a few stabilizing puffs into the open air, Fiona turned to face Joan.

"The Portland High Coven has publicized the ban against you. All communication must go through formal channels submitted by the Calvert coven, not you alone. Otherwise, any attempts will be ignored."

Assholes. Joan wasn't surprised, all things considered. The Calvert coven had tried similar heavy-handed tactics in a meeting the day before, suggesting Joan step down as lead, demanding she exile Leigh. They had no true leverage to force her to do anything.

She was the most powerful witch on their land, and they knew it.

"The Ruby Court guild of Black Rose City," Fiona continued, "requests all communication from Calvert come through Leigh Phan."

Elizaveta's doing, no doubt, in an attempt to keep tabs on Leigh.

Joan's overhanging favor had been addressed, and though she would be fine if she never had to deal with Elizaveta and Bartholomew ever again, Leigh's involvement was more complicated. Joan wanted to tend to the situation herself. Leigh had insisted she'd handle it, so Joan had to let her.

"You're persona non grata in the formal circles, but word

has gotten out about you letting a few of the road stragglers in without applications, and everyone else is calling Joan of Crows the People's Champion."

Joan grunted and tried not to roll her eyes. Why her name wasn't good enough all by itself was beyond her.

"One more thing," Fiona said, now uneasy.

Joan was unsettled by this nervousness in Fiona. She'd been so confident and sure in Black Rose City, though her unhappiness had been obvious.

"The way things have always been done isn't the right path for the future. I don't know if yours is any better, but I'd, um . . ." Fiona stood a little straighter. "If you can find a place for me, I'd like to stay here. In Calvert."

"What about your . . . position in Black Rose City?"

Fiona took a drag from her cigarette and pondered her boots. "I've been released from my post."

Hmm. More likely she'd been transferred here to Calvert by the High Coven to spy on Joan.

Another war witch in Calvert. One with experience, who understood the players of the region and that solutions would be shaded gray instead of black and white.

"Well, you know we've got open borders around here now," Joan said, and to make sure Fiona understood the bigger picture, she added, "I've got nothing to hide."

Not anymore, and word about Leigh must have reached the High Coven as well.

The sun's rays cut past the clouds on the horizon. She was grateful she could taste the air again, yet something unrecognizable left a bitter aftertaste on her tongue—not a threat, but nothing good either.

The silence of the street captured her attention. The last few houses had emptied out soon after Leigh had stopped using the glamour. Not a lot of folks wanted to live with a bloodling as a neighbor. Joan didn't like it, though she understood the sentiment.

Time to rebuild, to make something stronger, something new.

"The house across the street used to belong to-to my teacher." She covered the stutter with a cough. Joan didn't speak often of Gretchen Wilson, who had been murdered by a traitor to the coven and a servant of the vampire lord who'd held Leigh captive.

"She taught me as much if not more than my father did, about what it means to be a binder, about this land around us and the people here."

She'd also been hell-bent on holding to the outdated ways of doing things. Gretchen's trust in the wrong people had led to her death.

"The house has been empty since . . ." Joan couldn't say it out loud. "It's furnished, though you should feel free to make it your own."

After a long measuring look, and a heartfelt thanks, Fiona slipped her hands into her jeans pockets and crossed the street. She stopped for a moment at the end of the walk before she went inside without a glance back.

Maybe a life in Calvert was what Fiona needed. It had worked for Joan.

Leigh wrapped her arms around Joan's waist from behind, and rested her chin on Joan's shoulder.

"She gonna stay?"

"Seems like it."

"Hmm. Good. You need someone to back you up."

Joan had to grin. "I've got you." And Dayton. And his damned dog.

"One more won't hurt."

The sun slipped past the horizon, and dusk brought a chill in response. A single crow circled overhead before landing on a hedge in front of the porch. Perhaps it was a portent. She hadn't gotten far enough in Agnes's journals to practice those skills.

Then again, maybe it was just a crow sitting on a branch. Joan sent a mental poke for it to skedaddle and leave her be for once.

The crow flew away with a loud squawk.

If only all her problems were so easily resolved.

"That's enough for one day." Leigh tugged at Joan's hand. "Come back inside, lover."

The day's remaining light emphasized Leigh's open expression, the tension of the last few months gone without a trace.

When Leigh turned toward the house, pulling Joan along with her, Joan couldn't help but gaze at the darkening horizon. Judging by that odd taste on the air, some new problem would knock on Joan's door soon enough.

A warbinder would answer.

ACKNOWLEDGMENTS

This book has been damned near two years in the making and the list of people to thank is long.

Bywater Books, and Salem West in particular, gave me the time and space to craft the story I wanted to tell even as life decided to switch to hard mode. For months, every two steps forward resulted in only a half-step of progress. Thank you for your patience, encouragement, and willingness to work with me through those challenges.

Ann McMan's magic is well-known throughout our community, so I was thrilled yet not surprised to see *Incendiant's* astounding cover. Her mojo is unparalleled, and I never want to end up on her naughty list.

Thanks to Kit Haggard, editor extraordinaire, for her insight and guidance, shining light on my blind spots and strengthening the story's foundation. Thanks, Kit. You were right about everything.

Thanks to Heather Flournoy, editor magnifique, who showed me how much road I had for these characters, and what opportunities I might be missing. She also laughed at my jokes and made *me* laugh when I thought the tears might drown me.

A large Manhattan (perfect, up, with a port-soaked cherry) raised to Rey Spangler, Anna Burke, Melissa Brayden, Susan X Meagher, Milena McKay, Jenn Alexander, and Jules Revel.

Sapphic Lit Mafia has saved my sanity more times than I can count, and I hope to offer you all the same as you fight your own battles.

Thanks to the Whiskey Crab folks who asked me how the book was going, even though they knew I'd talk about it endlessly. The next round is on me. You've been with me every step of the way, and I love you all.

Thanks to Steph Yager and Quinn Clarkson, who read unpolished versions, helped me fill all the holes, and reminded me how books are supposed to work. And hats off to the Tech Spec Fic folks who offered their feedback on the prologue.

To my accountability partner, Shawn Marie Bryan: you're next! And thank you for those touchpoints to keep me moving inexorably forward.

To Christel Cogneau, thank you for your endless support of my work and for making sure everyone else knows about it.

To Mom, thank you for trying to get me to slow down. I'm sorry I didn't listen, but thanks for loving me anyway.

A special thanks goes out to Bruce Wyman, who, for *weeks*, texted me nightly to ask about my progress and encouraged me to keep going. You were always there when I needed you and celebrated every word of this book. I will never forget it. My thanks may not be enough, but I will keep trying.

For anyone I've neglected to include, please know I appreciate you and your support, and I apologize for the oversight.

Thanks to Chase the younger for always saying nice things about my writing, even though you don't read it. (Don't start now. It's best for both of us.)

And always, thanks to Kate. Words fail around you, so I don't know what to say, but I will always hold your hand. I'm eternally grateful that you squeeze it back.

ABOUT THE AUTHOR

Virginia Black is the award-winning author of *No Shelter But the Stars* (Bywater Books, 2024) and *Consecrated Ground* (Bywater Books, 2023), as well as several short stories. She was a Lambda Literary 2024 Fellow in Speculative Fiction. She enjoys strong whiskey, loud music, and writing about angsty protagonists, though not necessarily in that order. When not penning dark speculative sapphic fiction, she is almost always reading or lurking on RPG sites. She lives in the Pacific Northwest with her wife of 23 years (and counting) and their savagely witty teenage daughter.

Learn more at virginiablackwrites.com.

And follow her at:

Facebook: //virginiablackwrites
Instagram: @virginiablackwrites
BlueSky: @virginiablack.bsky.social

Bywater Books believes that all people have the right to read or not read what they want—and that we are all entitled to make those choices ourselves. But to ensure these freedoms, books and information must remain accessible. Any effort to eliminate or restrict these rights stands in opposition to freedom of choice.

Please join us by opposing book bans and censorship of the LGBTQ+ and BIPOC communities.

At Bywater Books, we are all stories.

For more information about Bywater Books, our publishing mission, authors, and our titles, please visit our website.

https://bywaterbooks.com

www.ingramcontent.com/pod-product-compliance
Lightning Source LLC
Jackson TN
JSHW021945080625
85606JS00007B/38